BLOOD CITY

BOOK TWO OF
THE MONSTER KEEPER SERIES

JEFF SEATS

SD PUBLISHING

Published by SD Publishing

Publisher's Note: This is a work of fiction. Names,
characters, places, and incidents are a product of the author's imagination.
Locales and public names are sometimes used for atmospheric purposes. Any
resemblance to actual people, living or dead, or to businesses, companies,
events, institutions, or locales is completely coincidental.

Blood City/Jeff Seats -1st ed.

ISBN: 978-0-9983896-2-2

For my 94-year-old mother and her five sisters, all in their 90s.

My immortal family.

Acknowledgments

Thanks to my daughter Elizabeth Seats and her friend Craig Riedler, whose core idea of a busload of people stumbling into a town populated by vampires led first to a screenplay and then to this novel. They provided me the rib with which I molded clay around to form the body and then breathed life into it.

Contents

Chapter 1

PROLOGUE

Portland, Oregon 1900

A WEATHER-WORN face reflected the warm glow of a lantern hanging on a nearby piling. The single source of light cast harsh shadows, emphasizing the many wrinkles that contoured his skin; making them read as miniature canyons on some distant island. He turned a timepiece towards the light to better see the dial, and watch the hands tick closer to the hour of nine p.m. and the high tide that would arrive with it; enabling his ship easier passage down the Willamette River and on towards the Pacific Ocean. Nervously, he scratched the gray stubble on his cheek as he inspected the pier for prying eyes. Then he looked down at the two men delivering an awkward bundle onto the deck of his ship. The first mate would see to the storage of the freight after they had gotten underway.

The ship's captain opened the gold cover on the pocket watch again. He was getting itchy to cast off. It was one hundred miles from Portland to the ocean, and there was no guarantee that they would make the next available slack tide that would safely allow his vessel to cross the Columbia Bar—the graveyard of the Pacific. If those two didn't hurry, his ship would get caught in Astoria waiting for the next opportunity to break out into deep water. He was a merchantman, after all, and the longer he stayed in port, the longer it would take to get the goods his ship carried to Shanghai, sold, and pocket the profits. Time being money, as an old saying went.

Besides, the longer his ship stayed moored in this city, the greater the possibility of the local constabulary discovering the bundle now being left on deck and the more out-of-pocket cash it would take to pay them off, or that his newest "hire" might even escape. And he was in no frame of mind to allow either to happen, not after all the trouble he had to go through to engage that local crimp, Joseph "Bunco" Kelly, to acquire the "sailor" in the first place.

As if on cue, the two men stepped off the gangplank connecting the deck of his ship to the dock and came to a stop in front of the nervous captain. Kelly, stepped closer, bowler hat in hand. The ship's skipper unfolded a sheet of paper and handed it to Kelly; one last task before the job was complete. Kelly reached into his coat pocket and pulled out a fountain pen and forged the signature of the new "crew member" agreeing to the terms of employment and the rules of the ship legally binding him to the captain and the vessel he would be sailing on.

"He's a bit under the weather at the moment," Bunco said in an affected Irish accent and winked conspiratorially, acknowledging that the bundle he had just delivered was a man who had been drugged. "But the lad'll be as right as rain come the mornin'. Now if you'll be upholdin' your end of the deal?" Bunco asked with his hand out.

The captain removed a large leather billfold from his inside coat pocket and counted out the bills, placing them individually onto Bunco's palm, one five-dollar bill at a time.

"—and thirty," the captain said, closing the billfold.

"If you would pardon the impertinence, but our agreement was for fifty dollars this time. You were in a hurry you said," Bunco stated apologetically, then grinned.

Exasperated, the captain pulled out an additional twenty dollars and stabbed the extra paper notes on top of the initial thirty already in Bunco's palm.

"It's blood money, that's what it is," the captain grumbled.

"Yes, and I wouldn't be gettin' paid now if you weren't needin' an extra hand. Would I?"

Bunco looked at the printed paper in his hand. He held the greenbacks up to the lantern to make sure they appeared authentic. He felt satisfied when he saw the red treasury stamp at the bottom right. It wouldn't do his reputation any good as a swindler if he were to be swindled himself.

The ship's captain turned, grabbed the lantern, and stormed down the gangplank, barking orders to his men. The flurry of activity on the deck disinterested Bunco and he turned to his friend, Stingaree Poe. "Now for the next delivery of the evening Poe, me boy." They spun the cart around and headed into the service tunnel that opened out onto the lower tier of docks lining the riverfront and pushed it back under the city.

The only illumination for Bunco and Poe as they moved into the dank tunnel came from a lantern that was hanging from a pole lashed to the front side of the cart. As the small wagon moved forward amber light radiating from the lantern, rocked back and forth across the brick walls, first it climbed the right side, swung around to the left, and down to the ground. Then the circle of light moved back up to the right wall again in a predictable pattern made only different by the speed at which they proceeded. After several minutes of pushing and pulling the cart, the sounds of the waterfront had fallen behind them, and they were deep into the dark passage under the city.

A step.

Splash.

"Ah hell!" Poe grumbled. "You'd think that by this time of year the tunnels would have dried out more."

"Quit your gripin', you old fool," Bunco said. "These tunnels connect to the river, remember? Rivers flood. The last flood was only a month ago. And we're talkin' about the streets above being flooded. Down here? Now that would have been a wee bit more than floodin', to be sure."

Bunco stepped under the swaying light and opened the cover of his pocket watch, checked the time, then closed it with a snap. Satisfied with what he saw, he put the timepiece back into his vest pocket and urged his partner to keep moving through the tunnel.

"What the hell was that?" Poe asked, wiping at his face.

"What?"

"That shit that just brushed across my face. Felt like a cobweb or somethin'."

"You drinking your own rotgut again there Poe?"

"Hey! I felt somethin' touch me."

A rustling sound came from above their heads.

"And what was that? The wind blowing through the bows of the trees?" Poe rubbed his face, trying to remove the sticky feeling. "This is disconcerting."

"Quit your grousing. We gotta get this one delivered and get above ground before sunrise."

As ordered, Poe shut up, and the two continued into the tunnel for several more minutes.

"We stop here," Bunco said quietly.

"Here? Where's here?" Poe looked around the extremely dark passage. In the lantern light, all he could make out was the same monotonous brick that lined the passage since they left the waterfront. "What are we—"

"Shush!"

The two partners in crime stood next to the cart, making no sound. Then Poe brushed at his face again, more vigorously than before. "Aack!" He said, spitting and rubbing his tongue. "What the hell? That web shit got in my mouth! What is it?" Poe asked, his voice tinged with fear.

"That is your signal to leave." Bunco pulled a partially used candle from his pocket, lighted it from the lantern and handed it to Poe. "You go and head on back to the saloon. I'll be handlin' things from here."

"You sure? You don't need my help with this?"

"Friend, believe me, I can handle things. And besides, you want nothing to do with this transaction."

"I don't understand . . .,"

"And you never will. Truth be told, I don't either."

They heard more movement coming towards them.

"Now get yourself outta here before you can't go nowhere no more!" Bunco said, pushing Poe away from the area

———————◆◇◆———————

STINGAREE POE TURNED and looked at his friend and, sometimes, business partner. He did not know what was happening, but when Bunco told him to depart, it was for a good reason. And besides, he always returned with a pocket of cash.

Poe usually met the ship captains with Bunco, but on these occasions, he wasn't allowed to observe. The first few times were not something he thought very much about, but these occurrences had been increasing in frequency. Whoever Bunco was doing business with was very secretive. Not that he would ever spill the beans; Poe's sense of morality was deeply attached to his desire for money. Drugging and selling stupid farm boys or drunk lumbermen to an all-expenses-paid voyage around the Pacific Ocean was relativity harmless. Sure, a few died from the occasional overdose, and a few more may have died while trying to escape before being delivered to their new employer, but that was the price of doing business. At any rate, everyone knew that if you entered this part of town, you were taking your chances with either the crimps, the faro dealers, or the whores.

As for those pathetic drunks who awoke in the basement after he and Bunco had spent the better part of a night collecting them for one of their biggest paydays ever, well, it wasn't as if he or Bunco had killed them, was it? Their stupidity did. Sure, they awoke from their drug-induced sleep a bit earlier than expected and the idiots tried to escape. But Poe had securely locked the cellar door, so they broke into the adjoining basement of the undertaker's looking for another way out, but that exit door was shut tight as well. And neither Poe nor Bunco had told them it was okay to drink anything they found lying around, either. Though those barrels of embalming fluid they found must have smelled a lot like the rotgut that Poe served in his bar, but still . . . .. He shuddered at the idea of drinking the stuff the undertaker used in his work. But drink they did. Instead of six "able-bodied" albeit passed out sailors to sell, they had six dead bodies.

Kelly didn't hesitate as his mind worked on a plan to profit out of adversity. They loaded the bodies into a wagon and made their way down to the docks. The bluster from the captain when he saw the six bodies piled on top of each other was quickly smoothed over by Bunco's fast talking. "You'll be findin' these lads had a bit too much of the strong stuff if you know what I mean, captain, but they'll be stiff as a mainmast come the mornin'."

Poe smiled. His friend did have a way with words.

Taking the candle from Kelly, Poe left his friend standing alone in the tunnel with the cart and the remaining "package." He did not know why they hadn't deposited this one onto the ship as well. But it was Bunco's business, and he was merely a partial partner, so if he wanted Poe to leave in the middle of this long, dark tunnel, that was fine with Poe. He walked beyond the light cast by the lantern, then stopped. Curiosity getting the better of him, he pinched out the flame from the candle blanketing him in a cloak of darkness and turned to watch what his friend was doing.

It didn't take long. Bunco stood exposed in the largest pool of light the kerosene fueled flame could provide. He turned his head and looked around the narrow space, anticipating something. The arrival of another? But from where? They had passed no opening from the time they had left the dock. The tunnel was lined with bricks from top to bottom, and the ground was solidly tamped down.

Then he heard the same rustling sound from earlier. Poe watched Bunco freeze. A touch of fear on his face—a look he had never seen on Bunco before. There was a slight rush of air accompanied by a creaking sound of rusted hinges. Poe strained his eyes. Just beyond the dimmest bit of lantern light, he could barely see a door opening in the wall he would have sworn was uninterrupted brick. Not that this surprised him. The tunnels were dark. Without the lantern, they would see nothing, and the brightness of the flame made all the darkness that much blacker beyond its bright cast circle of light. There could have been other doors and connecting tunnels, which he probably wouldn't have seen either.

BUNCO COMPELLED HIS eyes to seek the source of the sound. He tried not to let crippling fear overtake him when he heard the rustling noise Poe had noticed. At that point, he knew he had to get his companion the hell away from what was going to happen next. There was no time to contemplate anything else. But now, standing here alone in the tunnel, his thoughts went to how horribly this business transaction could go for himself.

To make matters worse, he had noticed the body in the cart was making minor movements, showing that the man was waking up. It was more art than exacting science, knowing how much of the narcotic to slip into a drink to knock a man out. Every person tolerated such things differently; too much, and he risked killing a man. And that was bad for his bottom line.

The grinding of rusty metal suggested that he had stopped in the correct spot. It still surprised him, the noise, even though he was expecting it. Bunco knew from experience that he would not see the man until it was too late, and already upon him. Man? That was a joke. But whatever he was, he looked like a man, and that was what Bunco needed to call him because to call him anything else was unthinkable.

POE STARED AT Bunco and saw him make a startled motion. Then he watched as black filaments, fibrous wisps of cobwebs, danced in front of his friend. Cobwebs! He absentmindedly brushed at his face one more time. The strands of black appeared thin enough to have seeped out between gaps in the brick wall, and they might have, but the door suggested someone or something else might also be arriving. He watched, dumbfounded. The threadlike filaments swirled around themselves and quickly formed into a shadowy, human shape. Then almost instantly the flowing fibrous body solidified into a man!

BUNCO WATCHED AS the man became solid. His heart pounded, but he remained calm on the outside. No need to draw attention to the fact that he was entirely thrown off his game every time this occurred. The secret to a successful business arrangement was not to let the other party see your discomfort. And this was undoubtedly the most uncomfortable he had ever been during a transaction. Well, this and every other time he had business to do with the shadow man.

"And a good evening to you, Joseph." A voice heavily laced with a Russian accent said.

"Evening Vladimir." Bunco returned, tapping the brim of his hat with his right hand.

Vladimir circled the cart and peered into the back. He looked up, disappointment in his eyes. "Our agreement was for two. Yes?"

Bunco swallowed dryly. He knew that this was going to happen. "Well, I . . . you see." He stumbled, trying to spin the best excuse. "I had an emergency order to fill. Ship's captain needed one, and the two were all that I had available. Had to be on board by high tide or the ship wouldn't be able to make their timetable getting out to sea."

"Yes." Vladimir contemplated the situation. "I can understand your predicament." He paused, appearing to think through the situation. "But we struck our agreement first. You didn't have to respond to the ship's captain, yet you did and left me with only one. I have many to feed. Tell me, how would you suggest I accomplish that now?"

The man in the cart made a soft moaning sound, and his legs twitched.

"I could save myself some money and give this one and you to my family. And I could take your friend too as a bonus."

Bunco's eyes flared. "Poe! Goddamn ye. Are you still out there?"

Poe stayed still and silent. He hugged the shadows ever tighter. But his fascination was too great to allow him to flee.

"Well, he's not here, so the least you'll get is this jaundiced piece of Irish meat."

A smile slowly spread across Vladimir's face. "A sorry piece of scrawny meat you may be my friend, but jaundice does not bother me in the slightest." He looked out into the dark direction where Poe was hiding and called out down the tunnel. "Do not worry Mr. Poe, both you and Joseph are safe tonight."

Both men relaxed a bit.

Turning back to Bunco, Vladimir continued, "But do not think that because our business arrangement is mutually beneficial, I appreciate being taken advantage of. My people and I also have needs, far more pressing than the sailing of a ship." He waved his arm, signaling.

From the open door, three people emerged and grouped around the cart.

"You will have to share tonight my family," Vladimir announced apologetically.

Bunco knew what was going to happen next, and he inched his way up the tunnel to where he thought Poe was standing. As he did so, he heard a voice coming from the bed of the cart. Then the man's head popped up over the side.

"Hey," he said, voice weak and groggy. "Where the hell am I—"

Vladimir's three companions rushed the man as he sat up.

"Wait! What? . . . Stop! *STOP!*" The man's screams echoed down the hard surface of the masonry-lined tunnel as they pulled him out of the cart and onto the ground where the feast commenced.

The lantern swung like a pendulum, back and forth, washing one side of the tunnel wall with light and then the other, briefly illuminating the horrid scene—claws and fangs tearing into the man—then hiding the blood by the passing shadow only to be exposed again on the return swing lighting the bloody gore one more time.

Poe reached out and grabbed Bunco by the shoulder when he had gotten close enough, and the two fled as far away from the carnage into the black hole of the tunnel as their feet would take them.

Vladimir called out after Bunco. "The next time when I ask for two . . .." Then he turned and lovingly watched his family enjoy their meal.

"Didn't you get the money?" Poe asked.

Bunco nudged his friend in the arm with his elbow. "He always pays in advance."

Chapter 2

ATTRITION

S AUNDERS REACHED OVER to the center console of the car Craig had signed out from the Mountain Home motor pool. "I don't know which bothers me more, that internet radio quack Dr. Gwen that you subject me to in the control room or this—" He pushed the eject button, and a CD slipped out of the slot. "—older than dirt music."

"A. She is not a quack. Her callers are the weird ones. And, B, this here is Twangy Duane Eddy. Without Eddy, there'd be no Hendrix. This is his debut album, 1958, and still my favorite." Craig showed the CD cover to his pal. The illustration showed Duane Eddy sitting on a guitar case, waiting for a ride. "*Have 'Twangy' Guitar, Will Travel.* A classic and you know the title plays off that TV Western, *Have—*"

"Yeah, yeah, yeah. *Have Gun - Will Travel.* Yes, I know. God, how I know."

"Fuck you, you ass-hole."

"Oh, now there's the educated adult in you coming out."

Craig replaced the CD lovingly back into its jewel case.

"Next time, no CD player in the car." Saunders half mumbled.

"Then you check the car out next time, and you can pick the options."

Saunders gave Craig a sneer, then opened a topographical map. After studying it, he stabbed his finger at a spot on the green printed page. "According to what I've read, we'll find our hold-out up Fisher Creek somewhere between here and an abandoned mine upstream a few miles. That-a-way." He pointed out the left side of the car.

"Just where along this creek, between here and the mine, are we going to find it?"

"And as I just said, *that* is something I do not know, but the mine makes the most logical location for her lair, so I suggest we get to hot-footing it. We've got a few hours before sunset." The best time to catch a rogue vampire was just after sunset, when it first emerged from its lair. The vamp would still transition from sleep to wakefulness, and they had discovered that was the best time to convince them to come to the reservation. CSC (Center for Specter Control) protocol, based upon the treaty, was to give the vampire the option. No outright killing them while in slumber, hiding away from the deathly rays of sunlight as was done in the vampire hunting days of yore. These rigid rules made the hunt a bit more challenging, if not altogether dangerous, for field agents. It meant approaching a vampire at night when it was out and in its element.

The two exited the car and went back to the trunk. Craig could tell that something other than his choice of music was playing through his friend's mind as Saunders slowly, deliberately, opened the lid. In awkward silence, they mechanically went about the business of "gearing-up" for the coming encounter. Kevlar stab vests were pulled over heads and snugly Velcroed into place. Side-arms were strapped on. Saunders preferred a holster that clipped to his belt, a holdover from his time in the Bureau, while Craig liked a tactical thigh holster that placed the handle of his .357 Magnum within easy reach. Finally, the agents removed two M16s, checked the magazines and slung the weapons over their shoulders where they hung comfortably; hands on grips ready to unload hot silver into any vampire that might be looking for a quick death. But before Saunders could close the lid, Craig turned and sat down on the edge of the open trunk.

"What's up?" Craig asked his friend.

"Up? Nothing." Saunders replied in a tone and with a look that said he got caught. Sylvester the Cat with Tweety Bird in his mouth.

"Come on. Spill it."

Saunders sat down next to Craig, not looking at him but staring out at the stream that was flowing by the parked car. "Okay . . . So . . .."

"So?"

"So . . . in case we come upon this vamp, and it uses its mind control tricks . . . what do you do? I do . . . what do I do to break free from it? I mean, what can I do? Is there anything *to* do?"

"Well, assuming it has no interest in listening to our offer of free room and board on the Rez—"

"Yeah, assuming that."

Craig's chin dropped, mouth opening wide with surprise as he realized what was on his buddy's mind. "Are you telling me that after all these years in the field you never encountered—"

"Yes. I'm telling you that after all this time—"

"Get out!"

"They only assigned me to take on the resisters. The ones who would not cooperate. My experience has only been daytime stuff; taking on the sleepers. You know; bust in, find its box, stake it, decap it, and then burn the fucker."

"Seriously, you never . . .."

"Yeah, luck of the draw, I guess."

Craig stiffened. "Lucky, right." He said incredulously. "Like how I always seem to choose the short matchstick when we got a shit detail to do. Luck of the draw, my ass."

"Hey! I don't cheat."

"In this case, at least, you sure didn't. Since this action is based on your brilliant research . . . you get point."

Saunders' face drained of all color.

"Payback is that bitch you've been avoiding for a very long time my friend," Craig replied unsympathetically.

"So . . . about what I was saying."

"Yeah, so, we've worked this out over the last few years when you've been shirking real duty. You take point, and I'll hold back by about ten yards and not in the vamp's line's sight in case you get 'vampnotized'. Hey! I just invented that."

"Great. Wait! Point man is a decoy."

"Yeah, but by the time the vamp figures out there are two of us—" Craig slapped the handle of his .357. "—bye bye vampire."

"Why doesn't it just 'vampnotize' you too?" Saunders added air quotes sarcastically around Craig's ridiculous new word.

"It's a line-of-sight kind of thing."

"What—"

"Don't worry about it. I got your back."

Saunders looked at his friend. "You know, you can be a pain in the ass."

A Cheshire cat grin was Craig's only reply.

"Okay." Saunders slapped his hands down on both knees and stood. "Thanks for the confidence building conversation. Close the trunk." Then he started walking up the trail.

Craig called out to him, "Aren't you going to wear the collar?" He was referring to the silver chain mail all field teams wore into such situations.

"That stuff itches when I sweat. I think it'll be more of a distraction than a help."

"I don't know about that."

"Go ahead, wear yours. Tell me how it feels in an hour." He turned and continued up the trail.

Craig shrugged and pulled up the collar of tightly interlocked silver rings around his throat, then snapped a full magazine into his rifle and followed, singing, "*Have Gun Will Travel reads the card of a man . . . .*"

Saunders looked back and shook his head. "Christ, why me?" Then he continued up the trail.

Agents Craig Wright and Ben Saunders were best of friends. At one time, they were partnered together as field agents for the CSC but as newer recruits came into the agency, they had to be split up, pairing more experienced hands with the youngsters. They were temporarily together again on this hunt for a "free radical" which wasn't all that far from the western headquarters of the organization created to round up such creatures. Wright came to the agency through the military, having served in Desert Storm. Saunders was straight out of the FBI. An analyst/profiler, he spent his time at the CSC checking out rumors of vampires and werewolves or mutants (the really hard ones to locate) and tracking down any information about their existence before sending out the "troops" to wrangle them in.

This particular bloodsucker they were after had been rumored to exist long before there was a government agency created to keep the world safe from said monsters.

Saunders had studied accounts, dating back to the earliest days of the Idaho gold rush, about supernatural occurrences from this area; centered somewhere along Fisher Creek. There had also been missing people reported, but those were old craggy miners and trappers who hadn't returned from an expedition or lone hikers who were too dumb to have trekked out into the wilderness alone and deserved what they got. Over the years, ranger and state police reports of bodies found, exsanguinated (bodies drained of blood) had piled up but figured it was just the work of scavenger animals tidying up the forest floor. So, there was no further thought about other potential causes of death and blood depletion and no red flags about these missing people, hence, no need for the CSC to pay any attention.

Not, however, until the attack reported a couple of weeks earlier. The usual horror movie scenario: college students went up into the mountains for a high old weekend of booze, pot, and skinny dipping. Out of a party of five, two came back and reported that their friends had been attacked. The rescue teams arriving at the campsite found plenty of gruesome evidence pointing to murder—lots of spilled blood and bodies found in various stages of dismemberment. The two survivors were still being held as suspects. No one believed their wild explanation of a beautiful woman tearing into their friends with fangs and sharp claws.

But the story caught Saunders' eye as he surfed the internet—which he often did when looking for such stories on his favorite conspiracy websites and grocery store tabloids. Backtracking through history, Saunders could connect the obvious dots. A rogue vampire must have been living in the mountains for over one hundred years.

Free radicals, such as this one, had resisted the call from Alexei Rurik—Kahn of all the immortal families—to abide by the treaty he had signed with Theodore Roosevelt (a peace treaty, of sorts, calling for the cessation of all hostilities between vampires and humans.) There were rogues all over the world who had been strong enough to oppose their Khan, and his agreement to be separated from humans in a vampire sanctuary. These rogues had learned to live in the shadows, literally, not drawing attention to themselves. Along with helping manage the reservations, CSC field agents hunted down these isolated vampires, eliminating them as a threat, either by bringing them back to live with the others or killing them.

After about an hour of steady progress up the hill, Saunders called a break. They sat on a fallen tree and drank some water. For a few moments, they just watched the stream burble past them.

Saunders looked at his friend, whose gazing fixated on a moss-covered rock. "You know . . . you can talk to me. Right?"

"About what?"

"Shit, you know man, don't make me say it."

Craig gave Saunders a blank look.

"Okay. It's not your fault that Vlad slipped off the reservation."

"Oh, it's not, huh? Were you there? Did *you* see what that son of a bitch did?"

"No."

"Exactly. Vladimir is no ordinary vampire who'll disappear and be content to hide in a . . . a—" He nodded up the hill, "—a fucking mine shaft or a ramshackle house. No. He hates us. I saw the loathing in his eyes as he held me by my throat . . . strangling me." His voice trailed off; then he shook his head. "Too many died that night."

Saunders cleared his throat and softly responded, "I saw the after-action photos. Can't imagine being there having to make the decision you had to make. There was no right action. Either way, people died. It was a Hobson's choice. But the deaths are not on you."

"What about the deaths of those that have occurred since he ran away? The ones he's killing *right now* to satisfy his thirst for blood? Who's to blame for those people's deaths?"

"Listen, buddy, I—"

"No. Talking is over. But thanks." Craig sealed the water bottle and stood. "We still have work to do."

They followed the stream for the rest of the afternoon and reached the mine entrance when dusk arrived. With the protective light of the sun gone, the two agents went into full self-preservation mode, wary of a likely attack from any direction. Saunders led the way with Craig following several paces behind. Teams never traveled too close to one another for fear that both might be surprised and killed before either could react. The moon was rising high in the sky by the time they arrived at the spot where the map showed the mine's location.

Saunders stopped near a large boulder, which blocked further view upstream. He held up his hand for Craig to do the same; then Saunders proceeded cautiously around the obstruction.

Craig must have been ten yards behind, slowly advancing when Saunders abruptly stopped again. This time, he did not hold up a hand to signal his partner to do the same. His friend just stopped, as though something had grabbed hold of him, freezing him in place. The hair on the back of Craig's neck rose as he sensed danger. Trying to get a view of what Saunders might be reacting to, Craig cautiously inched out onto the rocks until he was standing almost midstream and could see around his unmoving friend. And then he heard the voice of a woman singing; her supple voice harmonized with the splashing water of the stream as it wended its way around fallen trees and rocks on its precipitate migration down the mountainside.

Craig focused his eyes beyond his friend's back and saw the source of the music. In the shallows of the stream stood a completely naked Celtic goddess, resplendent in the light of the waxing moon. Her wet, alabaster skin glistened in the moonlight. The beads of water were a sparkling continuation of the stars in the night sky which merged, forming rivulets cascading down her shoulders and dripping off pert breasts which then rained onto the water's surface sending out concentric circles as a visual manifestation of how she was reaching into Saunders' mind. Her hypnotic, onyx eyes; bending his thoughts to her will, controlling him thoroughly.

It was a moment of a young man's fantasy or an old man's heart attack.

Fortunately, Craig hadn't been caught up in her mesmerizing trance as thoroughly as Saunders had, but her siren song was calling out to him now too, filling his ears with her arresting melody. He could feel her voice in his head—through his entire body—calling to him, "Come to me. I want you." But Craig remained unmoving, not sure if he too had fallen under the mental powers of the vampire or if he could not move from sheer fear.

Then Saunders lowered his gun and let it dangle from his hand before releasing it into the stream. He advanced towards the vamp, feigning acceptance of her invitation to join her for an intimate dinner. Craig tried to call out to his friend but found that he had no voice. Then his partner stopped within arm's length of the naked beauty. He reached for her, and she moved closer to him, pushing her breasts up against his chest. Saunders had no chance. He was a lamb led to slaughter. He arched his neck back, offering his exposed throat, as directed. The vamp opened her mouth, and dagger-like canines flashed in the moonlight and drove into his jugular vein. Saunders did not falter or flinch from the pain.

It took Craig a moment to grasp what he was witnessing and only when he looked down into the stream and saw the red of Saunders' blood rush past him did he realize he was watching a vampire killing yet another of his partners.

As she bit into Saunders' exposed throat and started sucking out his blood, she opened her eyes and looked directly into Craig's. Her red hair was aflame as the bright moonlight shone down on it. They had walked into a trap for certain. How long had this vampire lived in these woods? How many settlers, hunters, miners, timbermen had been uncontrollably drawn to such a perfect female form? He may not have been under her total control and could not hear her in his head, but he still understood what she was thinking. "You are next."

As if something had clicked a light switch on, he came back to self-awareness and brought his M16 up to his shoulder. The red laser sight flashed first across Saunders' chest as he walked it up and onto the vampire's forehead. She dropped his nearly lifeless body into the stream. An enraged screech erupted from her throat, and the beauty turned into an attacking beast flying towards Craig. Carefully, he squeezed the trigger once, twice, then a third time. Silver rounds found their target erasing the vampire's face and scrambling her brain.

What followed next was the death dance that all vampires experienced. The damage to her head insured that she was dead. There would be no way she could feel the body's inner juices bubbling up, releasing noxious fumes into the atmosphere through the hole that had been her throat. Nor would she feel her body bloating as gut and extremities expanded outward, threatening to explode like an over-inflated balloon only to implode on itself and collapse into a steaming pile of viscera. The cold water of the stream made the gaseous cloud appear to be a low hanging fog which hovered just above the surface of the fouled water.

His knees became instantly weak, and Craig sat on the closest rock, no longer able to stand. All he could do was watch the remains of the red-headed vampire around his feet as the stream washed them away. He became shocked by a sudden realization. When the vampire made eye contact with him, he felt like he was looking directly into Katherine's eyes, his last partner. This vampiric devil had indeed connected with his mind, maybe not strong enough to hold him physically in place, but so profoundly that she could plumb the depths of his soul. His last memory of that moment was of aiming his gun at her heart. Katherine's lovely face pleading with him to pull the trigger. "Please . . . I love you." She grit her teeth, "*Do it!*"

Then Craig was back staring at Saunders, on a stream bank in Idaho, knowing that he had to do the same again. He unholstered his sidearm, flicked off the safety and chambered a round. He felt himself on the verge of a moral crisis; having to kill yet another friend, another death that was his fault, and knew that this act could send him over the edge.

Craig had to deliberately shut out the memory of Katherine's death—at his own hands—and pull himself out of the spiraling vortex of doubt and the self-blame that he had more than abundantly heaped on his shoulders.

Saunders was too far gone from the vampire's bite to be conscious. Somehow it felt worse without his reassuring eyes confirming the obvious need.

He placed the muzzle of the gun close to his friend's heart and slowly squeezed off a silver round into his chest.

Blam!

Then he placed one more silver round into his skull.

Blam!

A magnet for death, that's what he felt he had become, and he wondered if there wasn't anyone he cared for who would not die in front of him.

He chambered another round and stared at the gun.

Maybe I should just . . ..

Chapter 3

SMORGASBORD

I T WAS COLD and damp. The morning temperature was a slight surprise because of the unseasonably warm spring-like weather the city had been experiencing. The early flowers, crocuses, and daffodils in some areas, fooled by the temperate conditions, had bloomed while their smarter neighbors were still playing it safe and keeping their heads down until a bit later in the season.

The boy, late teens, hard to tell from the hood he had mostly pulled over his head, sat in a recessed doorway, his temporary home for the night. He eyed a man coming in his direction, still a couple of blocks away and he might not even cross the kid's path, but it was game time, and he had to be ready for whoever might see him. The kid pulled a flattened cardboard box from under him, which had been insulation from the cold concrete but was now a sign. He turned it so that the letters scrawled in black Sharpie would be visible:

Seeking Human Kindness.

Homelessness is a scourge of twenty-first century America. For whatever reason, there are thousands of people who live on the streets of all cities, large and small. Unlike the thousands on the street because of mental health problems, drug addiction, or being flat-out broke, there is a subset of street kids who have found living in the dark crannies and doorways of the urban environment to be a rite of passage.

They subsist by any means necessary—from theft to pushing drugs, to selling themselves for sex. But panhandling is their number one gambit for filling their pockets with money. They position themselves in areas where a sympathetic person might see dirty, pathetic urchins as projections of their own children—God forbid. The marks were usually good for a buck or two. And then it was to the local Starbucks that some of these kids flocked; hovering around the entrance like fruit flies flitting around a glass of red wine.

Only the most intrepid of them were ready to ply their trade when the store opened at five a.m., but you had to start early to get enough cash before quitting time to afford a six-pack to help wash the Big Mac down. If lucky, one would sit holding a sign—

ANYTHING HELPS

need a real meal, tired of eating pigeon

out of money—STUCK, need ticket for bus home

—and guilt some cheap ass into contributing five bucks. Occasionally you would score a seven-dollar sandwich from one of the more bleeding-heart types; enabling all the cash accumulated that day to buy some pot and a sixer or two of Total Domination IPA, or any other of the local, higher alcohol beers—just because you lived on the streets it didn't mean you had no appreciation of the finer things in life.

This kid was one of the more industrious types, and if it would not be this guy, then it would be someone else. He heard the coffee shop door across the street close and got himself ready. This time he'd do the 'looking-down-at-the-sidewalk-not-saying-anything' routine. He felt a little added drama would seal the deal, so he reached into his pile and pulled a pathetic, weather-worn bongo drum into his lap and beat on it in his version of tribal expressionism. The kid cast his head down, pretending not to care if anyone saw him until he saw a pair of bright white Nikes in front of him. He looked up. A man held out a banana. *A banana? Shit!* And an overripe one at that. He hated overly ripe bananas. He nodded in fake appreciation, smiling as if the guy had done him a tremendous favor. The man continued to his car carrying a breakfast sandwich and grande mocha. *Fuck you! Cheap bastard.* But the earlier target was still coming in his direction. First, he stashed the banana; it wouldn't help his plight if he looked too prosperous. Then he uncovered a metal crutch, which he propped up against the door behind him—it never hurt to lay it on thick sometimes—and resumed beating on his drum with renewed vigor.

As his prey got nearer, it was apparent this man, too, had no sympathy for someone down on his luck. The guy walked past. But instead of looking away, like so many of the good citizens of Portland, he scrutinized the kid. For a moment the boy thought he recognized something in the man's eyes: desire. A look some of his friends on the street succumbed to; allowing themselves to be used in such a base way, if only for a moment in a warm bed and the semblance of being loved. The extra cash didn't hurt either. But when their eyes connected, the kid knew he was just being judged again. He stared back at the man. A look of contempt spread across the kid's dirty face, and he gave the man what he believed to be his best "fuck you, too" look. Just as the man passed beyond eyesight, the boy decided not to let that S.O.B. get away without some further input. "Thank you, *SIR!*" He spat out in his best sarcastic voice and flipped him the bird as an exclamation point.

Oh well, just another day at the office. He reached into his pocket and pulled out a pack of cigarettes. American Spirits. He lit one and inhaled deeply. If that asshole was any sign, this day was going to be another rough one. Well, at least he had made it through the night again. Not like so many of his mates. In the last year, nights on the streets had become very unsafe. Shelters that would sit half empty were now overflowing. People who refused to use them, except in the worst of conditions, now flocked to find sanctuary from the nighttime streets. Those who couldn't find a spot in the packed shelters crowded the sidewalks outside, trying to find a safe environment in which they could sleep, hoping that just the very act of being a part of a larger group would give them security, safety in numbers, and all that rot.

Inhaling again, the boy looked up into the overcast sky. The clouds were lightning, signaling the beginning of sunrise. He knew during the day he would be free from harm, at least from what was out there lurking in the night. Finding a place to sleep during the day, however, was more difficult, but he might get lucky and score an open chair in the library reading room. If he had any money, he could catch a few winks at the Starbucks across the street, but he knew the drill. No purchase, no sitting.

———◆———

THE SKY WAS lightning, and the man had to make it inside before the sun was entirely overhead. The overcast and rain helped keep the intensity of the sunlight from doing him too much damage, which was why he felt it safe enough to be out so late, or early as it would appear. He knew that was pushing luck, but he was a risk taker, always had been, even in the condition he was in; loaded after a night of reveling. Besides, along with risks came substantial rewards.

Continuing down the wet sidewalk, he spotted a pair of sneakers jutting from the recessed doorway of a small shop. The closer he got, the better he could see the telltale signs of a street kid: an unkempt pile of food wrappers, a couple of coffee cups, cut-up cardboard boxes laid flat to serve as an insulator from the cold concrete, and of course, a skateboard. The homeless youth was sitting cross-legged, beating on a small drum as though he were trying to conjure up the Street God of Cash. A crude sign pleading for assistance sat propped up against one of a ratty pair of Chuck Taylors that barely hung on dirty feet. He was staring across the street into the Starbucks window, willing someone to take pity on him.

The man grinned to himself. Too bad the kid didn't have the touch. That's what he liked to call it, "the touch," being able to make humans do his bidding through mental powers he had learned to use over many years, a favorable byproduct of his . . . condition.

He was close enough now to see the face of a boy—teenager—hard to tell from the hoody pulled over his head obscuring his face. As he passed the doorway, he and the teen made eye contact. The kid's eyes spoke with contempt at yet another Portland liberal walking by without giving him the courtesy of dropping a few quarters in his cup. The intensity of the boy's countenance made the man think maybe the kid could influence others' minds. But instead of bending them to take pity on his plight, he capably elicited a feeling of contempt toward the possible "Good

Samaritan." This visible attitude created in the Samaritan's mind a distaste for this street person and all the others who acted as though they deserved a handout, and screw anyone who passed by without dropping off a few shekels. Which was exactly the opposite outcome the kid had in mind.

Their eyes followed one another as the man passed the dry haven the youth had staked out. The boy's eyes flared with hostility. The man's eyes showed no acknowledgment of the kid's situation. He displayed no sign of moral judgment, but there was an assessment made; more like an appraisal as he passed, leaving no money.

"Thank you, sir!" the boy said, voice dripping with sarcasm.

The man continued past the kid, hands in his pocket and collar up. He came to the end of the block, stopped, and checked his pocket watch—an old timepiece from an earlier life and a younger, simpler Portland—time for the sun to rise. He'd had a successful night of it, and he really should get inside, but sometimes even after a filling evening he still was not sated. Looking around, he saw no one else around. It was still a bit early for the dog walkers or joggers. The Starbucks across the street was empty except for the two baristas and the old couple sitting with their backs to the window. Well, why call it quits when a nightcap was in order?

He reached into his pocket and pulled out a crumpled ten-dollar bill. The man never carried change; even today, the possibility of a real silver coin finding its way into his pocket and onto his hand was a pain he could do without. It was a bit like Superman carrying around a piece of kryptonite. He walked back toward where the street kid was smoking a cigarette. A disgusting habit. Well, at least he won't die from cancer.

When the man stepped back in front of the boy, he could see the kid had been fuming over being ignored. But, when he spied the greenback in the man's outstretched hand, the scowl vanished, and a slight smile made its way across his face, which grew broader in a metaphor for the sun rising and the dawn of a better day. The boy rose to his feet to accept the tenner and make his way across the street for some breakfast and shut-eye. But the man grabbed him by the shoulder and pushed him back into the shadow of the protective alcove.

"Hey! Get your fucking hands—" The boy's voice trailed off.

"*This will be so much easier on both of us if you relax,*" the man's voice echoed through the boy's head. But he no longer could respond or move.

The man reached for the zipper of the boy's hoody and pulled it down. A bandanna was wrapped around his neck, which the man discarded, revealing a dirty, yet invitingly youthful throat. The man so wanted to stroke the boy's exposed neck, to savor the moment, but he had a bit of a rush on, what with the sun rising. This was where the risk lies. Potential death by sunlight or discovery as he sucked the life out of the kid. Still, foreplay was for darker, more secure dining locations. The Adam's apple of the boy slid up and down as he tried to swallow away his fear. The man leaned over and opened his mouth, allowing the razor-sharp incisors to jet out and puncture the young skin.

Headlights from a car arced across the store entrance as it turned a corner. The man was cutting things close. He would not be able to drain the boy. Too bad. He found the street kid's blood had a certain flavor that appealed to him. He could always stop and bring the boy back with him—but no. The sun was dangerously close to causing his skin to burn, and the boy would hinder his speed returning to shelter. Besides, there were plenty more like him to be easily plucked from the streets. No, he could only drink enough to kill the boy and little else. He took one last swallow and then let the lad slump back to the cold cement, the ten-dollar bill still clutched in his right hand.

"Keep it," the man said to the boy. "You earned it."

The man pulled up the collar of his jacket and put on a stocking cap covering his hair. *Portland! I love this town. A meal on every corner, just like in the old days.* He picked up his pace with the brightening sky. He had over-celebrated the master's return. The overcast was unquestionably a lifesaver because this time he had absolutely pushed the boundaries of how long an immortal could be out after sunrise, which usually wasn't awfully long, but unquestionably not this long. The weather was why he loved the Pacific Northwest—such gloom for so much of the year—though that had been changing. He didn't understand the global warming argument. Of course, the climate was different now. Just ask someone who had been living in the region for nearly 150 years. They'd tell you.

The climate wasn't all that had altered over the years, either. Portland just was not the same wild west town that it had been when he first had strolled the streets in his hedonistic youth. Exiled by his stiff New England parents to the ends of the earth. They sent him to Portland with nothing more than a monthly stipend and a warning to behave himself. In 1878, Portland had a split personality. There was the north end where the upright, law-abiding lived and the area around the docks where the bars, houses of prostitution, and gambling halls clustered, ready to service the sailors, loggers, and ranchers who were looking to lighten their pockets of hard-earned money.

That was a much different Portland, to be sure. The kind of town where a young man with deep pockets could lose himself. He wasn't ambitious and had no desire to reform, as his father had hoped. The prostitutes and faro games and booze were enough to keep him busy for quite a while. And when all that became too ordinary, the opium dens in Chinatown provided new avenues to explore. That was where his ultimate downfall occurred. Or was it an awakening?

Stumbling out of one of those basement establishments, still in an opiate haze, he got himself turned around and opened a door he thought would lead to the stairs. But he found himself in a sort of hallway that angled into another. Instead of continuing straight, he took a left at the junction and proceeded until he stepped in a muddy puddle of water, where he stopped. He reached out to steady himself and touched a wet, rough-cut stone wall. Realization hit. He must have discovered one of the many tunnels he had heard whispers of—the passages first created for merchants to avoid busy muddy streets when getting their goods from the docks and into basement warehouses. He'd heard other stories of the tunnels as well. Stories of how crimps would use them to haul drugged loggers and farm boys down to awaiting ships.

Other passages were supposed to interconnect with these established tunnels and used for much more nefarious purposes. It was here where he met the Master. He thought his drugged, befuddled mind was still playing tricks when, out of the shadows of an already dark tunnel, black tendrils swirled around him. He felt sticky webbing like spiders' silk touching his skin. The filaments playfully danced around, engulfing him. Then they blended, merging and solidifying. At first, he could not understand what he was seeing. The more he tried to focus on the threads, the harder it was to see anything. When he let his eyes relax, however, he saw the fibrous wisps merge and form into the shape of a man blacker than the darkest shadows.

Then he heard a voice in his head.

"Eugene. Do not be afraid. I want you to join my family."

He surprised himself with his answer. "Yes, my master. I wish to join as well."

But that was long ago. Right now, the sun was dangerously high, and he needed to quit dawdling and get inside. His pace quickened as he turned the corner off of Hawthorne and rushed down the sidewalk towards safety. He paused in front of an old Victorian. The one with the overgrown garden. Eugene lifted the latch on the gate and scurried to the side of the house. He removed a key and opened a door. None too soon too. He had felt the back of his neck heat. The burning smell was unmistakable. The sun had started to do its work of cleansing the earth of his kind.

He closed the door and made sure the shade over the glass panel was firmly pulled shut. Then he turned left and went down into the basement. He enjoyed living in this part of town. First a working-class neighborhood, then one for hippies and drop-outs, now the home for hipsters, millennials, and drunk college kids as well as immigrants from almost every state in the union. He didn't over-abuse the easy access to the low-hanging fruit that was provided to him, that would draw attention. But then again, here they were. And the influx of nameless, homeless people sleeping in the doorways and under the shrubs made it a lot easier not to have to stray too far from home.

This part of Portland had always been good pickings. And he had a great location, far enough away from the stumbling drunks around the BAR-Muda triangle up Hawthorne at 49th, but still close enough to get anywhere in town he wanted to go. And Uber made things so much easier.

Eugene smiled as he lay back in the musty loam that lined his box. Vladimir was back in Portland. The days of isolation from his family were over. He smiled as he contemplated trying out one of those orange public bicycles he had seen. All he needed was the memory of how to ride one and a credit card—and all his were up to date with high limits.

It was a good life.

Chapter 4

THE REPORTER

THE WRITER FROM the *Emerald City Weekly* sat at the motel room desk. On the institutional green painted cinder block walls hung a couple of those ugly prints of landscapes these lower-end hospitality establishments used as decoration. However, since he was mostly self-financing this "expedition" and the fact he wasn't the highest paid reporter in the Northwest or California or Kansas or . . .. The bottom line was he had to watch his finances. He really needed to stop following *that* rabbit down *that* hole. It did nothing but depress him and make him resentful. At least this Executive Inn on NE Sandy appeared to be clean, or so he hoped. The 2.7 rating suggested something else, but the price was acceptable, and it was less than a five-minute drive from downtown. All things considered, what he couldn't see crawling on the ceiling after he turned the lights off was an acceptable risk.

He had been following a string of homicides for the past several weeks since he was first made aware of the two dead students in the university district. Those unfortunate kids, their bodies found with puncture marks in their necks and all blood removed. Soon after, there were more murders. More bodies found with missing blood, minor neck wounds, or throats ripped apart. And sometimes, limbs and heads severed from torsos. Each crime scene further and further south of the original, near the University of Washington. The killer seemed to be on the move—not "hunting" in the same area for a prolonged period—heading some place specific. And the dead left behind in his/her wake fulfilled some driving need. But what was it? He tried to stay away from speculative questions, because he knew dwelling on something that had no answers could only taint his objectivity as he unraveled the facts. But one thing was clear to TC, he was onto something quite horrible, yet exciting, and maybe even worthy of a Pulitzer. Knock on wood.

True Crime was not his specialty. In fact, he had never written about anything other than the mundane human interest stories that his editor kept assigning him. Although a big fan of Ann Rule in his younger days, as a writer, he was swimming in uncharted waters. Her breakout book about Ted Bundy scared the crap out of him when he read it for the first time at the ripe old age of seventeen. After that, he kept giving that nice, all-American-next-door-neighbor guy a wide berth. Otherwise, he knew nothing of the craft of telling the story of death.

Winning a Pulitzer might be dreaming, but even without the biggest prize in journalism, a story such as this could free him from covering all the boring stories his Seattle editor assigned him ever since he got laid off from the daily down here in Portland. They had downsized because of the publisher's never-ending desire to make it the most worthless newspaper in the country. Not merely worthless, but to make it a completely non-print publication, moving it entirely online.

The only reason they weren't successful at totally ending the print version to this point was that their subscription base comprised people over the age of fifty who had established morning routines and desired something to touch as they drank their coffee or sat on the toilet. Crossword puzzles, word jumble, Sudoku, and store coupons were more important than news. And God forbid if your favorite comic got removed!

He knew that eventually printed daily papers would cease to exist. It was only a matter of diminishing returns. As the old subscribers died off, there would no longer be a financial reason to maintain the show of publishing anything remotely recognizable as news other than as a platform for delivering advertising to readers. And it was cheaper to buy stories from a wire service than hire a room full of writers. Then there was the increasing use of AI programs, which would replace humans altogether.

The weekly, independent papers were quickly turning into the only game where journalists could find steady employment. But while he hated writing articles on city council meetings, beer tastings, and transit projects, he kind of liked making regular deposits in his bank account.

But now he had latched onto this story, beginning with the troubling deaths of those two university students late one rainy night. A story growing by the day, or rather, by night—since all the murders happened after sundown—convinced him he had uncovered a larger narrative possibly going back a hundred years.

Initial internet searches had led him to a similar killing spree in New York City in the late 1890s, which was compared to Jack the Ripper's activities in London. The details between the New York murders and those he was writing about were identical: the lack of any identifiable culprit(s), blood eerily removed from the corpses, some of the crime scenes were neat and business-like, while others a bloody mess. The first slayings of the co-eds were of the tidy variety, while others had run the gamut.

Headlines from the New York tabloids of the period were quite sensational but fit with the times. Though the name the press had assigned to the perpetrator surprised him.

The Night Stalker Kills Again!

•

Streets of New York Run Red with Blood!

•

Night Stalker. Will He Ever Be Caught?

•

Is the Night Stalker NY's Ripper?

•

Roosevelt to Form Night Stalker Task Force.

First-of-its-kind Detective Unit.

According to the articles, these murders happened in the dead of night, in alleys, dark doorways, cellars, and abandoned structures—just about anywhere secluded and off the beaten path. Most victims were from the unfortunate classes, the poor, street people, prostitutes, homeless children, and drunks. New York of the day had a never-ending supply of such targets. Oh, to be sure, society's upper crust hadn't been spared. It was the deaths from the privileged classes of Fifth Avenue that started the political fire under Roosevelt that motivated him to put an end to the carnage, or at least look like he was trying.

Another odd correlation research revealed between the two eras was, in the 1800s, there were several disappearances while the murders were happening. Many people went missing, seemingly vanishing off the face of the earth, never to be heard from again—no apparent reasons, no ransom notes, no unidentified bodies in the morgue. And while stories regarding people who had mysteriously disappeared were not as gruesome, and thus did not sell as well as murders, their numbers were significant enough to warrant coverage of their own, though never on the front page. Whatever the reasons, this was a mysterious side note to the main attraction of a Ripper-type psychopath on the loose in the Empire City.

Then, as if there were no more victims to be had, the killing orgy in old New York abruptly ceased a year after it had begun, as did the rash of unexplainable disappearances.

Further research revealed there had been similar murders documented over the succeeding years from across the globe: stories about bodies with blood removed, puncture wounds in necks, ravaged corpses, and strange vanishings. But these notices only reported on the discovery of a single body at a time; days, months, and even years, miles and countries apart and none duplicated the concentration of nightly butchery as during that one twelve-month period in New York City in 1895. Until now.

Since those first two deaths near the University of Washington, TC had followed this story, watching it morph into something more extensive than the homicides of two unfortunate college kids. Within days, several more had died in and around the university. Then the murder party moved south, ever so slowly—into Seattle's neighborhoods and mega-tech campuses; through downtown; into the Stadium

District; continuing south around Boeing Field, and then following I-5 into Tacoma. Tonight, he was sitting in the Executive Inn in Portland, Oregon, putting his notes in order, listening to the police scanner app on his phone, waiting for the next report and further material to support his slowly evolving theory.

He felt he was onto something big. Another "I-5 Killer," Randall Woodfield, or better still, another Ted Bundy. The thought of that guy still sent shivers down his back. Someone like that would get him some attention. But this killer would have to be given another handle. "Night Stalker" had been over-used too recently, with Richard Ramirez being given that title in the 80s; a shameless rip-off of the label attached to the murderer Roosevelt had to deal with. And obviously, The "I-5 Killer" was out too.

This title had to have some marketing punch as well. Maybe, "The Blood Drainer." Not drainer. Drinker? Siphon? Those would get attention, but he wasn't interested in his story sounding like something from the front page of the *Globe* or *Enquirer*. *Blood Drinker Strikes Again!* That could sell papers for sure, but he was following fact, not fancy. Though the missing blood angle was the crux of these deaths and the definite connection to those in old New York. "Blood Thief." Maybe just "Blood Killer." Maybe not. He'd have to think about this a while longer.

One nagging issue kept appearing as he continued to delve into what connected these murders. Motive. Were they cult-related ritualistic killings carried out to satisfy the demands of some worshiped god or demon, or just the manifestation of a bizarre mental condition? But the circumstances of all the deaths connecting across time and wide-ranging locations were too eerily the same to be merely coincidental. If not for the differences of when the murders occurred and where committed, they could have all been carried out by the hand of the same perpetrator.

TC was concluding something else was going on. Something he was finding hard to ignore. Every time he entered queries into Google, Yahoo, Bing, or any of the other lesser search engines, he invariably was presented with results pointing to times earlier than the 1800s. Links to stories from mythology, folklore, and legend offered as fact. These web pages suggested the atrocities he had been writing about for months, and those recorded since the dawn of history had one thing in common but were too fantastic to consider possible.

Vampires.

Chapter 5

ELLIE & PAUL

"HELLO CALLER, THIS is Dr. Gwen. You're on the air. How can I help you?"

"Um, yes, hi Doctor . . . I'm a little nervous."

"That's okay. It's just you and me here. What's your name?"

"Dana."

"Well, Dana, how can I help you?"

"It's my husband. I think he has . . . I think he isn't . . . I don't know how to put it."

"Sometimes just spitting it out is the best way."

"Okay. I don't think he is my husband. I mean, he's not the same man I married. I mean, I . . . I don't even think he *is* a man."

"Well, in this day and age, that wouldn't be all that surprising."

"No! I mean, I don't think he's even human. I think that he's been replaced—"

"Thank you, caller. Okay! I see that it's time for a break. More calls when—"

A buzzer filled the room with its annoying announcement.

Paul reached for the keyboard and turned the volume down on the internet radio feed and then reached under the desk to push the button, opening the electric lock on the door at the back of the room.

Bzzd. Click!

The door unlocked and was forcefully kicked open, banging heavily into the stop secured onto the floor. Ellie Struthers walked in balancing two large cups of coffee in a cardboard tray along with a bag of snacks. "Thanks for the help."

"Not a problem."

"Being sarcastic."

"Me too."

Ellie stepped through the door into Control-West and stopped. Con-West was one of three such control centers located across the country for the CSC to monitor their various reservations, responsible for the area west of the Rockies, at Mountain Home Air Force Base in Idaho.

The room resembled an amphitheater. The back of it was the highest point and was where the entrance was located, where Ellie was standing. From there, the floor stair-stepped down in four levels, with four workstations per level that facing a large monitor mounted onto the wall in the front. Right now, it showed two maps—the one on the right was of the entire United States and on the left, showed a more detailed view of the Western States. Multiple glowing dots representing the CSC's "monster reservations" were visible scattered across both displays. All were emitting steady green lights. Everything looked good.

Aside from Ellie and her workmate, Paul Mathews, the room was empty. They were the newbies with the agency, and so got the "honor" of pulling the worst hours. And with the recent decrease in staffing, they also drew more than their share of shit detail. Which, if one were to ask either of the two, they were assigned far more often than was fair. But no one ever said that military-like organizations were fair, and as far as super-secret government entities went, well, tonight's earth-saving duty was babysitting the control room.

The general illumination was set at a low, comfortable, almost intimate level. The ceiling fluorescents—used by the janitorial staff or on those rare occasions when the director called a pow-wow and wanted to see all facial responses—were turned off. Instead, the perimeter lights were dimmed so the side walls barely glowed, giving the space a warmth that belied the cold, tedious task of watching a dot on a map blink green. The only other illumination was the LED task light on the workstation, where Paul was sitting, creating a bright island in the middle of an ocean of dimness and the runway lighting embedded in the floor on either side of the center aisle which was more a nod to fire codes than room lighting.

Ellie checked the balance of the coffee tray before she proceeded further into the room. "So, what have you been doing while I was away getting coffee?" She asked, dropping the bag of pastries almost on top of his keyboard. She sat down in the chair next to his and removed the lid from her mocha, letting the steam rise into her nose, filling her sinuses with the chocolaty sweet aroma.

Paul nodded up to the big screen while he removed a treat. "I've been watching the wanderings of OR-7. A wolf that had been reintroducing into Oregon. He wandered south and seems like he's somewhere in California."

She sipped and looked up at the half of the screen showing a satellite map. A flashing red arrow icon labeled OR-7 was blinking somewhere near the Oregon/California border.

"That flashing yellow spot is where the state caught an image of OR-7 in the Siskiyou Mountains with a trail camera shortly after the battery in its tracking collar gave out. That blue flashing light is where they believe he is now, nearer to Nevada. And based on the photos, it looks like he has a mate and several offspring."

"Not what I was asking. And unless he's a lycan, not interested." She said as she moused over the internet radio button on his monitor. "I'm talking about this," and with one click the internet radio show was blaring through the room speakers, "—caller, you think that the victims of some recent murders were actually subjects of alien experimentation?"

"How else do you explain the missing blood? Vampires? Now *that's* crazy."

"Oh, look! The board is lighting up. More calls after this break."

Ellie clicked the mouse and the radio muted. She looked at Paul with an accusatory grin.

Paul looked at Ellie. "Hey! Craig had this station set, ready to play. I just thought I would see what he listened to on these long lonely nights in the Command Center." He took a drink of coffee. "And besides, it sounded like something interesting was going on." He grabbed the mouse and clicked the radio app back open.

"—sometimes I honestly don't understand why certain people call this show. Now, if there is anyone out there tonight who is interested in getting some serious help, I'm here for you. Line number one."

"Dr. Gwen."

"Yes?"

"Dr. Gwen—"

"Yes, this is Dr. Gwen, and your name is?"

"Dr. Gwen . . . sorry, this is Keith."

"Michigan State Keith? I told you the next time you and your frat buddies call this show—"

"I'm sorry. Yes it's me, but I have no one else to talk to . . . the cops don't believe—"

"Okay, Keith, everyone deserves a second chance . . . how can I help you?"

"That last caller . . . I think I saw the same thing!"

"Alright. I told you—"

"I was walking home from my bartending shift . . . in the shadows behind a truck . . . I saw two people. It looked like they were hugging, kissing. You know? And then the taller one, a guy, I guess . . . he, likes, starts kissing the other's neck . . . but the other, the uh, woman . . . starts struggling . . . then she goes all limp."

"If you believe you witnessed an assault—"

"I called the cops! I told you. The guy let the woman's body fall to the ground and, sort of, like, disappeared. The police came pretty fast, and I walked up to the car slowly so they wouldn't think I was a threat, but when I took them to the spot . . . the woman's body was *gone*! The cops thought I was crazy."

"I know how they feel."

"I'm being serious with you, doctor. I couldn't sleep. So when it got light, I went back to the spot. I found a silk scarf under the tires . . . there was blood on it!"

"Calm down Keith . . . I believe you. My producer will take your contact info if I put you on hold. I can refer you to someone who can help you in your community. Where do you live?"

"Vancouver. The one in Washington."

"Near Portland. Lovely area, now you stay on the line."

Ellie grabbed the mouse and clicked off the radio feed. For a long moment, she sat in silence.

"You know what that Keith guy was describing? Right?" Paul asked softly, not wanting to disturb whatever it was playing out inside Ellie's head.

"Some sort of vampire encounter," she replied in a trance-like fashion.

"Yeah. Like they were both vampires. The one feeding off the other, kind of like in-flight refueling the air force does. The woman was the tanker and the man—"

"Needed to have his tank topped off," Ellie continued his thought.

"That's weird though. Right? I've read nothing that describes this."

As if a light bulb clicked on in her head seeing all the pieces falling together, Ellie responded. "Unless you need every ounce of blood to strengthen up, but you have to do so without too much human carnage. Otherwise, we might catch wind and find him."

"God . . . What if it's Vlad?" Paul asked.

"We have to tell the commander."

"About what? Aside from a drunk college kid calling a radio shrink, we have no other info to provide. But now we have the haystack we're looking for, so we just dig deeper looking for that needle. Checking the more obscure sources like this radio show talking about gruesome murders would be a start."

Ellie paused and gazed into the cup of coffee. "God . . . I can still see Richard being torn apart whenever I close my eyes. There he is, held up by Vlad, eyes bugging out with surprise just before . . .,"

"Yeah, me too."

The conversation came to an abrupt halt as the two got lost in memories of a shared and horrific experience few would believe or understand, no matter how open-minded.

They both had been on a bus that broke down outside of RES SITE-ALPHA (a.k.a. Vamp Town), one of several secret government reservations overseen by the Center for Spectral Control—CSC—housing the various monsters that plagued the world. Vamp Town was the nickname for

SITE-ALPHA, which was the principal home for most of the world's existing vampires.

Ellie had been in an abusive relationship with her boyfriend, Richard Conroy. "Dick" to Paul and everyone else who had the misfortune of meeting him on that trip (or any time, Paul surmised).

Nine lost passengers stumbled into the oddly perfect, yet empty, small-town U.S.A., smack dab in the middle of the empty high desert of Eastern Oregon, searching for someone to help them, but there was no sign of any life. Only strangely out-of-place vacant buildings. As the sun set, they finally came upon a dive bar called the Bucket of Blood, which turned out to be an appropriate name for a joint in a town populated by vampires. Within minutes, it had become crowded with the locals, who hungrily eyed the passengers.

One by one, they culled away the lost travelers from the "herd" until there remained only four humans in a place full of blood-eaters. Paul, Ellie, her boyfriend Dick and Stephane. Steph was lost the moment Vladimir (a big shot amongst the local blood-sucking set) locked his eyes on her. Then Vlad killed Dick, in a none-too-pretty way, and allowed his followers to gorge on his remains; their first taste of fresh human blood in over one hundred years. Steph became a member of Vlad's vampire family.

The CSC had to send an Action Team and two agents, Liz Adams and Craig Wright, to rescue as many of the humans as they could. Ellie and Paul were the only ones who had avoided a grizzly demise, however. And their reward? Since the knowledge of vampires being real had to be kept in utter secrecy, they had the choice to either spend the rest of their days sequestered away from all humanity or join the very organization that had rescued them. (As long as they could pass the training program.)

That day, one bus driver, seven passengers, and three first responders died. Besides the heavy human toll, Vladimir Rurik fled the reservation along with several of his allies. The CSC had been looking for him ever since.

To fill the uncomfortable silence, Paul clicked the radio back on.

"—and my mother thinks the same way I do."

"That may be the case, John, but if what you just said was true, why are you still living with him?"

"But he doesn't really mean to hurt me. He's just frustrated with his job. He does love me. And I love him."

"There is no good way to say this, John, but you are being abused."

Paul quickly turned off the radio again. *That* was another smooth move on his part. Afraid of what he was going to see, he nevertheless looked at Ellie for her reaction. She had focused on the monitor in front of her, clicking through something on the internet. Face blank. Oh, he knew hiding behind that facade was raw emotion brewing. Not that he blamed her at all and not that he felt especially responsible. But damn it, there were times he could pick at a scab without even knowing it until he reopened the wound and the blood flowed again.

"So, have you noticed anything about Craig lately?" Paul asked, more like another attempt to change the subject.

The dark cloud that had been swirling around Ellie's head appeared to lift a slight amount. "What? You mean how distracted and moody he seems to be? No."

"The scuttle is that one of his brothers died. Maybe that's it. I really don't know him well enough, but I've also heard that before Liz he lost a partner in a hunt. Had to put her down. Then there was Saunders last month . . .." Paul's voice trailed off.

"Yeah, the Saunders thing was bad. They were supposed to be best friends. Been here together since their investiture, I heard. But didn't he die outright? I mean, Agent Wright didn't actually kill him."

"What's that got to do with anything? He still had to de-cap his friend. You think it could be easy?"

"I wonder . . .. " Ellie asked.

"What?"

"Well, it seems like there could be the possibility that at some point we may have to . . . you know . . . put down someone injured by a vamp or lycan down ourselves. I wonder if I could do it."

Paul deliberately looked into her eyes, then glanced away uncomfortably.

"Liz did on her first night on the job coming to save us," Ellie continued, "But he was someone she didn't know. Had just met him on the Osprey flight, in fact."

Then she looked Paul square into his eyes, probing deep as if she could see truth or falsehood. "Could you shoot me?"

"What the hell kinda question is that?"

"Could you? If I got bitten, could . . . you . . . kill . . . me?"

Paul shot up from his seat abruptly and turned away from Ellie. "I'm not answering stupid questions!"

"I think I could do it." She said with conviction. "I think I could shoot you."

"Glad to know," he said like a hurt puppy.

"You'd prefer to be turned into a monster?"

"I didn't say that—"

"Then what are you saying?"

He paused, not answering for a long moment. He opened his mouth to say something, but closed it and sat back down.

"I'm sorry, I didn't quite catch what you just said," Ellie poked at him.

Chapter 6

CRIME SCENE

T HE OLD MAN stood up from the table and offered his wife a hand. As she buttoned up her coat, he drained the last drops of coffee from his cup. Then both left the Starbucks, waving to the morning crew. Outside, they proceeded to the intersection. The man put a protective arm around his wife's shoulders and drew her in closer. This section on Hawthorne in the morning could be treacherous to cross, even when doing so with the lights were in your favor. There were too many people in a rush to get downtown to work, and a twenty-mile speed limit was simply too slow for some, tempting the hares to dodge in and out around perceived tortoises, seeming more like a NASCAR race than a morning commute. He looked twice before setting foot on the pavement, then ushered his wife across and towards home. Their path took them past the storefront where a street kid had staked out his home for the preceding night. They had seen him curled up in a sleeping bag as they walked past him an hour earlier. They stopped. To them, he was still asleep. The woman pulled out a couple of quarters from her coat pocket and gingerly dropped them into his cup, not wanting to make any noise that might wake the now sleeping boy. *Poor thing*. "You know there really ought to be a way to help these homeless people," she said.

"It's getting worse for sure," her husband replied.

The woman then dug her hand into her bag and found a few more coins. She pulled them out and took a step towards the slumped-over boy to reach for his cup one more time. She slipped on something slick that hadn't been there a moment earlier. As she reached out reflexively to her husband for support, the coins fell from her hand, missing the cup, and clattered on to the terracotta tiles of the entryway. Worried that she might wake the boy and then have to engage with him, she quickly stepped back. The woman clutched both her bag and husband tighter, not noticing the dark prints her shoe was leaving as they hastily departed.

Moments later, the headlights of an approaching car washed over the old couple as it pulled up to the curb near them. The car stopped. The passenger door opened, and a young woman leaned over and kissed the driver—her boyfriend—before she jumped out.

"Thanks for the ride. See you tonight?"

"Where else would I be?" He winked.

"Oh, shit. There's that kid again," she said, looking at the boy's dirty Converse sticking out of the doorway. "I told him he was trespassing and the next time . . .." She fished her phone out of her bag and hit the speed dial for the police's non-emergency number. "Hello. I want to report a trespasser. 3642 SE Hawthorne. Knit-Purl Yarns. My name is Lorie Laney. I work here . . . there. Opening shift. Yes. I don't feel safe rousting him. He got a little surly the last time. Yes, I can wait. Thank you." She looked at her boyfriend. "Cops'll be here soon, Don."

"If I had my way, these scumbags wouldn't be allowed to sleep wherever they wanted."

"You can't lock them all up."

"Why not?" His steely smile told her he was serious.

"When you become mayor, you can do just that," she responded jokingly.

"Among other things."

"Speaking of the city, you'd better get going, or you won't be first in line at the permit office. You hate waiting more than you hate the homeless."

He looked at the kid in the alcove, then looked at his girlfriend, then at his watch, and back at his girlfriend. "Okay, but wait in the Starbucks until they arrive."

She gave him a blank stare.

"Please."

"You're sweet," she responded, cracking his stone-face act with a smile. "I'll be okay." She closed the door and crossed the street, heading to the coffee shop, blowing a kiss as she did so.

Don smiled and waved back but stayed in place, waiting for her to enter the store. Only when she turned and shooed him away in an overly dramatic wave did he put the vehicle into gear. He deliberately drove slowly past the street kid and gave him a menacing stare-down in case he was awake. But the kid didn't move. Don then tapped the horn twice, saying goodbye to his girlfriend, and sped away.

Lorie waved again as he drove off, then turned to the counter and ordered her top-of-the-day, caramel mocha Frappuccino. No whip. It was the smallest of gestures to health and the desire to lose a few pounds before their wedding next fall.

"Was that guy across the street there when you opened?" Lorie asked the barista.

"Oh, Blunt? Yeah. He's there a lot."

"Tell me about it."

"That's strange." The barista had crossed to the window for a better look. "He looks passed out now, but when I got here, it seemed like he was awake and getting himself ready for 'business,' just like me." The barista shook her head. "My dad would disown me and let me rot on the street if I ever acted like that."

"Looks to me that has already happened to him."

The loud *BRURP* of a siren told them the police had arrived. Red and blue lights from the tops of two squad cars flashed across all the buildings and reflected in the store windows. One cop pulled up in front of the doorway while the other drove up onto the sidewalk a few feet back, then the policemen emerged from their cars and approached the offender.

"I guess they'll be wanting to talk to me. See you later," Lorie said and went outside and across the street to the yarn shop. She had expected to see the two officers rousting the kid to get on his feet, possibly arresting him. That was the deal. Register with the police, and place one of their *No Trespassing* signs in the window, and if someone camps in the doorway on your property, they can get arrested. She didn't want things to go that far, but she was tired of having to get him to leave the door unblocked so she could do her job. Not to mention having to clean up his night's worth of wrappers, half-eaten food, and God knew what else. Just because he saw no value in working didn't mean he should prevent her from doing so.

An officer had stepped away from the storefront and was speaking into the radio mic attached to his shoulder. She couldn't hear what he was saying, but she could see a bit more of the kid slumped in her doorway, and what she saw suggested he may never move on his own again. Overdose, she suspected, though she had never had to clean up needles as a part of his mess. The officer talking on a radio held up his hand to stop her as she got closer to the doorway. He gave her a look that said, "Be with you in a sec." And finished speaking into the radio. "Yeah, doesn't look good. We'll leave it for homicide." Then he turned his attention to Lorie. "Now. You, the one who called?"

"Yes. I'm Lorie Laney. I open the shop on weekdays." She looked around the shoulder of the policeman at the kid. "Is there something wrong with him?"

"Did he confront you in any way? Did he talk to you?"

"No. He was lying there just like he is now." Then she saw the blood oozing out from under the kid's body. "Oh, God! I ... I didn't see any blood before ... Is he dead?" Lorie stared at the body in disbelief.

"Looks that way."

"How?" Lorie's knees seemed like they were about to fold beneath her. She had seen dead bodies before: her grandmother in the open casket, her favorite aunt minutes after she passed in a hospital bed, that guy on the gurney who had gotten hit crossing the street a block away last year. But none of those dead had the graphic imagery of seeping blood.

"That's why we're talking to you. See anyone else around here when you arrived?"

"Um," she tried to remember. She got out of the car, saw the kid, made the call. "Yes, an older couple was walking past here when I got out of the car."

"Might explain the footprints leading away from the body. Just in case can I see the bottoms of your shoes?"

"Sure, I guess." Lorie lifted one foot. The cop directed his flashlight down at it, and then she brought up the other, which he examined as well.

"Clean. Those aren't your feet. Look, I'm going to have to ask you to stick around so you can speak with the detectives when they arrive. You may as well wait over in the coffee shop. You won't be opening the yarn store anytime soon, anyway."

———◦◦◦———

LORIE SIPPED ON the end dribbles of her Frappuccino and stared out the window. She watched the whole thing unfold across the street like it was one of the many crime dramas she liked on TV. It was all so familiar. First, the homicide detectives showed up, followed by the coroner. Someone shot photos of the crime scene. A bunch of other stuff happened—mostly masked by cops standing around, their parked cars, and the growing crowd of rubberneckers—and finally, the boy's body was zipped into a black bag, loaded into a vehicle, and driven away.

She had spoken with a couple of detectives and told them the same thing she said to the first officer, who arrived after her initial call. And now she waited to be released so she could get on with her day.

As she wondered who was going to clean up the blood around the entrance to the shop, a car with an Uber sticker pulled up. A man stepped out with a notepad and started taking pictures with his phone. Then he walked towards the crime scene.

———◆◇◆———

THE REPORTER GOT out of the Uber in front of the Starbucks. Across the street was a small yarn shop. *Knit Purl. Cute*, he thought. Streams of bright yellow crime scene tape cordoned off the area in front of the shop, with the police fully engaged in their investigation. The five-dollar scanner app on his phone had steered him to the right location again. TC thanked the driver and closed the car door. For a minute he stood and watched the activity, then turned and looked around, trying to gain some understanding of the crime scene and its surroundings. He set the camera on his phone to panorama and took a one-eighty degree shot of the area, followed by a quick video of the same scene.

Before crossing the street and asking questions, he paused and watched the action. He especially liked to scope out the bystanders and listen to them chat. Just the looks on their faces told him a lot about what had happened. In this case, a grisly murder, or so he had hoped. Not that he was ghoulish.

But if this turned out to be just another gang death or drug overdose, then he may have finally lost the trail of his big story. But, based on the talk from the gathered onlookers and what they were saying,

"Lots of blood."

"Neck wound."

"Horrible."

TC felt confident he was on the right path, so he walked over to the nearest cop who wasn't doing anything in particular. He had found asking the guys who were there as backup a question or two got better results. Now all he had to do was ask a few of the right questions.

Tapping on the recorder app for his phone, he stepped up to the officer he had targeted and held it up to his mouth, "TC Penner, Emerald City Weekly," he said, identifying himself.

The officer raised his eyebrow in acknowledgment that TC was talking to him, but said nothing.

"So, what happened here?"

"Street kid. Dead."

"Dead? No cause?"

"Well, a bit too early for that. But when I got here, there was blood pooling around his head."

"See any strange wounds?"

The cop thought for a moment. "I guess it was strange. Didn't hit me till you asked, but yeah. I'd say his neck had been bitten open if that didn't sound so F-ing crazy."

TC tried to see the dead body beyond the cop's shoulder. His eyes flashed wide as he caught a glimpse of the stiff's neck in the beam of a flashlight as they were zipping his remains into the black bag. Calling what he saw a bite wound was a bit of a sanitized term. What remained of this poor kid was ghastly—throat torn open, chunk of neck hanging by a flap of skin, and a mess of blood.

After viewing so many gruesome crime scenes these past few months, TC was almost missing the mind-numbing stories he had sought to be free of when he set out on this adventure. His favorite was neighborhood disputes regarding early morning garbage truck racket and their loud reverse beeping warning signals. Missing pets were also at the top of this list he 'loved' covering unless he got to write another 'expose' on why the monorail was a financial failure. But the keyword to that thought was—*almost*. He wanted to go back to writing those boring stories much less than seeing the aftermath of another messy murder, although the first couple of corpses caused him to deposit his dinner in the nearby shrubbery. Besides, he felt he was onto a story that needed to be told—seeing some nasty stuff along the way was just a part of the process.

"Anyone from around here see anything?" TC asked.

The policeman nodded over to the Starbucks window. "Yeah. I think that woman looking this way was the one who called it in."

"Thanks," TC called over his shoulder as he walked across the street.

He had lost the killer's trail after leaving Centralia, having followed this story from Seattle down to Tacoma, and Olympia with a side trip to Puyallup but mostly following

I-5 heading south. South beyond Centralia, though, there are few communities with significant populations and no reported deaths. If the murderer is still at work, he could have been leaving bodies stacked like cordwood in the forests and fields between there and Portland and no one would have found them right away, if ever.

If his hunch was right, Portland was the next large metropolis along the interstate to draw the killer he sought. TC had spent over a week in Portland without so much as a peep of any murder, and this call he heard on the scanner finally sounded like confirmation of his theory. At least this was the first one that the police had been called about. He had no way of knowing just how many more had occurred that went unreported, but he felt comfortable supposing more than just this one kid had died since his arrival; their bloodless bodies left in the dark corners of the city or the depths of the river.

Stepping inside the coffee shop, TC approached the young woman.

"I'm with the press. You found the kid over there?"

"Yes."

"Can I buy you another coffee?"

"Sure, thanks. Better make it decaf this time. I've already had more than enough stimulation for the morning."

"Anything to eat?"

"Did you see the kid's neck? No thanks. Won't be eating again anytime soon."

Chapter 7

ROAD TO HELL

T HE COOL LOAM he was lying on had done nothing
  to help Alexei sleep. Even secure inside the dark
box that served as his bed, he found his mind wandering,
worrying, rehashing all that had happened over the last few
months, second-guessing every action he had taken while
contemplating his next moves. From an intellectual point of
view, Alexei could understand what was keeping his request
to join the CSC from being approved. After all, how could
they trust a vampire to work with humans while not also
seeing them as a fine-dining experience? But it was urgent
they find Vladimir before he could repopulate the race. With
increased numbers, and him as their leader, he could finally
wreak his vengeance. Did the humans not see they were in
peril?

It was a miracle they had not locked him up as they
considered his offer. Instead, he was "allowed" to carry on as
mayor of Vamp Town, pending their decision. He just hoped
it wouldn't take too much longer. However, the prospect of
him staying pent up on this reservation was sending him in
the same direction as his brother. And if he, the reasonable
one—the Khan, the leader of all the remaining vampires, the
one who signed the treaty with Theodore Roosevelt placing
his race within this tiny town—was thinking along these

lines, how many of the others who remained with him were thinking the same thing?

Several had already left, in ones and twos, since Vladimir made his escape with a handful of confederates. That intake of fresh blood had empowered him to make the bold move. Breaking the intrinsic system of leadership his race recognized. Since vampires were a pack species, dominance could be challenged, but rarely was. Alexei knew he had lost his commanding strength after years of consuming only the packaged blood the government provided. His brother's vitality had surged after feasting on those unfortunate bus passengers. Vladimir's renewed strength undermined Alexei's authority, causing the ingrained fealty which compelled all immortals to respect, to be torn asunder, sending them teetering on the brink of civil war.

If Alexei was going to stand a chance at stopping his brother, he had to consume fresh blood, and not from the occasional animals the government also supplied. He needed human blood, not even the most recently harvested and bagged variety from a blood bank, would suffice. No, Alexei had to draw the fresh, warm elixir from the source himself. But his continued presence on the reservation prevented him from finding this much-needed ingredient. Something drastic was going to have to happen. Something the CSC and humanity would not look upon favorably.

It wasn't the first time, nor would it be the last, that Alexei thought about kismet and how simple actions could lead to world-changing events. Had a bus driver not taken an alternative route? Had the bus traveled five more miles before running out of fuel? Had the lost passengers walked in the opposite direction? If not for ten lost humans stumbling upon a town full of vampires, life would have remained boringly the same. But Alexei knew the bus was just a catalyst that had ignited long steeping unrest into a revolt against the status quo. A sedition lead by his brother.

Alexei found himself caught between doing what would violate his word given to Theodore Roosevelt in 1898—ceasing the killing of humans—and the necessity to hunt so he could regain the strength needed to neutralize, if not destroy, his brother and protect humanity. How could any mortal understand? Even Roosevelt wouldn't comprehend the predicament Alexei found himself in.

He was also concerned his ward, Cindra, was not coping with her transition. The unfortunate girl had been traveling with her parents when their bus broke down outside of Vamp Town. Upon seeing her, two of Vladimir's precious, long-time followers desired her to replace their daughter, whom they lost to cholera in 1851 and mourned long before joining the ranks of the immortals. The two feasted on her parents, Marion and Wilson O'Neil, as she watched. Then they bit into her pristine neck, stealing her innocence, starting the process of turning her into a vampire, making her theirs. It would have fallen to them to escort her through the change had they not been killed by CSC operatives, who had come to rescue her and the others. Instead of putting her down, as humans did after one of theirs became infected, Alexei took it upon himself to be her guide on the path to a life with no end. Such a foolish, noble idea.

To ease her transition from human to vampire, he chose to guide her through the transition process gradually—as the monk had with him and his brother when he had selected them as mere boys. Turning children towards an immortal existence was complicated. As Khan, he discouraged such things.

He could have turned Cindra faster, almost immediately, in fact. But then she would stay as a child in appearance for the remainder of her long life, even as her intellect matured beyond her physical form. The mind of an adult in the body of a child. More than one immortal had been driven mad by this combination. The insane ones proved to be the most devastating to the human population. Even the most aggressive of vampires (and Vladimir fell into this category) found no pleasure in seeing the aftermath of these crazed attacks. They thrived on the terror generated by the act, nourishment an afterthought. For those thus afflicted, feeding became synonymous with mutilation.

You could see the disorientation in her eyes. She constantly asked for her mother and refused to consume the blood from his wrists, which she had to consume to stay alive. As a result, Alexei had taken on the chore of force-feeding her. He would reach into her mind and compel her to open her mouth, directing her to bite into his wrist. But she swallowed little, if any. Most of it would drain out of her mouth and down her chin when he released her mind. Cindra had a strong will. And the process left him frustrated. He often wondered how human parents could manage such willfulness in their children.

Now she was growing weak. At this rate, she would die. It didn't help her fading condition when she had gotten into the stash of human food in the back room of the bar—the Bucket of Blood—food placed there when they built the town, ostensibly, to study radiation contamination from early A-Bomb testing. It made her sick. Most actual human food would make a vampire violently ill, and sometimes consumption could lead to death. An expired can of army rations must have been tempting to a hungry little girl even if no soldier in his right mind would touch the stuff, and that was when it had been first produced for the second world war.

Alexei slid the top of his box (he preferred "box" to casket or coffin—terms invented by hysterical authors trying to scare silly humans), off to one side. It was still too early for him to walk outside. Fingers of the setting sun were still sneaking their way around the edges of the closed door and window coverings, though he was confident that the intensity of the diminished light would have little discernible effect on him. But there was no need to push the issue. So, he made his way down the hall to check on his ward instead.

He brooded again on the events leading to this moment. If only he stayed in town the night the bus passengers arrived instead of going out to watch the stars rise in the evening sky. Circumstances would have been different. But he had become nostalgic in the two hundred some odd years since he had become a creature of the night, and missed the simple things humans took for granted, such as the sun rising in the east.

The early morning light gave a sumptuous, warm softness to the colors. What photographers called the golden hour. The golden hour also could bookend the day as the sun set—a beauty of nature that he could not fully appreciate at either end of the day. Wide-screen HD TVs only could show so much. But filmed images were not the same as experiencing the feel of warmth on the skin and the light glowing even through closed eyelids. Someday, perhaps sooner than later, VR headset technology would give a lifelike feeling to visual simulations. Then who knew? Maybe there will be a chemical breakthrough creating a stronger SPF sunscreen just for vampires. Ha! He could imagine the commercials for that product.

Pausing at Cindra's door, he chuckled again at the thought of the family of vampires with the overprotective mother applying an extra thick coating of the cream on her child before going out to play with friends—with its food. You don't live as a blood-sucking creature without a certain morbid sense of humor.

He turned the handle and entered. Her bed was empty. The room was small, but he searched it anyway. The girl was gone. Now he did indeed need to go into the setting sun. He rushed out of City Hall and down the stairs.

He knew where to begin the search—the Bucket of Blood where the food she craved was. Or at least she held onto a memory of craving human food. What she actually wanted—needed—was the *feeling* of having eaten, but her mind was still equating food with roast beef and peanut butter and apples. Not the earthy, coppery taste of blood. As he rounded the corner heading west, he could feel the sun weakly trying to bake the life out of him, but its intensity was such that it couldn't cause even the slightest of burns. Certainly not deliver the death blow it would have at high noon. Nevertheless, the last rays of the sun could still cause debilitating headaches.

The bar was empty. Not surprising at this time of day. The locals rarely arrived until after sundown. However, since Sean died siding with Vladimir, the place never had the same jois de vevre. No matter his political bent, he was one entertaining fellow. Obviously, someone had cleaned up the mess from the death that occurred here. The CSC must have come in during the day and cleaned the dried viscera of the human, though from the size of the mess it had to have to have taken several days.

He took in a breath; the faint sweetish smell of disinfectant was still obvious to the nose. Closing the door, he stopped. Didn't there use to be a bell? He turned and looked up at the spot at the top of the door where it should have been. The screw holes were there, but the bell was removed. He surmised the cleanup crew did not appreciate the constant ringing as they entered and exited the building. Too bad. He liked the tinkling of "hello" or "goodbye" every time the door opened.

Alexei proceeded directly behind the counter and through the dirty curtains hanging in the doorway separating the bar from the unnecessary kitchen. This room was where he had discovered a violently ill Cindra surrounded by empty cans of food for the first time. Having little personal experience with the after-effects of a vampire eating mortal food, he had to consult with one of his people, a rather prominent doctor in his day, a Russian Jew who had to flee one of the Tzar's pogroms. Alexei had turned the man who the Cossacks certainly would have killed. He practically begged for the chance to become immortal so he could avenge his people. Alexei wasn't sure about the vengeance part, but he recognized a valuable addition to his family.

The doctor knew right away the treatment for the ailing Cindra was to ingest copious amounts of blood to flush her system of the poison she had eaten. The violent nature of her illness was not a pleasant thing to witness. And administering the treatment, a monumental task considering her disdain for blood. Eventually, he nursed her through the worst of it. Since then, she had appeared to be on a more solid path towards an eventual and complete transition, or so he thought.

After such a violent reaction, he hoped Cindra had learned a valuable lesson and shaken the craving for human food, even the horrid stuff, in those surplus military cans. Maybe she had even turned the corner in accepting her new situation. Entering the kitchen, he saw what he had feared. *Why didn't I remove all this temptation? Or at the very least, the opener?*

Slumped on the floor in a corner was Cindra not moving. Eyes shut tight. Open cans around her on the floor. In one hand, she held one labeled—pound cake. There was a piece in her other hand with a bite taken from it. She didn't even look up apologetically, as a child would when caught red-handed disobeying. She no longer was the little girl he knew. Her body was bloated, skin stretched tight and red from the strain of trying to burst.

Instead of imploding as a fully realized vampire would at death, her body had expanded, then slowly discharged smoldering gelatinous fluid out of mouth and nose. At this rate, her remains would boil and seep out well into the night.

The girl was dead. He had failed to help her.

If vampires could cry, he would be on his knees in anguish. Instead, he merely watched her organs dissolve and burble out of the husk of a useless body and onto the floor.

Chapter 8

NO PLACE LIKE HOME

T HE SMALL HOUSE wasn't in shambles, but there were years of use written across its surface. The once bright-white trim was now a dirty gray. The siding had not received a fresh coat of paint in a long time. Only spots on the clapboard that had bubbled, threatening to expose raw wood, had received attention with liberal amounts of new paint being slathered over them, connecting successive layers of latex to one another in a never-ending stop-gap to maintain the plastic skin keeping the elements out of the interior. And there were many such spots. The resulting patchwork quilt effect gave the tired house the appearance of an old pieced together circus tent. The latest patches were a darker hue than earlier ones as ultraviolet light from the sun-bleached them all towards a shade closer to a light pink rather than the original rose color first selected in the sixties.

At first glance, the roof looked intact, but the undulating waves of the composite shingles suggested that there was at least one too many overlays. This last one showed its age; edges curling and moss growing between the seams. Hopefully, the rafters could handle another layer, but safety probably demanded a complete tear-off.

The same held true with the garden. The lawn had long ago lost its battle with the moss, which always trespassed in the grass and beds in this part of the country. But at least you didn't have to mow the moss and when all the other yards turned yellow and brown in the summer due to lack of watering, the moss still maintained a green hue with no further work.

The plants were well-established. One Doug fir towered over the yard, rising out of the ground at almost thirty feet. Several large rhododendrons and azaleas lined both sides of the property and partially obscured the two windows in front of the house on either side of the door. The azaleas were in their earliest stages of bloom, revealing hints of the colors they would display. The rhoddies were holding back, though, not quite ready to blossom, but when they did, the tropical looking flowers would turn this modest home into a visual Garden of Eden, distracting the eye from any of the flaws otherwise present.

Craig Wright placed both of his hands on the steering wheel and took in a slow, deep, calming breath. He closed his eyes and pictured the yard full of kids' toys: bikes, Tonka Trucks, bats, and balls. He remembered how his dad didn't take down the Christmas lights until about this same time of year. "I think they're pretty," he'd always say as an excuse. Translation: he had fun decorating the house, but when the holidays were over, he had no desire to get rained on while removing the over-the-top decorations, which got more elaborate each year trying to outdo himself from the year before. "Besides, who wrote the law saying we shouldn't decorate the house for Valentine's Day? Or Easter? Huh?"

The memories of his dad and this yard were very tangible. His dad was a yard guy, and despite his desire to dodge the chore of taking down the lights, he took great pride in how lush his lawn was. He used to manicure the shrubs with the artistic attention of a Bonsai master; trimming branches and pinching off new shoots to maintain the right shape of the plant, sculpting each one from season to season. He would spend hours clipping the Japanese maple that used to be to the left of where the front walk intersected with the sidewalk.

Craig could see his dad sitting on the garden stool next to the tree, trimming away the lacy leaves and new branches in the spring, opening the red canopy giving it a filigreed lightness. His trick, he said, was not to allow one branch to touch another. And he always would cut off the stubborn shoots poking straight up towards the sunlight or the subversive ones that would U-turn back and under towards the trunk. The result of his endeavors was the envy of the other gardeners in the neighborhood who couldn't grasp his approach or had no desire to take the time away from pursuing other life options.

Starting in late Spring, his dad would drag out the various garden products to spray the foliage with just the right amounts designed to encourage bigger blooms, kill pests, or strengthen root systems. His dad would fill his pump sprayer with this or that chemical and the correct measure of water, pump up the pressure in the container, and go into battle against the evildoers trying to destroy his handiwork. Craig shook his head at the memory of seeing him shirtless, skin glistening in the sun from the sweat of hard work, sprayer hung from his shoulder and ready for an ice-cold Oly. His reward for another hard-fought battle won.

It wasn't until his father's Parkinson's diagnosis that this image of the happy garden warrior, taking on the weeds and the insects with surgical strikes of poisons, like a

general laying out elaborate battle plans, came to him. The
doctor had told them there could be several potential causes
for Parkinson's. This guy believed the number one cause
was environmental. As in exposure to chemicals. Craig's
immediate first thought was of his dad spraying with no
shirt. Or gloves. Or mask. Inhaling the noxious spray as it
misted back onto his exposed chest and arms. And how
the fungicides and herbicides must have mixed with the
sweat on his skin and then rubbed into his pores when he
wiped off the excess moisture with the gasoline rag from the
lawn mower. His dad had turned his own body into a toxic
Superfund site and set up the ticking time bomb that would
lead to the debilitating end Parkinson's would bring.

"What's going on with you Craig?" Liz Adams asked from
the passenger side of the car.

"What?"

"You've been acting weird since Saunders died. And now this
visit to Eugene to see your mother. And you drag me along
with you?"

"You know my brother died."

"Yes, you told me, but how long has it been? And now you
decide to visit her. Did you even tell your mother that you
were coming?" Realization washed over Liz. "Just when was
the last time you saw your mother?"

"Huh?"

"When—"

"I call her every week," Craig said defensively.

"Do you talk with her?"

"Sometimes I call when she's out and miss her, but I leave a message on her machine."

"Well, I guess you *are* a good son," she said, her voice laced with sarcasm.

"Hey, I have another brother, you know," Craig growled at her. "Between my calls and his visits and calls, she gets lots of contact."

Liz turned her body to face Craig. He looked straight out the windshield, not making eye contact with her, his hands still grasping the wheel. She reached over to him and gently placed her hand on top of his. She could feel the tension but wasn't sure what was going on with him. Was the man who could stare down a vampire afraid of his eighty-year-old mother? A slight smile formed on her lips. Maybe there was another reason for his apprehension. She looked at the clock on the dashboard. It was time to break whatever spell he was operating under and get him inside. Otherwise, they'd run out of time and force them to rush to catch their flight.

"Come on, big boy. Let's go. Come on. We came here because of you. Now let's do it." She slipped out of the car without looking back to see if he moved.

Craig blinked a couple of times and turned off the engine and got out of the car, joining Liz on the front walk. He hesitated, holding his hand over the doorbell. Liz shook her head and pushed the button instead of waiting any longer.

His mother greeted them at the door, "Craig! What a nice surprise. And who did you bring to protect yourself from me?"

"I, uh . . .," Craig stammered.

"Hi Mrs. Wright, my name is Liz Adams."

In typical fashion, she greeted Liz like an honored guest and long-lost friend as she ushered them into the living room.

"I'll make some lunch."

"Sorry, Mom, no time to eat. We have to catch a return flight to DC. Can't keep away from the senator too long." He smiled weakly as he forced the lie out of his mouth.

His mother eyed him with suspicion, then glanced at Liz. "You work for the senator too?"

"Senator? Uh, no. I'm with the FBI." She gave a wink to Craig.

"I wish Craig had tried for the FBI. Seems like he's rather old to still be an intern for a senator."

"Mom! Not this again."

"I have a right to express my opinions."

"Yes, you do, Mrs. Wright," Liz said with a grin, having a bit of fun at Craig's expense.

"You can call me Rose," Craig's mother said, giving Liz's hand a gentle squeeze. "So, are you important people able to stay long enough for a cup of tea?"

"That would be delightful, Rose," Liz spit out before Craig could say something stupid.

"Craig, give your mother a hand," Rose said, moving towards the kitchen.

He followed her, looking back at Liz he mouthed something that she thought was "fuck you." She grinned in response.

"The kettle is on the counter."

That meant filling the kettle with water. Which he did, flipping up the faucet handle and watching the cold water enter the darkness of the metal pot. After he set the kettle on the burner of the stove and turned it on, he reached for a towel to dry his hands.

"That one is for dishes," he heard her say. "The hand towel is over there where it usually is."

He turned and rolled his eyes. Even with his back turned toward her, she knew.

"There is a difference, you know. I taught you better."

"Yes, you did." He reached for the red towel hanging on the lower hook.

"Now you have to throw them both in the laundry."

"Of course, I do." He sighed heavily and tossed them into the basket just inside the laundry room door, which dad had converted from a mud porch just off the kitchen.

"What's the special occasion?"

"What do you mean?" he asked.

"For the visit. I haven't seen you for—"

"It's only been six months."

"It's been eight months, three weeks, and two days."

These discussions never ended well for him. He clamped his jaw tight and grabbed the edge of the counter with his hands firmly. Slowly, drawing in a breath to mask his irritation, he responded, "Sorry. Eight months, three weeks, and two days. I call all the time," he added in weak protest.

His mom folded her hands and rested them over the top of her beloved crossword puzzle. Her eyes glazed over, looking straight ahead. "I know you aren't here because of Tim's death." Rose paused, trying to summon words that wouldn't turn Craig into a defensive ten-year-old. But there were things she needed to say, and now was the time. "Something is going on. You have something to say to me, but for some reason, you can't."

Craig turned back to the counter and moved the teacups around on the white surface; the square tiles became a chess board and his mother just opened with a classic master's move, honesty.

"I worry about you," she said in a voice overlaid with sadness.

She kept up the attack by moving her emotional pieces across the board, not allowing him to counter.

"I've never believed that aide for a U.S. senator story. I look for you sometimes on the news standing behind the important people as they make their pronouncements to the cameras. After all this time, I should have seen you at least once. You know, you never have told me the name of your boss."

"His name . . .," Craig only had his mother to tell his cover story to, and he had never thought that she would care enough, so he never came up with a senator's name to hide behind. "His name is . . .,"

She was now dangerously close to capturing his king, and he hadn't even made his first move.

"You know there's nothing to worry about," he said.

"I have had these dreams ever since you joined the army. I see you in danger, and I don't know from what. But my mother's intuition says that the danger isn't coming from the Senate floor."

Craig looked into his mother's eyes, dampness welling up, pleading with him to come clean. But he couldn't. *What am I supposed to say? That I came to see you one last time before I get my ticket punched by a vampire?*

The whistling kettle saved him from further discussion. He poured the boiling water into the teapot and his mom bobbed the tea ball up and down several times, then she hit him with a sneak-attack question, "So is that pretty thing your girlfriend?" She gestured towards the open doorway, looking out from the kitchen towards Liz, who was sitting awkwardly on the sofa. His mother had replaced her dour expression with a mischievous grin.

"Mom, no! We're friends. That's all."

"Well, not many boys bring their female friends home to meet their mothers."

Craig gave a sigh of resignation. "I give. Yes, maybe. We, um, haven't really talked about it. But yeah, I think . . . something is going on. I don't know."

His mother gave him a perceptive smile. "A bit of mystery makes things interesting." She finished pulling the tea ball out of the pot and walked through the door. "Bring the cups with you . . . please."

Liz turned as Craig and his mother returned with tea.

"Mrs. Wright, your collection of watercolors is very interesting."

"Those are my mother's. She started painting when she turned 60. Never took a class. They called her a primitive."

"Well, they are certainly very nice."

"Thank you." She took a sip of tea. "I hope you like chamomile." She smiled and turned to Craig. Now his mother seemed like she was ready to play along with him and his ruse. She sighed dramatically. "It wasn't much of a surprise your brother died when he did. His health wasn't all that great these past several years. Had to have been about his third or fourth heart attack, and I'm sure the MS didn't help matters much," his mother said in a wistful tone.

"Or the smoking," Craig added.

"Or the smoking." Her voice faded out as she got lost in a memory loop." Janice had him cremated. I told her to bring his remains home whenever she feels up to it and we'll have him buried with your father."

Craig shook his head. "We were never close." Taking a deep breath, he stood. "This tea has gone right through me. Be right back." He set the full cup on the side table and headed down the hall.

He had to get out of there. The memories of this place, and his brothers growing up, were giving him vertigo. Rounding the corner, he stopped outside his parents' room. On the wall, he could see the three photos of the boys taken in the late '60s each with their hair neatly combed, posed just so for the perfect vision of innocence and family harmony. The last time he looked at those was when he was helping his father get dressed one morning before he fell and had to go into rehab, then straight into the nursing home. "So, Craig, do you have any kids?"

"No, dad, I'm not married."

"Really? *Our* Craig isn't married either."

"Do you have any brothers or sisters?"

"Yes dad, two brothers, Bill and Tim."

"Really! Our Craig has two brothers named Bill and Tim."

"Dad. There. I'm in that picture there." He had pointed to the one in the middle, buzz cut with enough hair left in front to do a slight flip, kept in place with a dab of Butch Wax. His dad had been an old-school guy who brought his own fashion sensibilities to his boys.

"Thanks for your help. I wish our Craig was as good to me as you are." His dad said.

The comment had cut him deeply. Until that point, he saw the humor in this harmless exchange with his father and his demented mind. And even though he totally understood his dad didn't know what he was saying, it still hurt. A few months later, his father fell while Craig had taken a weekend off to go camping with friends. Caregivers need a break now and then. They took him to emergency, then a temporary stay in the hospital, followed by a required assessment in a rehab center. And then a permanent room in the nursing home. A few months later, he died.

He had helped his dad as well as he could, which helped his mother immensely. No point in dwelling on things that cannot be changed. Craig wiped the wetness from his cheeks and returned to the living room but stopped before he entered, appreciating the portrait of a mother talking to her daughter-in-law. A lovely view of a life that couldn't be.

"I guess we have to go to catch our flight," he announced as he entered the room, looking at his cell phone screen.

Liz looked at the clock on her cell. "There's plenty of—"

"No, you two shouldn't be late," Rose said. "It was a nice visit. Thank you for dropping by." She stood unsteadily.

"Nice to have met you, Mrs. . . . Rose," Liz smiled and warmly hugged her.

His mom returned the embrace. "And you too, Liz."

Craig stepped towards the door and gave his mother a stiff, awkward hug. "Love you, Mom."

"I love you too," she said, wrapping her arms tightly around her son, afraid to let go. Then she asked Liz, "Please make sure the 'senator' isn't too rough on him, will you? Craig is such a sensitive boy. And you be careful around those FBI agents." She winked. "You hear?"

"I'll call you next week, Mom."

She smiled, "You always do. Wait. I have something for you." He watched her go back into the kitchen and then come back out. She was hastily wrapping something in the crossword page of the newspaper and handed it to him. "You might need this. Now go, don't be late for your flight."

A couple more awkward waves and then Craig and Liz were out the door. Liz watched Craig take a quick peek at what his mother had given him. She couldn't see what it was, and Craig just as quickly wrapped the newspaper back around it. When he got into the car, he carelessly tossed it on the console separating their two seats. As they drove away, Liz watched his mother give a hesitant wave, then turn and close the door, not looking back. Switching her gaze to Craig, she saw he had a firm grip on the wheel, knuckles almost white, looking straight ahead. She thought he might be crying. Then she looked down at the console where the package was resting. Peeking out from the edge of the newsprint were the silver beads and crucifix of a rosary.

Chapter 9

NEWBIE

COMMANDER COLE, SAMANTHA, head of the
Center for Specter Control-West straightened her
desktop for the fifth time. Studying her effort, she seemed
satisfied this time; the tape dispenser was neatly in place, the
lampshade tilted just so, stray papers corralled and stacked
in the baskets or filed away, and pens lined up according
to their importance of use. She grabbed her coffee cup and
peered inside before putting it to her lips. Cold, but not
older than this morning, which was better than swallowing
the little islands of mold that sometimes formed when she
wasn't paying attention.

To say she was nervous might be an understatement. No
superior could make her nerves so on edge than the visitor
who was being escorted into the "Asylum" (the nickname
given to the extra secure, secret facility fenced off from
all non-authorized personnel that made up the regular
contingent of Mountain Home Air Force Base.) The phone
on her desk rang, giving her a bit of a start. Picking up the
receiver, she shook her head in a self-scolding motion. *What
is wrong with me?* She asked herself, as if she didn't know.

"Cole," she said bluntly. "Thank you. Please escort him in."

Hanging up, she grabbed the first piece of paper within reach and pretended to read it; showing how swamped with work she was. As the door opened, she noticed the document she had grabbed was the season schedule for the Boise State Broncos. And it was upside down. Too late. There he was, standing at parade rest in front of her. Cole looked up into those twinkling blue eyes. His beaming smile said it all.

Caught! She stopped being the commander of CSC West and was back at her enhanced training all those long years ago, with Master Sergeant Terry chastising her for some minor infraction of military etiquette. She stood and reached her hand across the desk.

"What? So formal? It has been a while, but you don't even have a hug inside you for your favorite drill instructor?" He asked, arms extended out, calling her into his friendly embrace.

Slightly abashed, she brought her hand back down and brushed it along the side of her pants; smoothing the nonexistent wrinkles as though that was her intent all along. Then she walked around the desk and instantly she was twenty years old, and this father figure of a man was warmly smiling; reassuring her all would be good just as soon as she would, "Stop *fucking* around and focus on your training, soldier!" The tenor of his commanding voice still rang through her head anytime she was about to make a bonehead move, and even louder after she made one. Samantha studied his face and saw none of the old, hard-assed drill sergeant she had remembered. Today she was no longer the sniveling newbie needing to be molded. Today, in fact, she outranked him. Even so, old instincts faded slowly.

Terry still held out his arms to her, determined not to lower them until they made contact. He smiled and wiggled the fingers of his open hands, calling her towards him. Then he gave her a wink.

That was all it took, and she stepped into his waiting arms, as a boat entered its slip, and wrapped hers around his back. His thick, muscled biceps immediately enveloped Cole's lighter frame, giving her a firm, reassuring squeeze. The bond was still there. They warmly hugged. Two genuine friends. Opening her eyes, she saw her assistant was still in the room, grinning from ear to ear.

"I'm sure you have somewhere you need to be, Henry."

"No doubt, ma'am, but this is much more entertaining."

"I think the Action Teams are practicing fast roping out of an Osprey in an hour. You've never done that, have you?"

Henry looked at his watch. "Oh, sorry! I didn't notice the time. I've gotta . . . Um . . . Yeah, you know . . . check on the . . ." He said, inching his way out of the door.

"Yes, please see to that."

Henry slunk out of Cole's office and closed the door quietly behind him.

Master Sergeant Terry smiled, "Still a fan of the smurf turf I see, Sam," he said; referring to the "paperwork" she had been pretending to read when he entered the office.

"Tell me, JR, if you think the Ducks will do any better this year?"

"With their new coach, I think it's possible."

Cole shook her head sadly. "You never went there."

"Hey! Have to support my friend from the hood. Mel Renfro lived down the street from us and went to my high school."

Cole rolled her eyes.

"Graduated form Oregon, 1960. College Football Hall of Fame running back? Pro Football Hall fame for the Cowboys? Well, he was a pretty big deal to us, and his brother too."

"We all have to have our heroes." Cole moved back to her chair and sat, indicating that Terry should take a seat as well, but he remained standing. "I was a bit surprised when I read the email informing me of your decision to return to the CSC. You've proved yourself. You could live out retirement as a normal human without all that crap about how the government owns your ass till the end of time."

Terry wandered over to the glass wall of the office overlooking the control room. A lot had changed since he had last been here. The room was the same institutional shade of yuck. The desks and chairs looked similar, but they had upgraded the technology. The CRT monitors on the desks had been replaced with LED flat screens. It reminded him of NASA mission control, though a smaller version. The lack of human activity working in the room surprised him. Back in his day, the place buzzed with activity. Now it looked like the staff was down to a crew of just a couple of techs monitoring the entire western operations. He turned back to Cole, concern on his face.

"And you wondered why I want to come back." He pointed with his thumb over his shoulder back at the control room. "I see you appear to be a few hands short in there. I would think that you would want the extra help. And at no cost to you. I've got a great pension plan. Thanks to our Uncle Sam." He winked. "I'm guessing the same situation holds true for the Action Teams and the field agents too."

Cole looked down at her folded hands resting on the desktop, defeated—unable to even pretend to be happy about anything, including seeing her old friend. "It started with the damned Congress dangling budget issues out in front of the last president to get concessions for the things they wanted. Of course, they knew nothing of the funding for this operation. Hell, none of them even know about us. They buried our funding inside other budgets. Since spending money in those departments seemed to be un-American, well, it didn't take long for some bean-counter to slash a percentage here and another there before it really affected how a secret program operates."

"And I thought the lack of potential recruits for enhanced training over the last couple of years was due to not enough qualified candidates." Terry said.

"Nope, we had to scale back across the board. Reevaluate how we even run the agency."

"Then my being here doesn't surprise you at all."

"It was my idea to reach out to all the retired members of the CSC. Just surprised that the one to bite first was you." Cole said.

"Hook, line, and sinker."

THE ODD THING for Samantha Cole was that she had pursued a military career. Her father Lynn was a Vietnam-era Baby Boomer who turned eighteen in 1968, the year before the first draft started. He was not from a military family, and there had been no tradition of signing up unless in a time of national emergency as his father, her grandfather, had done in World War II. Her dad was a comfortably situated high school student with better-than-average grades, attending a college prep school, which helped one get a better evaluation with college entrance officers. So, off to college and the protection it still afforded from the draft. The halls of the ivory tower offered the appearance of a freer life than the one he had left, so he fell into the routine of living as the others of his age. He protested the war, smoked some pot, wore beads, and grew his hair out longer than his mother's. He also met Cole's mother, Emily. Not being stupid, he also continued to study about as hard as he did in high school, which got him graduated and into the work world. He and Emily got married, settled down, and in 1976, out popped Samantha.

She supposed the idea of military service came through contact with her grandfather. He would never have encouraged or suggested she join the army. The army just was no place for women, certainly not his granddaughter. But over the years, she became fascinated.

Her grandfather was of "The Greatest Generation" (a title coined by Tom Brokaw), a designation he never accepted, much less talked about. Samantha knew her gramps had been in the army and served in a war from the box she found hidden in the attic.

In it was a bunch of black-and-white photos, of smiling men in various types of uniforms. But best were the colorfully embroidered pieces of fabric. Samantha would pull them out and stare at them, touching the edges, tracing the patterns with a finger, and turning them over in her hands. There were three of them: a red square with a blue ball with white letters—*AA*, a blue arch above this with the word—*AIRBORNE* in white thread, a small round blue patch with a white ice cream cone, and one with three stacked arrows. But the things that she like the most were the pins: a tarnished brass upside-down ice cream cone with wings, and the ones that looked like a series of colored stripes that reminded her of Pippi Longstocking's knee-high socks. One time she pinned them on her blouse and looked at her reflection in the old mirror, just as grams called her for lunch. Samantha skipped down the stairs, forgetting the pretty baubles she was wearing. When she sat down at the table, gramps, already two bites into his grilled cheese, was about to pour a spoonful of tomato soup into his smiling mouth when he saw her. His face went dark, and he almost dropped the spoon into the bowl.

"Where'd you get those?" He asked her, knowing the answer.

She touched the pretty pins on her chest. "Um, in the box in the attic."

Gramps then closed his eyes and slowly took in a deep breath.

Her grandmother reached across the table and gently touched the top of his clenched hand.

Without opening his eyes, he said in a quiet, deliberate tone, "That box is private."

"But...,"

"But I never told you that. Never said you couldn't look into it." He sighed and opened his eyes, now shimmering with moisture. "I wish I had never saved that stuff." Then he took an absent-minded bite of his sandwich.

With tears about to cascade down her cheeks, Samantha said, "I'm sorry, Grandpa."

"Nothing to be sorry about," Grams told her. "That box holds a bunch of memories your Grandpa doesn't want to talk about, but he can't—won't—get rid of them, either."

Samantha looked down at the red soup and stirred the spoon around, moving the bobbing oyster crackers like they were bumper cars.

"What you're wearing are battle ribbons. Pretty, huh?" Gramps finally said.

She nodded, not looking up, afraid of the trouble she was in.

"You know what war is?"

Looking up from the colliding crackers, she answered, "Uh-huh. It's when countries are angry and fight each other."

The smile returned to his face, and he chuckled. "Yeah, sort of. But the fight can get pretty big. The war I was in covered the world. It was called World War Two."

"Did you win?"

"Yes. *We* won."

From that point on, her gramps encouraged her to ask him questions about the war. Cole learned her grandfather was a staff sergeant in the Eighty-Second Airborne. The AA patch stood for All-American. He told her about the battles he was in, and what the pretty striped ribbons represented. And the ice cream cones? They weren't ice cream at all. They were parachutes, Gramps and his buddies used when they jumped out of airplanes and into battle.

As she got a little older, the black-and-white photos piqued her curiosity. All were of soldiers taken at different times and locations. Smiling men at camp, out on the town, or in combat gear against burned-out buildings. They were always smiling. Smiling as they leaned against a tank or standing by a jeep. Even smiling as one held a rifle pointing at a body laid out on the ground in front of him. Every so often, she would bring a photo or two down from their crypt in the attic.

"Who's this, Grandpa?" she'd ask. He would take the picture, stare at it, and usually lose himself for a moment. She let him, and never pushed him, knowing that this was hard on him but also wanting to learn more.

"Him? Smitty. Smitty Smith. Don't remember his first name. May have never known it. Always called him Smitty," he paused. "Lost track of him in the Ardennes. Someone said he'd gotten captured and killed in the massacre at Malmedy. All those guys executed by the SS"

And so it continued between her and her grandfather. As she got older, they'd watch war movies together. Not the documentaries. They used actual footage and were too much for him to see. But the Hollywood depictions were usually okay, except every so often something snuck in. Such as the scene in *The Longest Day* of an airborne unit (Eighty-Second) landing right on top of Sainte-Mère-Église. The Germans slaughtered those helpless soldiers. And the depiction, while not super bloody as a film might show today, was still hard on him. By far their favorites were the ones that stepped out of reality—*The Great Escape*,

Kelly's Heroes, *The Dirty Dozen*—but even those touched on subjects that could bring a tear to his eyes.

Samantha Cole's interest in the war and American history continued throughout high school. The stories she learned about the men who served with gramps inspired her to choose the army instead of going straight to college. Her determination to be as good as Gramps and his buddies led to her getting "noticed" and sent to a specialized, enhanced training program where her instructor was one Master Sergeant Terry. Aside from knocking some practical sense into her, it was Terry who observed her intellect and her focus on history. This got her to college paid by the government, and upon graduation, posted to the Center for Specter Control where they assigned her to the Action Team, then she moved into the slot of Field Agent, then into tech, and analysis, and eventually became the commander.

And now that she was one of the buck stoppers, she found herself in charge at the most challenging time in the organization's history. She hoped Vlad's escape—not an escape, literally, since he wasn't a prisoner, though he wasn't necessarily in Vamp Town by his own choice either—was the signal something momentous was about to happen. Another type of world war? For the first time since she had joined the CSC, Cole could see how pathetically inadequate the unit was in being able to contain the immortals for as long as they had without the active help of their Khan, Vlad's brother, Alex. But Vlad's departure showed that his brother's control over the vamps might have ended.

She caught her reflection in a brass wall plaque and wondered who might be looking back at her—one of those smiling men from the black-and-white photos in the attic, her modest grandfather, or the capable Master

Sergeant Terry? She hoped for everyone's sake that it was a combination of them all. Because the coming conflict was going to need leaders like them to stand up to what surely could be called an existential threat to the human race.

Chapter 10

SHIT DUTY

"FIRST, WE'RE ASSIGNED to the night shift in the command center," Ellie complained. "And then we get this detail." She turned around, looking at all the lockers in the room where the Action Team kept its gear. "As if I don't know hazing when I experience it. And believe me, you don't know hazing until the other girls on a cheerleading squad have hazed you."

"Well, at least you got what you asked for," Paul said as he reached deep into the smelly dark recesses of Sergeant St. Jean's locker with a cleaning rag.

Ellie looked up from the large table in the middle of the locker room, where she was cleaning a sword with an oiled cloth. "What the hell does that mean?"

"Ah, you know, when you asked if we would be assigned together."

"Oh! That."

"Yeah, that. But who thought w— would do this grunt work instead of being out in the field going after Vlad? It's been six months since we finished enhanced training. I was a god-damned fucking lieutenant in the god-damned U.S. Army. I got a purple heart in Durkadurkastan, for

Christ's sake, and they got me doing this?" He pulled out an extremely dirty pair of undershorts from the interior of the locker and held it up in disgust with two fingers.

"Well, as you recall, your former rank holds no weight around here. You and I are lowest on the totem pole, and we need to prove ourselves." She turned and replaced the sword on the wall at the end of the table. A handwritten sign above identified it as the—*Wall O' Hurt.*

"This shit reminds me too much of high school." He flung his rag toward a bucket of sudsy water.

"When we first met on the bus, I didn't know you were such a whiner," she said with a grin.

"Sorry, I whine when I'm bored. And this bores the shit out of me."

This section of the CSC they had been "burdened" to clean was the locker room/ready room/equipment room for the Action Teams and agents. Before any of them headed out into the field, they would first gear-up here. Open-faced lockers, familiar to pro athletes, lined both sides of the space. Inside the lockers were all manners of body armor—various modified versions of Kevlar vests, silver chain mail to be worn around necks and wrists, and helmets. Not to mention clean ACUs, belts, pouches, boots, and other necessary items, the use of which depended on the monster du jour.

And as Paul had discovered, there were the occasional dirty undergarments tossed in the deep recesses awaiting discovery and cleaning. He felt especially lucky he had only found dirty underwear in St. Jean's locker. This time. The disgusting possibilities of what else was lurking back inside were endless.

Down the center of the room ran several long tables lined with various types of chairs, stools, and benches. They used these surfaces for everything but never for any one thing. They were workbenches for cleaning weapons and repairing gear, or they became impromptu mess tables for last-minute dinners as a team prepped to fly out. The tables could take on the resemblance of college study hall desks with laptops, stacks of research materials and paperwork scattered about, including letters home and updates to last wills. The flat surfaces even became conference tables for pre-action plans of attack—displaying support materials, such as maps and photos—or post-action reviews of how well things had gone, or how not to fuck things up the same way the next engagement.

When the time between actions was tight, the tables became makeshift bunks. There was even a story of a onetime "thing" happening on one between Ortega and Ellingson. But it was only a rumor, and never spoken of out loud. At least not around Ortega and Ellingson. Rounding out the furnishings was a large flat screen TV on a rolling cart that usually played action movies or sporting events, but often displayed feeds from the control room.

The "Wall O' Hurt" was at the end of the room where Ellie was standing. The wall held a multitude of weapons and the ammo required, ready for quick selection, based on whichever monster needed managing.

The lockers had a small chalkboard placed at the top with handwritten names of the current users. A survey around the room showed erased names on several of these lockers. Con West had the capabilities of fielding three Action Teams with seven members each. There were twenty-one lockers for them as well as six more for the three, two-person teams of field agents. By Paul's count, there were eight empty lockers. Some users had retired out of the organization, though more had died in the line of duty. Four lockers still displayed fallen warrior memorials honoring those who had died most recently.

The oldest of the four had been killed by a lycan escaping from SITE-DELTA. Two others had had their tickets punched in Vamp Town, Susan Todd, and Eugene Evers, trying to rescue a group of ill-fated bus passengers. Ellie and Paul represented the only human survivors of ten who had ventured into the vampire reserve. And the most recent, Ben Saunders, died just a week earlier. Ellie and Paul had been with the CSC long enough to have gotten to know Agent Saunders, and they keenly felt his loss. Fresh flowers continued to be placed in the locker next to Saunders' photograph, presumably by his best friend Agent Craig Wright.

"Who would have thought that less than a year ago we had to fight for our lives in a town full of USDA certified vampires," Ellie said, then paused and became more reflective. "And we were the only ones to survive."

Paul saw Ellie slipping back into that night in Vamp Town, which was never a good thing. They both had the unpleasant experience of watching her boyfriend turning into pulp as several vampires feasted on his bloody remains. As much as Paul hated the guy, he knew that a death sentence was not the appropriate punishment for being a dick.

Trying to distract her from the memory, Paul said, "How about that cheesy film they showed during investiture? I mean, the guy who played Theodore Roosevelt may have been some old-time Hollywood great, but it sure seemed like he dialed in his performance for the government paycheck.

That Teddy Roosevelt grin of his was a bit over the top. Don't you think?"

Eager to be rescued from her dark place, Ellie gladly took the lifeline. "Oh, and the person playing Alex, talk about an over-the-top performance. And they made no attempt at trying to make him look anything like he really does. Heck, he looked more like George Hamilton than Alex."

Paul looked at her sideways, not understanding the reference.

"*Love at First Bite*? George Hamilton plays Dracula in the . . . haven't you watched any of the vampire movies in the library?"

"Yeah, saw it with you, remember?" He gave her a wink and a smile. "I thought he looked more like a young Khan."

Now it was Ellie's turn to give him the questioning eyes.

"You know. 'Khan!'" He yelled out emotionally. "Ricardo Montalban. *Star Trek Wrath of Khan*?"

"Oh, wouldn't that be an irony?" she asked speculatively. "Using an actor, who would later play a character named Khan, to play the role of the Khan of the vampire race. Thinking like that can twist the brain."

"So, where're the Action Teams? All of 'em seem to be off the base today."

"Full moon tonight. They were all sent to DELTA to help contain the lycans."

"That sounds like less fun than . . .," he picked up a dirty sock from the back of St. Jean's locker, "Phew! This one's ripe!" He tossed it into a bag.

"Yeah, but at least it would be doing something important," Ellie said, brushing away a lock of her hair from her eyes.

A phone on the wall rang.

Paul was closest and moved to answer it.

Ring. Ring. Ring.

"Yeah, Yeah. Hold on. I'm almost there." The fourth ring was about to sound when he picked up the receiver.

"Paul's cleaning service. No job too . . . Oh! Commander Cole . . . Yes, Ellie's here too . . . Yes, ma'am. We'll be right over, ma'am." Paul hung up the phone and turned to Ellie, slightly dumbfounded.

"Yes? And?"

"We've gotta go over to the boss's office right now," Paul responded as he removed his cleaning gloves.

"I told you your sense of humor was going to get you in trouble. Now you're taking me down with you. Okay, what did you do this time?"

"Nothing." He said with some indignation in his voice. "She has an assignment for us. A real one. Okay?"

———◦———

COMMANDER COLE SET her pen down on the desktop when she heard muffled voices coming from outside the office door. She stared at the wooden surface as though willing it to open would be enough. Not even vampires could move inanimate objects through mere thought.

The doorknob turned slightly, then stopped, drawing her out of her musings. This time she stared even harder, not believing, but hoping the force of her will could motivate them to barge right in or at least to knock, anything to get beyond this silliness. Maybe the pins would pop up out of the hinges, and the door would miraculously fall to the floor. When she was growing up, she had often practiced mentally willing someone's head to explode. Not the undeserving. Just the girl who took her Barbie. Or the jock in high school who thought he could grab her breast as he had backed her into the open locker. Later on, she had identified at least one drill sergeant who seemed to ask for it, too. She would give the back of her target's head an intense glare, believing that if she hit the correct frequency—or whatever it was—the head would pop outward, spreading its watermelon-like innards around the parade ground.

Knock. Knock. Knock.

Progress! Thank God.

"Enter!" she barked. Best to put a commanding voice in the mix to speed up things.

The doorknob rattled a bit, then turned, and the door swung open. Agents Struthers and Mathews stood on the opposite side. Paul had his hand stretched out gallantly, allowing the lady to go first. Ellie was having none of it. And so they both stood unmoving.

It was an odd thing, she thought, how formal titles terrified some people. She didn't know what to expect from Ellie and Paul, but she wouldn't have put her money on this behavior.

"Oh, for the love of... Move your asses in here. *Now!*"

"Yes, ma'am!" Paul stated as he launched himself into the office ahead of his partner and then came to rest uncomfortably in front of the commander.

Cole felt a certain vibe coming from the agents as they stood in front of her and realized that the foolishness of entering her office was not natural for an experienced military man or the bright young lady. She couldn't tell what it was or why it had manifested itself in such a way, but Mountain Home was a small place and the CSC even smaller. Whatever was going on between these two didn't bother her as long as they performed.

"Alex has asked for a face-to-face. As you know, Craig and Liz are away for the weekend, and you two are the only ones who are available," Cole said.

Ellie and Paul looked at one another in surprise.

"Unless you'd rather continue with the more important duties you have been performing?"

"No, ma'am. I dare not speak for Agent Struthers here, but I had enough of locker room clean up in high school."

"It means going back to the Rez. You two ready? I know you experienced a lot when you were last there. It would be okay if—" Cole asked.

"Yes, commander, I'm ready," Ellie stated firmly.

Cole nodded. "Good. Nothing like climbing back onto the horse that threw you. An osprey is warming up right now. See you tomorrow on your return." She stood up from her chair.

Paul and Ellie snapped a sharp salute.

Cole smiled and held out her hand. "We aren't strictly military around here, remember? We're civilians. Saluting is not required."

Ellie took Cole's outstretched hand and shook it, followed by Paul, and they both turned and left the room.

Chapter 11

ENCORE

G RACEFUL FEMININE FINGERS reached around Vladimir's shoulders, firmly gripping him as he finished. When she was confident he had had his fill, Stephanie stepped around from behind and pulled the body off his lap. She looked to the perimeter of the dark chamber, into the shadows, and nodded. Two figures emerged, grabbed the husk of the girl that lay at Vladimir's feet like an empty dress, and dragged it back to where the others huddled, waiting. It would now be their turn to feed on the "table scraps."

Stephanie turned her attention back to the master. She nuzzled her nose close into Vladimir's neck and licked the blood that had spilled out of his mouth and down his throat. Stephanie worked her mouth around Vladimir's face as a lover would during foreplay, tasting the areas exposed to the air before he allowed her to swirl her tongue around his lips. Then she reached her tongue into his moist mouth; drinking in the last swallow of blood, which he held for her.

The pleasure she felt at this moment reminded her of another life—one filled with sexual gratification as she used one man, then another, and another. But this wasn't sex. Vampires didn't have sex, not in the human understanding of the act. This was far more intimate and passionate. She had never felt so connected as she did when sharing another's life fluid with Vladimir.

——◆——

VLADIMIR SAT ON the ratty old armchair, eyes closed, allowing Stephanie to remove the residue of the sweet girl—sweet, as in taste. He did not know what type of disposition she possessed. It was irrelevant at any rate. But what of all those tattoos and piercings? That was something he was going to have to get used to. It appeared most of the youth in this time found the need to color their skin with both agreeable and horrendous art; poor design made even worse by an unskilled tattooist's hand. The ink may not have been aesthetically pleasing, but it didn't block his access to her jugular, nor had it tainted the blood as it flowed out into his mouth. Some things he could excuse.

At this moment, he felt contentment. A rare occurrence, to be sure. But here he was, safe, surrounded by his clan, fawned over by a beautiful woman. What else should it be called? He was glad his decision to turn Stephanie quickly had been a good one. Instead of making her his familiar, or draining her outright, he had gambled she would be a good fit for his new family. And Stephanie had not proven his instincts wrong. If his judgment had gotten rusty during his years in captivity, then he would have finished her and not had a further thought about it. But she had proven to be loyal and suited to an immortal's life, adapting to every aspect with a wild abandon. Right now, however, she was annoying him, and he brushed her away.

Vladimir opened his eyes and surveyed his new home. It had been many months of feasting since he and his small coterie left Seattle and worked their way south, never staying in one place for too long. His single-minded purpose was to increase his strength for the inescapable confrontation with Alexei. The only way for the outcome to be favorable to him was to consume as much fresh human blood as he could. And to achieve the level of dominance required to best his brother, Vladimir had been gorging on blood to the point he found the red liquid disgusting. Well, unappealing. Almost.

Seattle had been fruitful. There was an overabundance of wealthy, naïve youth with too much mommy and daddy money to make them cautious. All they had to do to entrap these terminally pampered kids, was suggest there might be some new, and possibly barrier-breaking drug on the market, or no-holds-barred/after-hours club, or kinky sex party to attend. And like the Pied Piper of Hamelin, they would lead their willing prey to the nearest dark corner for a good bloodletting.

This country had changed so much since he had last trod its streets. Oh, he was aware of the metamorphosis from the popular media that flowed freely through the reservation. But it was a different matter when confronted with it up close. Did people have so much money they substituted what it could buy for actual child rearing? Was providing your child with the newest car, the best technical gadgets, and the most expensive clothing the way to raise a human? Perhaps a tasty one, but he couldn't drink all humans dry, though the thought was enticing. He felt he must have gotten soft in his old age to be thinking of frivolous novelties, such as how humans raised their offspring. Microsoft and Amazon millionaires, you could take the lot and drain them. Provided that a few of their gullible children remained for snacking on.

If one wasn't too careful—and careful was not quite what they had been—the best way to get caught by vampire hunters was to languish in one place for too long. They had turned Seattle into a killing field, so it was time for Vladimir and his merry band of immortals to pull up stakes and head to the one place he felt he could call home. A place where they could be careful, blend in with the unseemly underworld, and cull the herd with more discretion than they had in Seattle. The smaller cities and towns along the Interstate Five corridor were just convenient rest stops on the way to his favorite hunting grounds, Portland.

Before his brother had forced the families to abide by that one-sided treaty and move into the revolting reservation, Portland was a boisterous, lawless town. 1880s Portland had been rough around the edges but was by far and away the best place he had ever lived, providing a seemingly endless flow of blood—surpassing the likes of more sophisticated cities such as London, Paris, Rome, Moscow, and New York. For that, he happily would give up a few of the more refined things in life.

From the time of its founding, Portland may as well have been the ass-end of nowhere compared with the rest of the cities in America. To get there, one had to have the toughness of a mountain man, or the endurance of an immigrant crossing a continent. Or be willing to sail down one ocean and up almost the entire length of another and then travel up two rivers, seventy miles inland, to reach it.

Because of its isolation, Portland had a reputation as a place to get lost in. To start over. To hide. Or to send your stupid child before he made yet another mistake to sully the family name. The local police were unscrupulous. Gambling and prostitution were unchecked. Mind diverting substances—such as alcohol and opium—were in abundance. And the raucous lumbermen, sailors, ranchers, and farmers with paychecks burning holes in their pockets were easy prey as they headed into the "wrong" part of town in search of some release from the hard circumstances of their lives.

Men seemed to disappear nightly. Whether their knifed bodies had been dumped into the river, or a crimp ensnared them and sold them to a ship's captain needing crew. He may even have sprouted wings and flown away for all anyone knew. Anything seemed possible. Nothing was surprising, and few cared. With the table set in such a manner, whatever Vladimir and his followers did was hidden by a reality that was commonplace. One more dead or missing person was tallied up to life as usual on the streets of Portland, Oregon.

Not that Vladimir didn't feel a little jealous. The crimps, white slavers, cardsharps, and whores received far more credit for all the missing than they deserved. But he was still here while the likes of Bunco Kelly and his crony, Stingaree Poe—such colorful names—had long since rotted away in their graves. Given his immortality, he could overlook this minor slight.

Now, though, he was back in what he liked to call his "hometown." He didn't have any misconceptions this had remained the wild west town he loved. Old he might be, but ill-informed he wasn't. He was aware Portland was going through a growth boom with new people streaming in monthly. Many of the new residents were young and restless souls looking for a place that understood them. They had read Portland opened its arms to those who identified as creative, weird, different, or just unemployed or unemployable. The building boom brought in many itinerant construction workers and illegal aliens looking to fill service jobs. And, as in a lot of cities, there was a sizable and growing homeless population. The circumstances were different, but the net result was the same: there was a significant population of disconnected who wouldn't be missed right away, if at all. A flock of sheep ripe for the slaughter.

This chamber Vladimir had established as his refuge was dank and dark. The porous brick walls did nothing to keep out the moisture that saturated the ground around its location so near the river. And that this chamber was under the streets of the city made it damper than what one might imagine for it being relatively dry at this time of year. It was connected to a network of passageways he had been familiar with the last time he was in residence in this city. Out of sight of what law existed, the tunnels served as convenient locations for anything benefiting from being hidden from the bright light of day.

As the city grew, so too had the web of shafts. By the end of World War II, the rough and tumble world the tunnels had hidden from view disappeared as post-war prosperity arrived and they razed old buildings to make way for highways and parking lots. Knowing the tunnels represented a lurid past the city fathers wanted to sweep under the carpet, the government made it an unwritten policy to erase evidence of its seedier past when opium dens, gambling joints, and speakeasies existed comfortably next to—actually below—churches, schools, and confectionery shops. City managers instructed municipal street crews to fill in any below-grade voids located during maintenance and repairs. As new buildings replaced old, robust concrete foundations blocked off passage connections turning what was once a pedestrian subway, with access to almost any location on the west side of the river, into a maze of dead-end tunnels few people knew how to navigate through.

Historians have had an ongoing debate about the existence of the "Portland Underground." In recent years, it had become a popular marketing ploy, acknowledging a history that had been actively white-washed, and asserting the city's unique place in the world. Come to Portland, home of craft beer, bicycles, donuts, and Shanghai tunnels. The debate usually acknowledged the existence of some tunnels used for commerce. But doubters questioned whether they had ever been turned into a refuge for criminal activities used by crimps, drug dealers, and white slavers. And there were the pure disbelievers who universally disregarded the notion of any tunnels existing below the surface of the city and saw them strictly as the work of myth, legend, and speculative fiction.

Vladimir sat slumped in the ratty Victorian armchair surveying the chamber, the last of his lairs. When Alexei made the ill-fated agreement with Roosevelt and sent out the call to come to him, Vladimir believed he might never again set foot in these subterranean passages. Fearing his brother had signed away too many vampire rights, he went on a week-long bender and drank as much of this town's lifeblood as he could hold. The hangover was epic, surpassing even those of his first year of immortality when he had no reign on his addiction and no gauge to his limits. These tunnels had served him well, providing protection from the killing light of day and allowing him to negotiate the city at will.

The sound of quiet sobbing emanating from the darkest of the shadowed corners of the lair interrupted his musings. Vladimir stood and approached the source. Huddled on the floor was another girl. Her hands were grasping a stocking cap, pulling the knit hat down as far as she could over her head and face, trying vainly to hide. Vladimir bent over and offered her a hand.

"Please, stand, Annie," he said in a voice that seemed to tranquilize the girl.

He gently pulled the frightened girl out of the shadowy perimeter of the chamber and into the warm light of the oil lanterns hanging from the ceiling.

"I am Vladimir. Join me," he said, smiling, ushering her to the armchair. His throne.

Vladimir sat first, then urged her to sit on his lap.

"I do not wish to hurt you," he whispered into her ear as he stroked her neck. "Just relax." He bent towards her exposed throat and opened his mouth.

Chapter 12

TARGET ACQUIRED

"THIS SURE BEATS another wasted night in that sterile control room." Paul threw out to the only person who was sitting near to him.

Ellie kept her eyes glued to the laptop on her knees.

"I said . . .," Paul raised his voice to be heard over the drone of the propellers. "Sure beats control room detail."

Ellie continued to sway in her canvas seat, remaining fixated on the screen in front of her.

A little miffed, Paul tapped her shoulder and spoke again, "*Hey!* I said . . .,"

Ellie finally looked up and saw that Paul's lips were moving. She shook her head and pointed a finger at her headset. "Use the intercom."

For a second, he didn't quite understand, then the finger gesture, and the mouthed words, seemed to register. He toggled the switch on the chord. "Sorry. Never could get used to these things."

"What did you want?"

"I was saying that a flight west is better than wasting time on control room detail. Right?"

Ellie gave him no response, keeping a focus on her laptop.

"Or fishing out rank underwear from a smelly locker." Still, Paul got no sign that he had spoken, so he switched his headset on and off, on and off. "Helloo? I said—"

"Christ! I heard you. You can be so annoying."

"Sorry. You didn't answer me."

Ellie looked up from the monitor and into his petulant face. "I don't know what you do with your spare time, but I try to make myself useful."

"I work on the computer just like you."

"You surf the web."

"Right, just like you," Paul said.

"I'm not looking for nacho recipes."

"It was nacho pie, and you liked it, as I recall. So, what are you looking for?"

"What we talked about?" Ellie shifted the laptop so Paul could see the screen better. "I searched more alternative news outlets for anything that might lead us to where Vlad had gotten to. A handful of vampires would need to feed every so often and they couldn't have done so without *someone* taking notice of the aftermath and reporting."

"Like the Dr. Gwen show."

"Yes, and other media outlets," Ellie answered. "I ran a search for any news reports about strange murders. Stuck them all in here." She started clicking, and opening file folders. "Let's see. Is this it?" She opened one and scrolled through the contents. "Nope. Oh, this one. No . . . Yes! See, all these articles are from the New York Times archive about those Night Stalker Murders when Theodore Roosevelt was police commissioner. You remember, from investiture."

"Yeah, yeah. They ended up being caused by a nest of vampires. The CSC was created on the backs of the detectives Roosevelt put together to hunt them down." Paul sat back with a satisfied smirk on his face. "I paid attention. But you might figure out a better way to name your files, so you don't have to go through this Easter Egg Hunt again."

Ellie playfully stuck her tongue out at him. "I know what I'm doing." She clicked open another file folder. "Here's another one." She moused over one JPEG, clicked, and a scanned image of a newspaper article appeared. Not an old one from the Times, but a contemporary clipping from a Seattle paper, the *Emerald City Weekly*.

UNIVERSITY STUDENTS DEAD

Bloody Crime Scene

and another—

BODY FOUND BEHEADED

Drained of Blood

and another—

HOMELESS MAN DEAD

Blood Removed

There were a series of such articles, all written by the same reporter. The locations of the murders suggested this murder spree seemed to have its start in Seattle with several University of Washington students. The trail of death then moved into downtown and Pioneer Square and the stadium area with Boeing field next and continued into Fife, Tacoma, and Olympia.

The voice of the crew chief came over their headsets, "Vamp Town in five."

Paul looked at him, giving the thumbs up sign.

"Let's show these to Alex. Maybe he can shed more light on where Vlad might be."

———◆◇◆———

THE TWO NEW field agents stepped down off the rear loading ramp of the Osprey and looked east toward the town they had had the misfortune of visiting once not too long ago. They would leave the flight crew to patiently wait for their return and the trip back to Mountain Home. Before they had split up, Ellie and Paul coordinated their watches with the pilot so everyone understood the craft would dust off at sunset, whether they were on board. The pilot gave the pair an icy stare to emphasize neither he nor his crew would remain on the ground of a vampire reservation after dark, no matter what the reason or who it was being left behind. Paul could tell the pilot would leave even if ordered to remain. But knowing the town's inhabitants, who wouldn't?

"Copy?" the pilot asked earnestly.

"Oh, yeah. We sure as shit copy!" Paul gave Ellie a slap on the shoulder. "Don't we partner?"

"Fo shizzle!" Ellie gave Paul an exploding fist bump, checked her watch one more time, and headed toward the town. "Come on! We're burnin' daylight." She called back as she quickly headed towards the city limits, leaving Paul behind.

When he caught up to her, he asked, "The fuck's a fo shizzle?"

"Don't like Snoop Dog? Means 'for sure.' As in 'I'm for sure as shit, *not* staying the night here.' The flight crew understood."

They continued a few more yards and came to the edge of a street. The last time they had approached this same pavement encircling the four-square blocks making up Vamp Town, they were passengers of a lost, out-of-gas bus looking for help. Back then, this was just an answer to their collective prayers. Now, they knew what lay within those buildings behind the covered windows. They felt reasonably optimistic the blood-sucking inhabitants would treat them differently than the last time. After all, it was broad daylight. And, more important, Alex, their leader, had sent his reassurances they would be safe. Not that they were concerned, but not that they weren't either. They both checked the time again. Sunset was at 7:42 p.m., and they wanted to be halfway back to the base by then.

"I wonder if the rattlesnakes ever get this close to town?" Paul asked, grinning.

Ellie's response was to stop in her tracks. "Rattlesnakes! Where?" She cautiously looked around until she saw the look on Paul's face. "Asshole." Then she punched him in the arm and crossed the blacktop, entering the town.

"Ow!"

The building Alex had directed them to for this meeting was one they were familiar with and had been inside during their previous visit. The sign on the exterior said this was the city hall/police station they had excitedly entered, hoping the local authorities could assist them. Ha! The joke was on them. Instead of walking into a functioning police station circa 2016, expecting to find at least a couple of small-town cops, they had entered a simulation of the interior of a police station straight out of the 1960s.

The room had desks and chairs, paperwork, desk lamps, wanted posters, and even telephones. The presidential portrait of JFK was a nice touch. But when they looked at the paperwork, the pages were empty. The files were full of blank paper. The phones had no dial tone. The utterly unsettling aspect of the room was its lack of humanity. There were no personal items on the desks, no family photos or kids' artwork, no sports team swag, no "World's Greatest Dad" cups with dried coffee stains, not even pencils with teeth marks. It was a lifeless showpiece—like a museum diorama or a film set.

Ellie and Paul stopped inside the building entrance and looked at the door to the police station and then at the one for the City Hall across the foyer. Paul couldn't remember seeing this the last time they were here. Obviously, like a flock of lost sheep, their first course of action was to go to the police. But finding none, their next thought was to head back outside and scour the area looking for anyone who could help. They ignored the entrance to the city hall in the mad dash to get out onto the street. Today they knew there was nothing behind "door number one" and Alex had summoned them to this building to meet. So "door number two" had to be it.

Paul reached for the handle and turned it, popping the door open. "After you," he gallantly said, sweeping his arm in a grand gesture as he bowed to Ellie.

"Chicken?" she fired back as she entered.

The first thing that wasn't hard to notice was the lush, dark fabric drape covering the opening from the inside. Once through the doors and beyond the curtains, they found themselves in a disorienting, black void. Instinctively, they both reached out, trying to feel something in their moment of blindness. Then the darkness swept away as another drape in front of them was pulled aside, revealing Alex holding the curtain open for them.

Ellie and Paul slowly stepped into a dimly lighted room. The expressive sounds of a piano and sultry sax greeted them; blending perfectly with deep shadows created by multi-colored lamp shades and directional spots tightly focused on selected works of art.

"Oh! Agents!" Alexei expressed surprise as they entered.

"You remember us, don't you?" Paul stated. "We're from the bus. You saved us."

"Yes, yes."

"I'm Agent Struthers, and this is Agent Mathews," Ellie said.

"Of course, Ellie, I remember you and you as well, Paul. Welcome to my home," Alexei announced graciously.

"You were expecting Liz and Craig. Weren't you? They were away, and Commander Cole thought you wanted to talk immediately."

"She was correct," Alexei said, readjusting himself to changing expectations. "Please, make yourselves comfortable."

"Wow," Paul said as he gawked at their surroundings.

"This is quite the place," Ellie added in agreement.

"You were, perhaps, expecting a vampire's lair with dripping stone walls, flaming torches, and cobwebs?"

"Is that Ellington?" Paul asked, ignoring the remark by focusing on the music playing in the background.

"Thelonious Monk. *Round Midnight.*"

"OOOh, yeah," Paul answered as though he knew, but had momentarily forgotten the name of the musician. But he didn't.

Alexei went over to the stereo and held up the album cover. "*Genius of Modern Music.* 1947. Not that Ellington is anything to sneeze at, but I'm partial to the bebop."

Ignoring the album cover altogether, Paul moved in to check out the sound system and whistled as he touched the tuner. "Marantz 4270 Quad. Nice." Then he looked at the turntable. "Dual 1229. Sweet."

"I have a fondness for quality," Alexei stated. "I see you do as well."

"My dad had a great set-up. Mom never got newer equipment after he died, never needed to. I listened to some great audio growing up."

"There is a certain richness and warmth in the music when listened to through tubes. Not cold and precise, like that digitized noise available on CDs or MP3 files."

The room they were standing in was the complete opposite of the police station next door.

This room, City Hall, was packed with many fascinating objects—not objects, possessions. This was definitely a place where someone lived. The variety of the items showed someone with eclectic tastes who had assembled this collection lived here. And while the room was quite full, the items were not placed haphazardly. Everything looked to be set in a specific location, precisely for an intended purpose.

The general decor included a hodge-podge of various, comfortable-looking furniture types. All classic designs from French Empire to Art Deco to Mid-century Modern. Expensive Tiffany shade lamps, and artfully crafted oriental carpets. Floor-to-ceiling shelves lined the perimeter of the room, filled with volumes of books, both new and old, some appearing ancient. The windows were covered in dual layers of richly brocaded, heavy, dark-colored fabrics, which kept all sunlight from sneaking in from the outside. Impressive pieces of bric-a-brac cluttered tabletops—globes, clocks, semi-precious stones and geodes, pinned butterflies, dried flowers, and pressed leaves.

A small museum's worth of paintings were scattered about the walls, set on easels, and propped up against pedestals, which supported many sculptures, from ancient to abstract. In a corner was a modern desk with a flat screen monitor and a computer tower. In fact, there was so much to see they completely forgot for the moment they had entered a vampire's refuge.

Noting the agent's reactions to his environment, Alexei said a little defensively, "I *have* been living here for quite some time."

"No! Nothing to apologize for," Ellie blurted out. "It's just that—"

"You didn't expect a blood-drinking monster to be interested in the things that make life worth living." He held up his hand to halt Ellie from interrupting. "Because even though you don't want to acknowledge this minor fact, I am *alive*. My people, here, in the confines of this reservation, *live*. Vladimir and his followers are *living*. Vampires, for all the hurt and pain they bring to humans still are *alive*. However, you are partially correct in your misguided perceptions. Sadly, we vampires seem to focus on that which sustains us physically. But humans—humans bring so much more to the world.

"I and others appreciate these gifts, even though we cannot contribute." Alexei rotated around in his comfortably cluttered home; arms outstretched. "These paintings and sculptures, literature, music, films, and objects of science and the natural world I have assembled here are all the result of the creativity and curiosity humans bring to life.

"You are probably not aware of this; how could you be?" He paused, standing in front of a small painting on an easel and admired it for a moment before continuing. "Some of the world's greatest art collections were assembled by vampires. Being a long-lived group, we have accumulated vast amounts of wealth, which has been used to collect and save many valuable treasures. We have donated pieces and some collections to museums all over the world."

"So, how does that happen when all of you are here?" Paul asked, trying to understand.

"Please, you know full well not all the immortals heeded my call to honor the treaty. Some of those 'Free Radicals,' which you call them, were among the most ancient members of the families with the largest fortunes. And while respecting my authority, they remained comfortably ensconced in the safety of anonymity in the outside world, keeping out of the spotlight. Others used 'familiars' to manage their affairs while they remained in residence with me. They saw, unlike me, that the pendulum would swing back one day and vampires might again walk freely out in the world."

"Okay . . .," Paul ignored how some vampires could avoid the treaty's obligations. Instead, he focused on what was around him in this room. ". . . but I'm not sure I understand why you seem to have a soft spot for humans."

"It is sad, Agent Mathews, that you choose to only see us as the enemy."

"You exist by drinking human blood."

"Point taken. But that does not mean we do not value the contributions humanity brings to the world."

Paul didn't like this answer; justifying why vampires are good for human life. He could just as easily argue that Fascists, Nazis, the Khmer Rouge—or any number of strongmen—also sought to control people for the betterment of humanity.

"I know what you are thinking. Yes, Vampirism is a scourge brought upon humanity eons ago. But vampires are not born, we are created. We remember our lives from before. And in a slight gesture to that life not lived, some have taken advantage of our immortality and payback, in small ways, for the lives we must take to sustain our existence." He hung his head for a moment and continued in a more distant tone. "And, yes, others have taken a darker path."

Ellie opened her mouth to interject, "But how about—"

"Please let me finish the lecture. Agents Wright and Adams have heard it, as well as the ones before them. Now, as new members of the CSC, it is your turn."

Paul looked to Ellie and mouthed the words—more shit duty.

"It may sound pedantic, but it beats the alternative." He smiled and winked, showing the slightest tip of a fang protruding below his upper lip.

"Take all the time you need," Paul quickly replied with a nervous grin.

"Thank you," Alexei said, hoping they understood his joke. "Not even we know the origins. Perhaps we have always been competing species since the first tetrapod dragged itself onto land. But answer me this. If vampires had wanted to wipe out humans, don't you think we could have done so centuries ago? And probably should have too. But it is in our self-interest for humans to thrive. Yes, blood is in that mix. But in retrospect, none of these achievements that I can appreciate would exist without human creativity. You see, some of us were painters, composers, and poets before we turned into vampires. But when we became immortal, we lost the creative spark. We can appreciate it intellectually. We can even still practice those varied arts and crafts. But the thing that makes a painting beautiful—worth appreciating—*that* is lost to us for eternity. Without the ability to create, which humanity brings to this world, then there would be no Monk, Beethoven, Leonardo, Balanchine, Shakespeare . . . Slim Whitman," He smiled. "Joking aside. An existence without all this would be like living in a bloodstained slaughterhouse. A slaughterhouse, I am sorry to say, my brother now wishes this world to become."

———◆◇◆———

"WHATCHYA GOT GOING on over here?" Paul asked as he and Ellie walked over to a couple of rolling pinboards and a large layout table. The surfaces were covered in layers of clippings, illustrations, and photos of the sun and the moon, along with technical data and astronomical charts. It looked like a cluttered police detective's office, with all the clues and photos of the victim and suspects splayed out to always be in view. In fact, this was what was missing in the lifeless police station on the other side of this building. Its disorderly existence was startling in this museum.

"A small passion of mine," Alexei said as he joined them. He turned on a light to illuminate the boards. "Over the past several years, I have been yearning to see a sunrise. I mean, not just watch it, but experience the sun as it fully develops out of the east and climbs high into the sky without the fear of immolation. My insufficient substitution is to go out and witness the millions of stars—all suns in their own right—as they appear in the wake of our setting sun. When you and your fellow passengers stumbled into this town, I was watching the moonrise seventy miles east on top of Vinegar Hill. But the sun . . . the sun is the focus of my imagination."

He closed his eyes. "I can still feel its warmth from when I was a child, before . . . well, at any rate, I cannot experience the sun as you can. However, do you see this? This is the path of the next solar eclipse," he said with some excitement and uncovered a map buried on the table. Alexei traced the path of the sun with a finger. "Totality will pass almost directly over the reservation here. It is my chance for two whole minutes to look up and stare directly at my nemesis."

"You sure that's a good idea?" Paul asked with genuine concern.

Alexei walked closer to the collage of photos and pointed to one of them. "This is what the sun looks like in totality when the moon fully covers that big dangerous ball of burning plasma. Only then can I safely stand outside during the day without being wrapped in layers of protection. In fact, at the precise moment of totality, I will be surrounded by a three-hundred-sixty-degree sunset as I look straight into the sun's corona. Well, not without these." He picked up a pair of paper-framed dark glasses. "My eyes are more sensitive than a human's and the chance of blinding is even greater."

He touched one photo depicting a total eclipse, almost lovingly tracing the filigree of tendrils swimming in the cosmos from behind the moon. "I have been alive for so long. It is amazing. I have been nowhere close enough to see this wonderful phenomenon. But then that would have been when I was younger, and my thought processes revolved around staying focused on the future and not dwelling on a past that cannot be reattained." He stared at the photos. "Imagine standing outside during the day . . .."

Ellie cleared her throat, not wanting to interrupt. "I'm sorry, sir, but I'm pretty certain that this is not why you called us here."

Alexei snapped out of his fixated trance and came back into the moment. "Of course, you are correct." He stepped over to a chair and picked up a ragged stuffed duck. "I asked Craig, Agent Wright, to get this for me to give to Cindra. She was having such a difficult time adjusting, so I thought maybe this toy would help her." He turned the yellow bird wearing a short green shirt over in his hands, then let a wistful smile cross his face. "He chose this duck. Said it would bring her luck."

"Oh, how is she doing?" Ellie asked. "Can we see her?"

Alexei didn't answer. He looked everywhere except at the two agents before he slowly spoke in a low tone, "I am sorry to say she . . . died. The transition was too much for her. Humanity had a powerful grip on that child. I found her dead in the back room of the bar. She was sitting on the floor with several open food cans around her. A piece of pound cake still in her hands." He grinned weakly. "A sweet tooth." Alexei caressed the duck lovingly, imagining Cindra being there with them, and handed it to Ellie. "Please give this back to Craig and let him know. She always had it with her. I found it on the shelf with the canned food."

Ellie took the plush toy in hand solemnly.

"But Cindra's death isn't the only reason you asked for face-to-face. Tragic as it is, you could have sent that message by email or on the phone," Paul suggested softly.

Alexei roamed around the room. Wistfully, he touched objects as he passed them, contemplating; clearly wanting to say something more, but hesitating. He continued to wander as though he was taking a mental snapshot of all this he had accumulated. He paused in front of a painting of a meadow in the late afternoon, pulled a book off a shelf, fingered the hand-tooled leather cover, and stopped at a globe of the earth. He slowly spun around by walking his fingers over the surface. The table lamp next to him cast light up onto his face, illuminating it with a warmth that belied his pale white skin.

"Do you know of my request to join the CSC as a part of the effort to locate my brother?" He asked hesitantly.

"They haven't mentioned it since the time you appeared in the CSC compound and asked Craig in front of the two of us," Ellie said. She looked at Paul for any different information he might have heard.

Paul shook his head, "no."

"I was hoping for a new partnership with humans in the spirit of the treaty I signed with Theodore . . . I am not surprised, but I can wait no longer. My brother is a danger to us all. I know where Vladimir is, and I plan on stopping him."

Ellie leaned in closer to Alex. "He wouldn't be in Portland, would he?"

"What makes you say that?" he asked, surprised.

Ellie smiled, "Lucky guess."

"Please inform Commander Cole that change coming. The status quo is over."

Chapter 13

FACING FACTS

COMMANDER COLE SIGHED heavily. There was no point in waiting any longer. She had let a few months go by, hoping they could find Vlad and put back into his bottle, or staked through his putrid heart in his coffin, or wherever the hell he slept during the day. But if an organization operated on hopes and prayers, not much would get accomplished, whether you believed in a higher power—higher than the country you swore an oath to serve, defend and protect—or not. However, an organization also needed funding to maintain its mission. And the organization she worked for was in danger of having its budget cut. With limited funding, it would be all but impossible to protect the population from the spread of Vladimir's plague. It would be akin to turning the power off to the refrigeration units in the CDC and watching all the killer bugs let loose into the world.

Since its founding, the Center for Spectral Control had done a reasonably good job of keeping the blood-eaters apart from the suppliers. They had successfully relegated the principal offenders to the fictional worlds of folklore, urban legends, and pop culture amusements made famous by the likes of Anne Rice, Universal Studios, and the *X Files*.

But it took money to maintain the status quo. And while it was good the general population could live with the fantasy version of vampires, werewolves, and mutants, the number of people who knew the actual story, and kept funding flowing, were becoming fewer. It was foreseeable that at some point, those with the institutional memory of the horrors hidden away across the country could disappear from government service. No more funding meant the fantasy monsters that had been a construct of the entertainment industry could return as an all-too-deadly reality.

During her stint as a field agent, Cole hadn't noticed the shrinking budgets. Frankly, the cuts were microscopic back then. Who cared if the office furniture was a hodgepodge from different eras? Heavy metal desks from the forties, old oak behemoths from the thirties, or those nineteen-sixties avocado Mid-century-modern numbers all blended comfortably together and seemed to make the place homey and not as institutional as one would expect a secret government organization to be. Her boss, Commander Wilson, was a skillful juggler of finances; making sure his people never felt the pinch. The latest in technology and weaponry was always available. And in the end, that was what kept people alive, and the monsters safely tucked away from the world.

But when they promoted her to the position of commander, the financial realities hit her smack in the face with gale force winds. The belt-tightening became obvious to all in the organization. But Cole found the managerial skills she had no idea were needed for this job and didn't know she possessed.

Cole became a master at shifting dollars from unimportant things (such as the newest projectors or copy machines), to things her people needed, like the latest body armor and detection gear. The workstations in the control room may have been ten years old, but they connected to a state-of-the-art mainframe that was always kept in top shape. And, in keeping with the tradition of her successors, the office furniture remained the same. Any replacements came from the same government warehouse they stored the Ark of the Covenant, or so it seemed, judging from the layers of dust on everything.

Cole herself sat at the same wooden desk all directors had since the 1940s. Ditto for the facility itself. Nothing had been updated since the early 70s. The color schemes in many of the common areas still had the institutional green many mental health facilities seemed to use, not that there was any connection between the two. She did, however, secure the two Ospreys, which were essential to managing the network of reservations. (A not inexpensive feat from an acquisition or maintenance point of view.) With the longest running wars in U.S. history going on, there was also a great opportunity in snagging equipment listed as "damaged" and out of commission at substantial discounts (aka, free). It helped to know people who knew people. Cole even knew how to get her hands on a couple of tanks too, but as fun as that would be, she acknowledged it would be overkill. With her adroit management, the work of the mission carried on and never took a back seat to anything else. Until now.

Faced with a spending freeze, she could not hire replacements for the devastating loss of several longtime operatives. It was now time to be that stick in the eye to her superiors. A usually bad career move, drawing all kinds of negative attention to the person who complained, getting labeled as "trouble." But her career wasn't what was important at this point. It was beyond time for someone to poke the bear and she decided it was up to her to do so.

Cole pulled out a sheet of paper and stared at its stark white emptiness. She picked up her pen and began writing. She would later digitize and encrypt it, but for now, the old-school-pen-to-page gave what she was about to write more weight, and a slower pace to better consider her word choice.

General Marcus Aurelius Bryant

Director, CSC

Washington D.C.

Sir:

There are several developments regarding CSC West I wish to address in this letter. Not the least of which is our continued budget deficiencies, and my concern about further cuts to funding based upon public statements made by our new President. As frightening as it is to learn that the science of the EPA, NOA, and NASA may be considered questionable, it is hard for me to believe the CSC, which monitors all things about as unscientific as it gets, wouldn't be considered in budget readjustments.

Our agency is essential to national security but is hidden within the Bureau of Land Management and further masked under the Department of Indian Affairs. We are at serious risk. I say this considering how poorly congress has funded that department over the years. It would not surprise me to learn the new administration planned to defund it all together and let Native Americans go it alone.

She paused and reread this last part. Yes, a pen was a good idea. No way would she send this with the opening statement intact.

Before I address the actual accounting details, I would like to give you an overall assessment of how I currently see the agency.

When Theodore Roosevelt established the Center for Specter Control, he was only considering the vampire threat to humanity. While there was some sign he also was aware of the existence of other monsters, he best understood what vampires could do to a city and, by extension, to a country—reference his stint as NYC Police Commissioner.

It didn't take long after the establishment of the CSC for this agency to confront the other "specters" that terrorized the earth. Of the three main varieties of monsters—mutants, werewolves, and vampires—it is with the vampires we have seen the reservation system unable to adequately handle, as they call it, their captivity.

Mutants require constant human monitoring. They must be held in cells that would resemble zoos in the outside world. Werewolves seem to understand the need for their confinement and are grateful to live without the fear of harming innocents. The only time we see activity that needs increased human presence is during full moon cycles when they have no control over their affliction. Otherwise, they can be left in their communities to enjoy a life of leisure. Many of them have found farming, handicrafts, and the arts as fulfilling as a hectic life in modern society.

The vampires, however, are a singular problem. These beings are immortal. The ones who were initially brought onto the reservation had already lived more lifetimes than their mortal guards, protectors, and providers of food (blood supply). While it might have been expedient in 1890 to agree to the treaty to—

Cole paused again and rubbed her tired eyes. She shook her head, realizing what she had written so far was all too well-known by the general. Some serious editing was in store for this before it saw the light of day. Staring at the words, she wondered where this letter was going to end up. What was she writing anyway, a resignation letter? A damaging failure had happened on her watch. The most ruthless vampire, Vladimir Rurik, was loose and threatening to bring the fragile CSC down around them.

A knock on her office door took her out of the letter-writing mode.

"Yes? Come in."

Ellie and Paul entered the room and stood in front of her desk.

"Ma'am, we know where Vlad is."

Cole smiled for the first time in days.

"And Alex has a message for you."

Chapter 14

MANIFESTO

W ITH COFFEE FIRMLY in hand, Ellie idly spun her desk chair; pivoting around and around, kicking her legs up as though she were a little girl again in her grandfather's office. "We told Commander Cole where Vlad was, and she sent us back here to the control room like she's punishing us for something we did wrong." She launched herself into one more rotation in the swivel chair. "All this tension is getting to me."

"You don't look very tense," Paul observed as her face turned away from him.

"This is how I deal with it."

"You could do more internet research. Maybe other news articles could help pinpoint his exact location."

"My mind is just too distracted. Can't focus," Ellie said.

"We only told her this morning. Besides, Craig and Liz won't be back until tomorrow. I don't think Vlad will be in any great hurry to leave Portland, even if he knew we were on to him. That cocky son of a bitch."

Ellie kicked out her legs, causing her chair to spin around one more time.

"Okay, then think of something not work-related and see if that helps."

Ellie stopped her merry-go-round and sat perfectly still. Then a sly smile came across her face. "So, have you given any more thought to where you want to go for dinner on Saturday?"

"No." Paul turned his attention back to the monitor. "It's too far away for me to be thinking about shit like that." He kept his eyes dutifully on the screen, scrolling through images and clicking on files.

Ellie put her coffee cup down with an emphatic clack, "It's Thursday."

A playful smile formed at the corners of his mouth, yet he kept his eyes focused on pretend work. "Anyway, how many good places are there to go in Mountain Home? Applebee's should have plenty of room. No need for reservations if that's what you're getting at."

She rolled up close to Paul and placed her mouth near his right ear. "If you think Applebee's is what you promised to celebrate our anniversary of joining this outfit, then you, sir, were sailing under false colors when you made it!" She then pushed against his desk and shoved herself back over to her workstation.

"By the way, technically, our anniversary isn't until June. So, Applebee's will do perfectly well," Paul said with a devious grin. Then he pulled up an email screen hidden behind some work on his monitor and hit send. Instantly Ellie saw an email had arrived for her and she opened it. She scrolled down and was looking at a mouthwatering picture of a plate of baked cod. Below that was the name—Epi's Basque Restaurant.

Ellie smiled. This place had been all the talk from others in the CSC though it was in Boise, not Mountain Home.

"It'll be a long drive at night after a couple of bottles of wine," she threw out playfully.

"Keep scrolling."

Another picture moved up into view. It was an artist rendering showing the Idaho state capitol building in the upper right and a hotel in the foreground. A red sign stood out against its French-styled roof. It read—*500*. Ellie continued scrolling down the screen, looking at a few pictures of the nicely appointed interior. The last photo was of a room labeled "Standard King."

A wary smirk broke across her face, and she turned to see the beaming grin on Paul's face. "You shit. How long were you thinking you could keep me hanging?"

"Just about as long as you took. I was kinda afraid you might begin to get violent, and *I did not* want you to hit me."

She turned back to her monitor. "Inn at 500? You seem to be mighty confident, soldier."

"Well, I thought . . . it's not as if we haven't . . . Oh, hell." Now he was the one who was being played out on the line.

She rolled herself back to him with the grace of an astronaut on a spacewalk, gently shoving off from the side of a shuttle. Leaning her head on his shoulder and grabbing his arm, she replied, "Got-ya!"

A loud ping came from the room speakers, drawing their attention immediately to the large monitor at the front of the room. The maps on display had disappeared and the screen had gone completely black.

"What the . . .?" Paul's voice trailed off as he looked down at his work screen and saw that his monitor had gone black as well. "What the fuck?"

"It looks the same on my screen too," Ellie said, as she scrolled her mouse over the intruding blackness trying to click out of it. "What's going on?" In fact, all the other dormant monitors at the other workstations in the control room had snapped on, all showing the same black window.

"I'm no IT guy," Paul said, not knowing what to do. "Haven't the slightest . . ."

Then the frozen image of an out-of-focus face abruptly replaced the black screens.

A moment passed, and then the head moved. Its facial features remained blurred and became grossly distorted as it shifted closer to the camera lens—first showing a big fuzzy eyeball, then an oversized nose, making the whole thing appear to be a student's avant-garde video art project.

Then some background sound was broadcast through the speakers. A nervous cough. A shifting chair. And then a whispered voice.

"Master, you're too close to the camera."

The blurred face turned away from the screen and asked, "What?"

"You are too close to the camera lens. That round thing at the top of the monitor. See that inset image of you at the bottom?"

Blurred eyes glanced down at the bottom of his screen, "Oh!" The face became more defined as it settled into the appropriate spot and then came into complete focus. A handsome man in his late twenties with pale white skin, strawberry blond hair, and pupils of onyx was staring into the camera. He smiled.

⸻◆⸻

SIMULTANEOUSLY, ELLIE AND Paul turned to each other. The last time they had seen that face—now smiling at them from every computer monitor in the control room—was on the night when they walked into that little town. At first, it appeared to be a godsend. It ended up being a portal to perdition, with no divinity in sight.

And now they were looking at the face neither wanted to see again, digitally or not. Vladimir Rurik.

"I apologize for my lack of understanding of this technology." Vladimir smiled. "After all, I was born before the discovery of electricity." He made a deliberate show of composing himself. "Though I do not understand such things, I am told I am live-streamed to you via a cloud server. No chance for editing. All my flaws laid out before you," he smiled.

"H-o-l-y-s-h-i-t!" Paul slowly croaked out in a throaty whisper.

Vladimir looked away from the camera at the unseen voice. "You're doing great, master. Perfect!"

Vladimir smiled again.

"I desire to send your country a message. I would be most appreciative if you were to pass it along to your leaders." Vladimir paused. He adjusted himself so his body was fully centered within the frame of the screen, then continued in a coldly sober intonation.

"Your way of life will not end because of the impoverished immigrants streaming across your borders seeking a better life for their children. Islamic radicalism will not do it either. A war on drugs? Same-sex marriage? These are distractions your leaders use to blind you from seeing the real threat—the undeniable menace that can and will topple your civilization."

Vladimir took a dramatic pause. Then stared right into the camera, apparently now more than comfortable with the technology.

"I, Vladimir Rurik, am that threat." Again, he let that sink in.

"I make you humans a simple offer. You desist from hunting my people and me. Allow us to live as nature intended, or you will see exactly how your world can come crashing down on you."

Vladimir nodded to the unseen person off camera, and the screens turned crimson red. He continued his speech over a quick succession of images: a pile of Tutsi bodies butchered with machetes by Hutu tribesmen, CIA operatives attaching electrodes to the gentiles of prisoners, row upon row of Jews slowly filing into a gas chamber, a Serbian nationalist beating in the head of a Muslim woman with a hammer. The screen flashed a bright white, then grew into the image of a mushroom cloud roiling into the sky, dissolving into a photo of a little girl—a burn survivor from Nagasaki.

"For centuries, you have hunted immortals because of the untold horrors we have supposedly inflicted upon your kind. Ha! The irony is, immortals have been responsible for the deaths of an infinitesimal number of humans compared with how many humanity has slaughtered! Hitler, Stalin, Pol Pot, Idi Amin. Death on an industrial scale. And you are afraid of us?"

The string of bloody images stopped, and Vladimir's face reappeared.

"I have been inspired by the recruiting videos ISIS has created and posted online. But we have added our unique twist that should get our point across to viewers. I think our version to be more effective." Vladimir nodded again.

A new series of images flashed on the screen, this time showing vampires feasting on humans—messy pictures of gore pouring from ripped throats, heads being torn off by rampaging vampires, ghastly mounds of bloody internal organs, and hopeless humans screaming in pain and fear.

Vladimir's face reappeared, and he let out a laugh. "I believe we might even scare those ISIS pretenders."

After a pause, he solemnly continued, "You cannot stop me. Not this time. Your best hope is to agree with my conditions. I demand a new treaty between humans and vampires. And I alone will set the terms."

Vladimir folded his hands on the tabletop in front of him.

"My proposal is quite reasonable. You have one of two paths to choose from. The first leaves your world relatively unharmed. You will provide an uninterrupted supply of humans to feed my people. As simple as that. I will even allow you to select who you will send to us." His demeanor had become magnanimous, as though he was offering a tremendous gift. "Your choice for whatever the reason or criteria. We are not as selective as you are." He smiled at his own little joke.

"This avenue leaves you humans free to live your lives, chart your affairs, make war, build cities, go to the moon, raise families—whatever you want. Of course, as my family grows, so too the number of humans provided will need to be increased to sustain our needs. Think of it as a way of controlling your burgeoning population." Vladimir grinned.

"Or take the alternate path." His face solidified and became dark and fierce. "We will enslave humans. We will keep you like cattle. Your only purpose will be as food on the hoof. The earth as you know it will cease to exist."

He stopped as if putting an exclamation mark on the last statement.

"You do not have to decide today, tomorrow, or next week. But choose, you must. We have time, centuries, in fact. Immortality has a way of helping one to 'play the long game,' as you say. However, the practicalities of negotiating this agreement throughout the years with such fragile beings necessitate a speedier response. So alas, I must insist upon your decision within one month.

"Until then, you will immediately stop your search for me. This is not negotiable. By so doing, I can promise a reasonable approach to our hunts—no children, for instance. No berserker bloodsuckers running through the streets.

"Bring your agents home and tend to the lycans, mutants, and the other misfits you call *monsters*. If you refuse to call off your dogs, I will inundate the internet with the images I just showed you. Every single person will learn exactly what fear looks like. I wonder how many 'likes' I will get."

Vladimir stared into the camera with malevolent intensity. A wicked smile broke across his face, his image winked out, and the screens went blank.

———————◆◇◆———————

COMMANDER COLE STOOD in her office, looking through the window and down into the control room. Vlad's eyes seemed to drill directly into hers with an energy she wouldn't be able to resist if he were standing in the same room. When her computer monitor went black, she thought it might be a glitch in the system. She stood up to see if the same thing had affected the control room. When she opened the blinds, she found herself looking at Vlad's malicious face, just coming into focus. His visage was not just looming from the big screen, but looking up at her from every monitor in the room. The effect was unnerving.

Her knuckles went white as she gripped the sill of the window, steadying herself while Vlad outlined the ground rules for his new world order.

She had always felt that should anything or anyone try to upset the tenuous balance between the CSC and the vampires, he would be at the heart of it. His discontent with the treaty and confinement to the reservation was more than clear while she worked the Rez. He always taunted her and tested her searching for any weaknesses he could exploit. If it weren't for how vampires functioned on an instinctual level as pack animals submitting to the will of the strongest among them, Vlad would have laughed in his brother's face when Alex had struck the deal with Roosevelt. Fortunately for all, Alexei was not only the most formidable of the immortals. He had wisely recognized the vampire race was successfully being hunted to extinction. Without such a treaty, both he and Vlad, as well as their whole species, might have been staked to the ground and decapitated long ago.

But here was Vlad, in all his sanctimonious glory, threatening the very existence of humanity; smugly self-assured that he was safely hidden and unable to be unearthed.

Vlad had just declared war on humanity, and while Cole knew it was a war humans could win, it was indeed a war no one would want. However, she also knew humans had instinctual behaviors, too. Chief of which was an instinct for survival, and when push came to shove, humans would not relent. If war was what he wanted, then war he would get.

Chapter 15

RETURN FLIGHT

C RAIG CHECKED HIS watch again. Anything to take his mind off the visit with his mother. Of course, they loved each other, but speaking with her in person gave him no believable excuses to cut the conversation short and escape like he could with a phone call. So the full button-pushing mode had gone into effect with enough time for her to let out several of her classic lines. Emotional misery was its result.

He hated having to lie to his mother about his job. Even more, he hated his lack of creativity in inventing a believable enough lie that she would accept. "I'm an aide to a U.S. senator." Enough said. But now, now he had the ominous feeling he was the next one to have a fallen warrior memorial sitting in his locker. He wanted to tell her everything, so when the time came she could at least find solace in the fact he died serving his country. Of course, Liz used the "I work for the FBI." line like the others almost always did. At least Benji Saunders *had* been an agent for the Bureau.

In all honesty, however, he did not like how their relationship had evolved. Her role as "mother" and his as "son." She had forever imprinted in her mind that he was her little boy. If she knew what he did for a living, she'd probably ask him before he went out on a hunt if he had on a stain resistant jacket. "You know how hard it is to get blood out of clothing?"

He squeezed the rosary in his coat pocket. Mother's intuition? Did she sense this might be the last time they saw one another? Was she so aware of things she would deliberately give him a tool that might help save his life and a silver one to boot?

Now, finally, in the air, he rechecked his watch, making sure they would be on time for the meeting. Liz was sitting next to him, engrossed in a magazine she picked up at the Eugene airport, leaving him to his thoughts. And the only ones he could muster up were those of work or his mother, and he had enough of thinking about her to fill him for a while.

It had taken Craig the better part of the past ten months since the Vamp Town incident to convince Commander Cole and her superiors that bringing Alex into the CSC was not only a smart thing to do, but the only thing to do. How they couldn't see the logic was baffling to him, and the longer they took to come to the only reasonable decision, the further underground Vlad would burrow and the more time he had to repopulate the vampire race.

Craig was certain Vlad would not be content with living out his existence, hiding and lurking in the shadows. He was convinced Vlad was preparing to pay back humanity for the injustice he believed was done to him. Craig knew Alex understood this about his brother as well, albeit not soon enough.

Craig neurotically checked his watch one more time. The lack of direct flights between Eugene and Boise—lack, as in none—gave him extra time to reconsider his arguments for Alex joining the CSC. It was a little maddening that they had to first fly north to Portland, and then east to Boise, as opposed to the quicker, more logical straight-line route looking at any map would suggest.

First, Alex had intimate knowledge of how his brother operated, how he hunted, where his hideouts were, and most important his potential weaknesses.

Second, Alex was still in control of most of the remaining vamps. But his grip was tenuous, with one or two slipping out every week into the general human population ever since the incident.

Third, a policy of locking up vampires for all eternity may not have been realistic. Even Alex had expressed discontent with how his life was playing out. Without engaging him in a way to challenge his mind, there was the actual possibility he, too, would call it quits. The gates to hell would then open and who knew what carnage hundreds of hungry vamps set loose on the world could do? And while the number of vamps was nothing compared to the overwhelming size of the earth's population, the question remained: How long would it take to turn mere blood donors into an army of vampires?

Liz closed the magazine and held it in her lap. "This meeting, what do you think it's about?"

Craig shrugged his shoulders. "I don't know. Maybe it's about Alex and his request." *Or maybe it's about why I let Vlad escape.*

"You still think that there's a chance they'll let a vampire into the agency that keeps them in check?"

He frowned. "No, honestly. It has been too long, and I know Alex is getting anxious. You heard him. Even he has tired of being confined to Vamp Town."

"Whatever the meeting is about, it's been on the calendar for weeks. Long enough for you to have that touching family moment with your mother."

Craig looked into Liz's eyes. "You know what I'd say to Saunders if he said that?"

"Let me guess: Fuck you!" she said with a smile and opened her magazine.

Craig tried to resist the feelings pushing their way into his empty shell of a heart. Aside from the accepted idea that dating one's partner was a professional no-no, there was the practical side to consider. He was forty-nine years old. Liz, barely thirty. At least his former partner, Kathrine, had been closer in age, but then he had allowed the excuse of professionalism to get in the way as well. It just seemed easier to keep his feelings to himself—that is, up to the very moment he pulled the trigger, ending her life before she could transition into a vampire.

Even after Kathrine's death, he kept those feelings under wraps, ashamed he had never told her, sad he never gave her the opportunity to reject or accept him. Now, with Liz, he felt like he could face the same scenario, and maybe he might have to kill her one day as well. It was too much to contemplate. A shiver ran down his spine as though the hand of the reaper was resting on his shoulder.

Juggling all his anxieties had drained Craig. He was exhausted. He adjusted the seat back to recline and closed his eyes. *Breathe in. Breathe out. Breathe in.* Sleep overtook him, hitting the pause button on the playback of the visit with his mom, losing Kathrine, the fear of losing Liz, and his own mortality.

———◆———

LIZ LOOKED OVER at Craig. He was dead asleep. She doubted even a crash landing could have awakened him. He had gotten himself all wound up about seeing his mother, which had to be exhausting enough, but she could tell there was more going on that he was not revealing. She was reasonably sure he hadn't been sleeping all that much since Vlad had gone to ground. And losing his best friend probably didn't help, either. What Craig needed was a long uninterrupted period of relaxing sleep. Likely, what he really needed was a different job. As if *that* would ever happen.

She fished her phone out of her coat. They had been boarding the plane at Mahlon Sweet Field in Eugene when it vibrated, and then she heard the buzz, and the follow-up notification, but she could not look at it as they crammed themselves into the narrow rows and tiny seats—even small for her frame. The airlines kept trying to figure out how to squeeze in more passengers per flight. *Assholes,* she thought.

The aggravation of boarding the plane had distracted Liz from checking to see who had tried to contact her. Now that she was settled in her seat, she saw Ellie had sent her a text:

Think we found V :)

This got her attention, and she mentally kicked herself for not looking at it when the message she first received it. She briefly thought about waking Craig, but saw he might actually be sound asleep, and let the idea pass. Plenty of time to tell him after he woke up.

Now, more than for comfort's sake, Liz wished there was enough of a need for a direct flight between Eugene and Boise. But both cities were not large enough markets, so they had to fly through a hub city to get to any other destination. At least they got the flight connecting through Portland and not Seattle.

Looking back at Craig, she was happy she hadn't bothered him. Calmness seemed to have finally descended over him, smoothing out his face and, if not for the stubble of his beard, she could see the cute little boy he once was.

She studied his features. He was a young-looking forty-nine. She had thought about him and her as an item, briefly. But the age difference between them was a barrier, at least for her, and him too, she supposed, since he made no moves to suggest otherwise.

But Liz felt he was interested in her the first time saw her in the lecture hall where, as a newbie, she learned of the CSC's mission. Craig did not have a good poker face—she could tell by the way he got flustered and tongue-tied the moment they had first locked eyes, surrounded by the other recruits and agents. Even the act of *not* answering her questions signaled his attraction. It seemed cute.

Craig shifted in his sleep, smashing his face up against the window. *Well, so much for the angelic face,* she thought. But even in its distorted appearance the kid she had seen in all those photos at his mother's house was still there: his baptism, first communion, as a boy scout in full uniform—merit badge sash loaded with colorfully embroidered disks of achievement—his brothers. It was odd to her how he seemed almost embarrassed by his family; at least his lack of talking about them gave that appearance. But his mother was a lovely lady. Liz couldn't see why he got so worked up about visiting her.

On the other hand, no one could understand the relationship she had with *her* mother, either. Liz accepted her eccentricities, but there would be no way in the world she would want Craig to witness her mother dancing around naked in the backyard with her Wiccan lady friends ushering in the solstice. To each her or his own but, occasionally, it was best to keep some things private.

She continued watching Craig. This was not the top agent she had first met. That man was intense and unforgiving in how he approached the job and demanded others followed suit. She knew it was mostly because of the work. People died when they let their guard down around any of the monsters—especially those that had a need to feed on human blood.

But this man, the one sleeping next to her, had changed, had lost his edge. Recently, when they were in Utah hunting free radicals, she got first-hand confirmation his concentration was off. He seemed more preoccupied with her safety than the mission, which played out in near disaster for them both.

It was high noon when they arrived at the unfinished housing development snugged up to the base of the Oquirrh mountains south of Salt Lake City. A tumbled-down sign read:

Welcome to

Brigham Canyon Estates

View Lots

Starting in The Low 100s

The developers apparently had big plans for this property until the Kennecott Copper Mine fell into financial troubles in the early 1980s. Located just up the slope from Copperton, Utah, they believed it was going to be the "in sub-division" for the entire region. Now paved streets leading to empty lots were all that remained. Stakes, some still with survey tape clinging to them, separated one parcel of land from the next. An occasional electrical service drop dotted the area—resembling submarine periscopes—sprouting up out of the sea of brown prairie grass.

Further up the slope stood several unfinished houses. Some with just the beginnings of a foundation poured, others stood with their 2x4 skeletal frames silhouetted against the brilliant blue sky, looking like the carcasses of long-dead mythical beasts.

At the top of the abandoned subdivision, tattered triangular flags, colors long since faded, fluttered in a breeze celebrating the cul-de-sac of four finished model homes. Weathered—*For Sale*—signs still stood waiting to attract the right family.

A drop in the world copper market may have foreshadowed the end of the developer's big plans. But the rumors of the area being haunted, along with the unexplained deaths of workers, county inspectors, and real estate agents, kept the unrealized neighborhood undisturbed.

Crowning it all off at the top of the slope was an ancient, slouching two-story farmhouse, standing as a silent guardian over the entire site. Its gray Dutch lap siding harkened back to the early homestead that once dominated this land. The old farmhouse seemed a more likely location for a vampire lair, but their information pointed to the show homes.

They entered the first of the four houses and found it stuffy, dark, and empty—as in no furnishings or any slumbering vamps. They brushed the rotted curtains aside; stirring up dancing dust particles in the beams of sunlight just in case any surprises were hiding in the shadows but didn't even scare up a mouse. Same for the next two houses.

Craig took point as they entered the last house and, in an overly dramatic hand gesture, told Liz to remain by the door. This pissed her off, and she was going to give him a piece of her mind about his patriarchal attitude when they finished the job, but then a small girl wandered into the room in front of him. She was a cute little thing, if hungry looking, which Craig couldn't see or was being mentally manipulated into lowering his guard. He must have connected her to the girl from the bus and her plight.

Unbelievably, Liz watched Craig follow the girl further into the dark recesses of the house as if she were a normal child. That was when four women entered wearing flowing, tattered dresses, more like ball gowns from the 1800s, and surrounded him. Then, out of the blackest shadows, a male materialized from a cloud of swirling black fibrous threads.

Immediately, the scene reminded Liz of the old Hammer Dracula movies. There was Christopher Lee, commanding his harem of beautiful vampires (in various degrees of undress) to attack the unwitting human. With arms outstretched in a stereotypical Hammer Films way, the females moved in closer to Craig. She could almost hear them chanting, "I vant to suck your blood!" But not quite.

And yet, for some inexplicable reason, Craig remained motionless, not responding to the threat. He seemed mesmerized by the girl, or the male, or all of them. Another thought crossed her mind. Craig, seeing the overwhelming numbers, offered himself up as a decoy so that Liz could escape.

Liz wanted no part of his skewed heroics. It was clear there would be no reasoning with this family of vampires. No convincing them of retiring to Vamp Town. Whatever Craig was really doing was not her concern. Living was. Instantly, she threw open the door and dashed around the interior of the house, tearing down the curtains and opening other doors to let the afternoon sun stream into the darkness. Her quick action caught most of the vamps by surprise; exposing enough of their skin to the burning UVR of the daylight for their innards to combust. She helped those that didn't immediately react to the light along with silver 9mm rounds straight to their hearts; leaving Craig surrounded by five burbling piles of putrefying goo.

And somehow the little girl still stood, unharmed, between the crisscrossing beams of light, reaching out her hand towards the unmoving Craig. Then the girl advanced towards him, visibly salivating from the hunger that must have been consuming her. Liz did not hesitate. She rushed in and pushed him aside while kicking the child through an open door and out onto the porch. Her eyes flared open with shock as her organs vaporized and roiled out of her nose, mouth, and ears. The look of fear on her face was all that Liz could remember as her body distended and then imploded on itself into a seething mess of red slop, joining her father and mothers on their journey to hell, or wherever vampires went when they died.

The intel on this family of vamps included a daguerreotype of the entire group. A proud man with his four wives and seven children in front of their two-story house with white-washed Dutch-lap siding.

It didn't take long for them to find the other six children still at rest in their boxes, lined up in the basement of the big house. Craig seemed to be lost in some sort of moral crisis, or whatever. But it didn't really matter what it was called. He was useless. So, she left him in his stupor, outside in the afternoon sun, while she performed the rest of the dirty work, staking each one in the heart and cutting off their heads. They may have each been over 100 years old, but to Liz, they looked like kids sleeping sweetly in their beds of soil. It was grizzly work, and she could not wash the images from her mind.

Yes, something was sure going on with her partner, but he wasn't talking. What was she supposed to do the next time? Because there would be a next time, and another, and another, until they found Vlad and put an end to him or, God forbid, he put an end to them.

Chapter 16

MEETING

T HE DOOR TO the conference room stood open as an invitation to directly walk in. Still, Craig hesitated just a few paces away. Yes, the meeting had been scheduled. Yes, he knew that Vlad may have been located. Yet things didn't seem right. He couldn't put his finger on exactly why he was so skittish about almost everything lately, but surprises usually lead to death. And he was tired of seeing his friends die. Of course, it was irrational for him to expect a sneak attack from a monster in the conference room. But he had never been called to a meeting with Commander Cole in any other room except her office. She usually preferred the office where she could hide behind her big old wooden desk like it was Fort Apache, the one in the Old West or the Bronx. Take your pick. For her to choose the most formal room in the asylum had to mean something. And he believed it was nothing good. Government overseers? Was the CSC going to be shut down? Were they going to be sent into exile? Did they finally blame him for letting Vlad get away? He certainly blamed himself.

"This is fucking silly," Craig said to himself, forgetting Liz was next to him.

Liz turned to him. "What?"

"Oh! I . . . uh . . . I said that this is where Saunders would pull out those damned matchsticks and force me to draw one," Craig said.

"What did that do?"

"The one who pulled the short stick would go first and take the initial brunt of the bad news or have to be the one to stand up in front of the newbies during investiture." Craig sighed and shook his head. "And I usually lost the cheatin' bastard."

"Calm down, big boy. I'll be happy to take point." Liz knew Craig felt he was to blame for Vlad and his followers leaving the reservation. Not that it was really his fault. He had to weigh the risk/benefits of dropping the MOAB; killing them, the Action Team, and the good vamps, just to keep a handful of disaffected vampires from heading out into the world. Everyone understood not all the vampires heeded Alex's call to join him and accept the treaty. That was why there were still rogues out there that needed to be found and stopped. The addition of a few more at large in the general population shouldn't have been that big of a deal. But then there was the Vlad factor, and there was no telling what kind of shit he intended.

Liz and Craig had just gotten back to the base and were the last ones to arrive. The door stood open, beckoning them to enter. They heard drifting out of the conference room—small talk, some laughing, no apparent indications of trouble. Liz grabbed Craig by the sleeve and gently pulled him towards the conference room. She knew he thought disaster lay just inside. But she was curious, and besides, what choice did they really have? Craig resisted the gentle tugging on his jacket.

"Aw come on, you big baby. This can't be worse than a MOAB or a vampire bite—or your mother." She grinned devilishly.

He mouthed two words in her direction, "Fuck you," and with reluctance, loosened his leg muscles and followed Liz through the gaping mouth of doom. He kept his focus strictly on the back of her head, as he followed Liz into the conference room; forestalling the inevitable eye contact with the boss and whoever else was there waiting for them, and abruptly ran into her as she came to a halt halfway through the opening.

"Master Sergeant Terry!" Craig heard Liz exclaim.

———◦———

THE BIG MAN stood from his place at the polished wood table, smiled, and extended his open hand towards her. "Liz, it's good to see you again and doing so well." His hand was still extended toward her, but she remained frozen by the shock of seeing her former DI standing in front of her.

"It's okay to shake my hand, Agent Adams. Not looking for a hug." He winked at her, referencing the awkward moment when an exuberant trainee lost control of her emotions upon learning she was to become a member of this top-secret organization. "But then again, giving an old friend a hug would not be out of line, either. I'm no longer your superior." He reached for her hand and pulled her into his friendly embrace. This man had been like a father to her. Not like her dad, per se, but a guardian and mentor. She could tell he cared about her, recognized her potential, and shepherded her through the rigors of the enhanced training program. And as a result, rode her like he rode no one else.

"What are you doing here?" Liz asked after she freed herself from his grasp.

"We'll be getting to that soon, Agent Adams," Commander Cole said.

Craig, recognizing he probably wouldn't get roasted—this time—reached out his hand towards Terry. "I've heard a few things about you, Master Sergeant. Nice to put a face with the stories."

"Well, I have touched many lives who have wandered the halls of this facility." He and Cole exchanged nods of recognition. "Won't ask you what they had to say. I have a good imagination."

Terry took his seat at the conference table. Liz moved to an empty chair, the surprise at seeing her former DI still on her face. Craig took the last open seat. Also present at the table were Ellie and Paul, as well as Captain Smith, overall commander of the Action Teams.

Cole addressed the entire group. "Master Sergeant Terry, retired U.S. Army, will join us at Mountain Home and be a welcome addition. My good friend JR is not new to the CSC. In fact, he knows this organization well. He not only had the job of identifying the best of the best to fill our ranks," she looked directly at Liz, "but he served a stint as an agent when he was a *much* younger man."

"Hey now, let's not get personal," Terry said, smiling.

"JR was recruited to our 'unique outfit' not too long after his service in Vietnam. He worked RES-SITE-ALPHA."

"Coined the name Vamp Town," Terry interjected rather proudly.

"Then, after ten years serving directly here, he was reassigned back to the Regular Army to help find and develop the talent that fit the Center's mission."

Terry leaned into the table and clasped his hands together, fingers intertwined. "I'm retired now, from the Army, that is. I know the budget cuts are affecting you." Taking a drink, he continued, "So I offered myself to be used by the CSC as Commander Cole sees fit. I've always been a part of this loony bin. It'd be a shame to let the knowledge I have," he tapped his skull, "go to waste. Besides, I hate golf."

"And we need all the help we can get too," Cole said, sitting down. "This whole thing with Vlad escaping has spooked all our international allies. They had been content with our handling the vampire threat—complacent is closer to the actual truth—and have let their guards down over the years. If we don't get this thing contained, we will be forced to reach out for their help.

"Right now, the Catholic Church is the closest to ramping up their hunting efforts. The Vatican has said they are reconstituting their Swiss Guard unit no matter what, but I want to quash this before we must involve a Pope or any other flavor of religious leader.

"So, with that hanging over our heads, we need to get a handle on this situation ASAP." She looked directly into the eyes of each person sitting at the table. "I just used military jargon. I hate military jargon. I suggest we get this issue behind us because if I use that lingo again, heads will roll." Cole made a long and deliberate pause. Then she let a smile crack across her stern face. "I believe you get my point." She gave a sly wink to Terry.

Cole continued, "Today, however, finding Vlad has become more urgent than ever. Yesterday, we received a video message from him. Ellie, Paul, and I are the only ones to have seen it. Now it's your turn. Paul?"

Paul tapped a key on his laptop, and a wall screen came to life. The blurred image of a man's face quickly came into focus.

VLAD FLASHED HIS corrupt smile, then disappeared with a blackout. No one who had just viewed that video felt untouched by the intensity of his eyes. Each felt Vlad's gaze as a personal violation, probing into the dark recesses of their minds.

The gathered sat staring at the blank screen, stunned by the intensity of the message.

For Master Sergeant Terry, this was like an unpleasant family gathering, learning that the pervy asshole of an uncle was indeed coming to Thanksgiving dinner. Accepting the unpleasant reality of the situation, he sucked in his breath and tried to blink away the bloody imagery, focusing instead on Vlad's words and the unambiguous threat he had made.

Liz saw this as a call to arms. How could those in government do anything other than react to this with alarm, and immediately order to quash Vlad before anything serious could happen? Serious, as in the whole fucking world could end! Having Terry with them was a good start. She knew him to be a fierce warrior, but there was no way age had not diminished his physical abilities. His best contributions now were knowledge and wisdom. But while he was not decrepit, he wasn't spry and young either, which was less than ideal for fighting vampires. Even Craig, she feared, was questionable. She looked across the table at her partner. His face was drained of color, as though Vlad had sucked him dry through the digital ether.

Craig just sat staring at the screen as if there was still something on it. From the first moment he saw Vlad's face come into focus, he only heard the vampire's voice speaking directly to him; mocking him for being so gullible as to have allowed him to flee. "You won't drop that bomb on those survivors from the bus—innocents that they are. What kind of human are you? All we want is to be free to live out our lives like you." Sucker!

Panic threatened to consume him. He felt the blood drain from his cheeks. His breath became short and shallow. Craig sensed the room closing in and could feel all eyes probing him for weakness. But as he glanced around, he saw that no one other than Liz was paying him any attention. The others were in animated, sidebar conversations, each arguing their own theories of what should be done. Then he heard Commander Cole's voice try to exert her authority over the room. The calmness of her words took hold over him as though she too was reaching into his mind, asserting her will over Vlad's. "Calm down, Craig. Breathe in slowly, deliberately. I need you. Do not run away from this fight." He felt her words rather than hear them.

Craig slowly opened his eyes and saw Liz had recognized his moment of trepidation, but no one else had. Even Cole paid him no attention. Hadn't she spoken to him? Clearly not because she had her hands full, getting everyone else in the room to come to some order. Whatever was going on inside his head was a convoluted maze that wouldn't be solved soon. Now he had to subdue his anxieties and lock them back into their box, far away from his conscious mind. But not entirely gone. Something he might bring along to a visit with a shrink at some later date. He gave Liz a slight smile and a wink. Then he blurted out, "Hey! Everyone. Shut the fuck up and listen to the boss."

The room went quiet. Now all eyes were for sure trained on Craig, but at least everyone had quieted down.

"Thank you, Agent Wright," Commander Cole said in a wry tone.

Everyone broke into laughter, cutting through the nervous tension that had permeated the room.

Cole addressed the unit. "Vampires are immortal blood eaters. From the beginning, we relied too heavily on their instinctual pack animal behavior to ensure compliance with the treaty. We were naïve in thinking Alex would be Khan forever and we didn't need to do much more to keep them in control. So, we focused our limited resources on the others that required more hands-on attention.

"We have become a weak reactionary force, only responding when something bad happens. And until the Vamp Town incident, that had not occurred with the reservation vamps, ever.

"With Vlad defying his brother's authority, issuing threats that are tantamount to war, it's time to become more proactive. And contrary to what I have said in the past, before this is all over, we just may need to realign with the religions of the world, our former allies, in this age-old struggle."

"And the treaty?" Asked Liz.

"I'm afraid that may have been an instrument of another era which has long since lost its value."

Craig stood, "This whole thing is way bigger than how many bodies we can throw at Vlad. The hatred we all saw in his eyes spoke of his contempt for humans. Maybe it's our fault for making him feel like he was a kept prisoner. I don't know. Maybe, if he had remained a human, he might have ended up as a psychotic murderer. Who knows? The fact is, we just watched him declare open season on humans. Either we do everything we can do to crush him now, or we go along with his demands and become his dairy herd and milked dry of our blood.

"Call the Pope? Hell yeah. Because this affects all people: Catholic, Muslim, Jew, atheist. But that is for the long term. We need to take Vlad on today!" Craig paused a moment, all eyes glued to the crazy man as he ranted. He cleared his throat. In for a penny, in for a pound. "Commander, I think now is the best time to reconsider bringing Alex in to help us—"

"What?" Terry said, almost spitting out his coffee. "Alexei Rurik, a vampire, a member of the CSC?"

Cole turned to Terry. "You can relax, JR. Already ran that idea up the mast and they almost hung me off the yardarm. Not that I disagree with Craig about the urgency we face in dealing with Vlad."

"The Director didn't know about Vlad's threat when you last asked." Liz inserted. "Maybe this video will change his mind. Alex has been dealing with Vlad for over a hundred years."

"Yeah," Craig said, "That has got to have some value."

Terry sat back in his chair. "Yeah, his insider knowledge was highly useful when Vlad challenged him for superiority. And won."

Craig shot Terry an evil eye for what he felt was a cheap shot.

Cole took the stack of papers in front of her, picked them up and straightened them in a tamping action, signifying an end of the discussion. "Sorry, you two," she said to Craig and Liz. "Not going to happen. The topic is closed."

Craig sat silenced.

"Ma'am?" Paul spoke hesitantly.

"Yes?"

"My impression . . . Our understanding," Paul looked at Ellie, who nodded, knowing what he was about to say. "when we saw him in Vamp Town . . . he uh . . .," Paul stuttered as he realized he hadn't told Cole this in their after-action report upon returning from their visit the other day. "Alex told us he was going to leave the Rez and find his brother. This is with or without our organization." After a pause, "At least that's how I understood his comments." Then he looked at Ellie for support.

"Right!" Ellie coughed out in agreement.

Commander Cole stared at the two new agents. "And this is the first I have heard this? When the dust settles, I think we shall discuss how to present the information thoroughly during a debriefing. Just the three of us. Yes?"

"Yes, ma'am!" The two embarrassed agents blurted out.

Cole resumed addressing the entire group. "Alex remaining on the reservation is not our current concern. If he helps in stopping or eliminating Vlad, then great. But know this. If Alex gets in our way, we will hunt him down, too." She smiled with determination. "Now, as for taking the fight to Vlad, Agent Struthers has pieced together his movements." Cole looked down the length of the table at Ellie. "Please continue."

"Thank you, ma'am." Ellie opened a folder and looked down at her notes. "Paul . . . uh, Agent Mathews and I have been searching the internet for stories that might point to Vlad's location. And we stumbled across a series of articles from a weekly out of Seattle. A reporter has been following a series of bizarre murders. Established news sources are calling it a potential serial killer. The police had found all the victims with throat injuries, bites, or worse, and most of their blood missing. That is, what blood that wasn't spewed around the crime scenes. At any rate, the amount of blood present never amounts to the amount of blood in a human body."

"That sounds like a vamp to me," Craig said. "So, we go to Seattle and—"

"Not in Seattle anymore." Paul interrupted. "The reporter for this paper seems to have a jones for this story. He has followed the killings as they started in North Seattle around the U District, down into the Skid Road area around Pike Place Market and the ballparks, south to the industrial area and Boeing Field, and on into Tacoma, and Olympia following I-5. Murders have also been reported in Centralia. Beyond that, there are small towns but no deaths. The killings seemed to stop."

Cole asked, "When was his last article written?"

Ellie flipped through the clippings in her file, "Oh." She held up one. "This last week."

"Portland . . .." Terry said, staring off into space.

What did you say, JR?" Cole asked.

"Portland. Vlad's in Portland."

"Yeah and then Salem and Eugene," Craig added enthusiastically.

"No. Portland is a favorite hunting ground for him. The closest that he called home amongst the many that he has had."

"And how do you know this? I mean for certain?" Craig asked incredulously.

"Vamp Town was my assignment when I worked here after Nam. I got to know both Alex and Vlad, but I think Vlad took a shine to me because of my recent war experience. All the killing he thought I did. Our chief topic of conversation. I'd tell him about some poor VC I watched buy it and he'd pull a story of his own out to share and compare."

Liz gave Terry a disapproving look, shaking her head. "That sick mother—"

"Language Adams," Cole said as she gave Craig a stern glare.

"What? What did I do?" Craig asked with mock innocence, knowing full well that he had the rep of being the resident potty mouth and was being accused of influencing his partner.

"I guess the lack of killing his own food kind of was getting to him. Anyway, I learned a few things, and Portland was a favorite location for him."

"And why Portland, Master Sergeant?" Paul was interested.

"You can call me JR, or Jackie. Terry works too. I'm retired from that other title." He smiled at everyone. "Back before the treaty, Portland was Vlad's last playground. The rest of America considered Portland the ass end of the country, where people came to disappear from their troubles back East. Portland was also a port where sea captains came to fill out their labor needs. Ever hear of the term being Shanghaied?"

Some nodded understanding, but Liz and Ellie both shook their heads.

"Well, it was a criminal way of getting a few needed bodies for your ship. You'd contact a local crimp who would, for a price, find you just the man you needed. What all this meant was that people went missing all the time. And they were usually alone, with no one to notice what happened to them. Not all the missing wound up on the high seas."

"Vlad." Liz realized.

"Yep. He feasted and gathered family members. He'd never had it so good. Then, when his brother signed the treaty and ordered all the remaining vampires to assemble for protective internment. Pissed Vlad off, but he could not fight the strength of his brother's will. Until now."

"And Portland is again ripe for harvest. Street kids, homeless, young creatives wandering the streets drunk at night," Paul said.

"A target rich environment." Craig agreed.

"A perfect place to hide and strengthen up for whatever lies ahead," Cole said with authority. "Liz, JR, and Craig, you three will head there in the morning. Sorry, but you know I can't spare any other bodies right now."

Craig stood with purpose. "I guess we better get packing."

Chapter 17

FOOLS RUSH IN

T HE REPORTER LOOKED down the dark street behind him. The noise he thought he heard must have been a cat or even one of those big Norwegian rats that seemed to infest any waterfront. A chill ran down his spine as he pictured one of those filthy rodents. Quickly, he turned back to the woman he had been following. He spotted her taking a right turn around a corner and picked up his pace, not wanting to lose her. It had taken him months to track her down, not her exactly, but he believed she had a hand in the murders he had been investigating. TC had followed a trail of death from Seattle, south, from one community to the next, always a step behind the perpetrators.

His quest had started months earlier following a lead regarding university students being found dead and drained of blood. The police had no clues and no motive. But those first two kids were just the precursor to the many other murders that followed. Mostly, the deaths adhered to the same pattern of bodies left in back alleys. All the assaults occurred at night. The only marks on their bodies were curious puncture wounds in their necks. Blood drained dry. Well, dry was just a figure of speech. Other bodily fluids remained; the after-death seepage that happens (before or after or during the onset of rigor mortis) was evidence of that. The strangeness of only the blood being removed from the body elicited speculation of a supernatural occurrence or diabolical testing or alien abduction.

The surgical precision of the wounds, two holes neatly located over the jugular, showed that whoever or whatever caused these deaths could tap directly into an artery and quickly remove the life force from the victim.

But that didn't explain the other deaths. Messy affairs; throats that were savagely torn apart and heads nearly removed. In these instances, blood also had been removed from the victims but not "drained dry" as in the other murders. Not that blood wasn't the goal. It was just that this killer appeared to rush his/her way to get at the red prize as quickly as possible. Tear open the primary artery between the heart and the brain and let the heart pump it out. Effective, but extremely untidy. It was as though the perp had been raised with no sense of "table manners."

TC always had to squash down those types of speculative ideas. His editor harbored no desire to even hint at the idea that these deaths had anything to do with blood consumption. So, he kept them to himself until he could prove something more substantive. He could write about the bizarre nature of the deaths, the missing blood, and even speculate about alien abductions or ritualistic ceremonies. But blood consumption—off limits. Of course, if the victim's blood was being consumed, then only one strong possibility existed who the consumers might be.

A chill ran down his back. Even he chose not to say that word out loud. The very thought that he was on the trail of vampires made it hard for him to fall asleep at night. He grinned, thinking about the garlic he kept in his hotel room and of the "made in China" plastic crucifixes he had bought the other day. He knew vampires were a construct of uneducated peasants and amplified over the years by popular fiction. No, whoever was doing this was just a sick motherfucker. Sicker if he/she drank the blood, but sick and human. However, it never hurt to be prepared. The Boy Scout motto.

Still, no one knew where the missing blood was. That was a mystery, and an obvious answer was what the authorities seemed to close their eyes to, either deliberately or merely out of the notion that the actual truth would be too much to believe. A truth that he acknowledged was hard to accept, even after all he had learned.

So, TC reviewed what he knew to this point: two methods of extracting blood; one brutal and messy, the other tidy. Was there one perpetrator or two? If two, were they working together or alone? It would be highly coincidental for two different killers to be operating simultaneously in the same locations, seeking the same prize. No, there had to be two or more killers working together. But why?

He stopped. There was that noise coming from behind again. This time when he turned to look, he saw the faintest of shadows—dissolve? He squinted his eyes to see better, but there was nothing, not even the cliché cat running out from behind the trash cans. *Fuck! Why did I follow this story again?* He returned to the task at hand and watched the woman slip into a door at the back of an old brick building that formed one boundary of the parking lot he was standing in. At least Portland, unlike Seattle, had done away with alleys years earlier, which made him feel less likely that he was being lured into a trap.

TC looked around the deserted parking lot one more time, to be certain. Mercury-vapor security lighting shed a harsh white-blue glare across the asphalt and the few parked cars. The bright illumination produced a sharp contrast between lighted objects and their cast shadows. The stark difference made it even harder to see into the dark areas and identify any signs of trouble. Seeing none, he returned his attention to the heavy metal door, which stood partially open. Dim light seeped out just enough to serve as an invitation for him to continue the pursuit. He stopped just before entering when he noticed some Chinese script along the side of the opening. He didn't know if it was Cantonese or Mandarin, or some other variant of the language, but he could tell that it had been there for quite some time.

Slowly he pushed on the door, listening for it to make a sound signaling his entry, but it swung open as though the hinges had recently been oiled. Again, he listened for sounds coming from the interior. There. Footfalls on wooden steps, heading down. A green glow of light from an exit sign above another door pointed the way and down he went.

Echoing footsteps kept drawing him down the stairs. At the bottom was a profoundly dark void that the green glow of the exit sign above his head could not penetrate. TC leaned into the black emptiness and let his eyes relax, trying to see the slightest outline of something. He held out his arm as a blind person might do when entering a new environment and swept it left, then right, then—bump—his hand touched a rough wood surface. It was a large crate which he felt his way around and then slid his foot forward, slowly inching it along the surface of the floor, probing for more obstacles that he might trip over. Then a faint light switched on, and a previously hidden archway glowed in front of him, beckoning him forward—another breadcrumb to follow.

For a moment, he considered using the flashlight on his cell phone but discarded that idea. You can't follow someone surreptitiously by advertising that you are behind them. Patiently, he continued his snail's pace across the floor, arriving at the arch. Then a creaking of rusted hinges came from below him and light washed up another set of stairs. He could hear footsteps faintly echoing off some hard surface as they receded, taunting him to follow. The open door provided enough illumination to negotiate the steps heading down as he collected more crumbs.

Somewhere along the line, he should have been thinking about how this woman might be leading him on. Surely, she had been toying with him, leaving the clues that allowed him to "barely" keep up with her. It was all a little too convenient that a light would come on just when it seemed he had lost her trail. But TC's curiosity had the better of him and his overwhelming desire to discover more buried any sense of caution he should have.

At the bottom of the stairs, he entered an unevenly lighted space. A quick visual scan showed this basement was the storeroom of the last resort for items that had outlived their usefulness. Stacked around him were more crates and boxes, piles of old office furniture parts, space dividers, retail displays, file cabinets, and other odd remainders of once useful items in the world of commerce. A forest of regularly spaced columns as large as tree trunks grew out of the heaps of junk.

Calling the large square posts "tree trunks" was not an exaggeration. In the 1890s, in both Seattle and Portland, old growth Douglas fir trees were almost literally within spitting distance of everyone's back door. That overstatement aside, their natural size and strength made them the no brain's choice for large-scale construction. This six-story brick building rising above him used solid tree trunks for pillars and beams. Despite the wooden structure, this type of building would never be destroyed by fire—these timbers could survive the hottest of blazes and still be structurally sound, but the fire's heat or an earthquake could turn the masonry walls into a pile of rubble in a manner of minutes.

TC looked around for an obvious path the woman could have taken but saw none. He had reached a dead end. Then he heard a tapping. A sharp, hard tap, like the sound of a ring being deliberately banged against a hard surface. He snapped his head to the sound and there she was. Standing in the opening of yet another door. She stood leaning against the frame. One arm extended high towards the header as though she were patiently waiting. A finger on her hand that was touching the frame above her head moved, and the ring on that finger tapped the frame once again.

Tap. Tap. Tap.

The woman he had been following (or had she been leading him) was standing under a bare light bulb clinging to a piece of conduit above her head. For the first time, he could get a good look at her. *Wow!* She was a dark-haired beauty. Another light behind her inside the space silhouetted her, perfectly highlighting all the appropriate curves. She was looking right at him, no longer pretending she didn't know she was being followed. Her eyes invited him forward. To keep following. And he obeyed.

He followed her into the next space, which was the landing to a stairwell that only went one direction, down, into a sub-basement. At the bottom of the two flights of stairs, he stopped. This level was almost entirely black. Instinctively, he brushed his hand against the wall, looking for a light switch. But none existed, or, at least, in the dark, he couldn't find one.

Tap. Tap. Tap.

TC heard her call echoing to him. *Where the hell is she?* Then a match flared, and he could see her milk-white face as she lighted a lantern hanging from the wall. She was standing in front of a heavy-looking wood door at the end of a brick-lined hallway, or tunnel. He shook his head. He did not know exactly where he was anymore and hoped that he could remember how to get out of this rat's maze later. But for now—*Got-ya!*

He heard, rather than saw, her pull out a ring of keys, insert one into a lock that sounded like it needed oil, and opened the door. She turned back to TC and waited long enough to see that he was still following and then took the lantern from the wall and walked through the opening, leaving the door ajar.

He watched the only light recede into yet another tunnel along with the woman leaving him in the dark. Now he pulled out his phone flashlight and directed it at the faint glow that showed through the opening. At the door, he saw more of the Chinese script painted on the surfaces surrounding the frame. He briefly wondered if these were words of welcome, or possibly a sign for business, an opium den from years ago? Maybe there was a warning hidden in those pictographs. He saw the lantern had stopped its movement. Waiting? He needed to get moving. Before pocketing his phone, he took a picture of the writing—for later research—and made his move to catch up with the woman.

TC stepped through the door and into another brick-lined tunnel. He guessed that by now they had to be beyond the building's foundation and under a street heading towards another basement. In the process of mentally mapping the area from when he had first entered this rabbit hole to now, he had lost track of the woman. He briefly panicked but saw that the lantern was still waiting for him. Good. In fact, it had stopped moving, and as he got closer, the light became brighter, almost blinding him from the intensity as it hung from a hook on the wall. But the woman had vanished. He grabbed the lantern and swung it around, trying to find her or see if there was another door to go through. Several paces further into the tunnel, he came to its abrupt end at a pile of construction rubble that closed off the rest of the passageway.

Stymied by the blockage, TC went back down the tunnel to where the lantern had been hanging. Only then did he notice that the floor directly under him was not the dirt caked concrete like the rest of the passage. He was standing on a wood planked square, and he could see light leaking out from around the edges. Setting the lantern down and getting on his knees, he found a fingerhold on the surface and lifted. He looked down through the trapdoor and saw another lighted lamp. Then he heard the rodent noise again from behind and peered through the lantern light and the darkness beyond, looking for the source. Had it followed him as he followed the woman? Looking back and into that gloomy boundary between illumination and shadow, he thought he saw the silhouette of a man—materialize? *Shit, I must be really spooked.* He returned his attention back to the trapdoor, then felt something like the strings of a cobweb touch his face.

Tap. Tap. Tap.

There she was, calling to him again. He looked down but didn't see the woman, but she wasn't too far away.

He brushed the webbing aside, then proceeded down the ladder to a lower layer of subterranean passages.

What the hell is this place? He asked himself as he peered into yet another dark tunnel, though he knew the answer. He had stumbled into the infamous Portland Shanghai Tunnels. Not the cellars that the tourists saw, but the remnants of the mythical network of passageways that were reported to have crisscrossed the entire area. *Ain't this somethin'*, he thought as he grabbed the lantern from the wall hook.

Tap. Tap. Tap.

A door opened in the black and an inviting, warm light streamed out from the room beyond, framing the outline of the woman he had been following. As if the first view of her figure had not been seared into his mind. Now the golden light gave her body a radiance that was all but angelic.

Tap. Tap. Tap.

Inside his head, he heard her words, *"Come to me, TC."*

Not able to control his muscles, TC felt himself moving towards the woman. He tried to resist but found that he couldn't. He wanted to tell her to leave him alone, but the words would not form. When he reached her, he stopped. With the most deliberate of actions, she lowered her face into his neck. Blood surged through his body. His throat pulsed as his heart pumped hard to feed the brain. Then she took in a deep, languorous breath, inhaling the intoxicating scent of his humanity.

"*Welcome to our home.*" The woman took TC's hand and led him into the glowing golden chamber.

From out of the shadowy recesses black filaments swirled around TC. The dark threads spun around him in a pirouette of an age-old dance as the strings merged into the shadow of a man sitting in a relic of an armchair in the center of the chamber.

"My name is Vladimir." He stood and walked towards TC. His smile revealed a pair of sharp fangs. "Please do not be afraid."

"You're a . . . a . . . vampire!" The words came stammering through TC's lips.

"I prefer immortal."

Chapter 18

INTO THE STORM

L IZ, CRAIG, AND Terry gathered in the locker room/armory to gear up for an eventual encounter with Vlad. Did that mean capturing or killing him? They didn't know which, but they wanted to be ready for either option. Though if polled, the majority sentiment would be the elimination of the problem altogether. The team members stood at the end of a table closest to the "Wall O' Hurt," selecting weapons to take along on the hunt in Portland.

The arsenal held a variety of arms, ranging from contemporary to traditional to ancient. As with human-on-human combat, the choice of tool was personal and based on the abilities and expertise of the user. Some preferred the size and weight of a 9mm Beretta, with a fifteen-round capacity, and the ease to reload quickly by slamming in a new magazine. Others liked the heft and stopping power of a .44 Magnum, otherwise known as the 'Dirty Harry' around the Asylum. Of course, if one desired stopping power and quick loading, there was an excellent selection of the trusted and revered 1911 '45s.

Several military-grade rifles were standing ready for use, from M4s to MK18s and HK416s. Most had variations and attachments specifically intended for use against many monsters. There were also scatter guns of various sizes, mostly with pistol grips. A shotgun was effective in close quarters fighting. Of course, ammo for all the firearms had some amount of silver content.

A favorite, when the possibility of confronting an amassed group of vampires or werewolves, was the Milkor Riot Gun. Initially designed as a grenade launcher, the Milkor had been adapted to fire gas canisters to disperse rowdy crowds. Since the idea was not to kill but subdue rampaging monsters, the CSC had adapted the canisters to distribute different repellents. For vampires, a mixture of garlic and holy water would aerosolize when the shell burst open after firing. The recipe for werewolves was similar, but wolfsbane (an herbaceous flowering plant) replaced the garlic. The resultant effect was to stun and thus overpower the offenders. Everything would depend upon the initial encounter. If it looked as though the monsters seemed amenable to being brought into the reservation system, then repellent was a soft use of force to help subdue and restrain them.

Since catching monsters was more an art than a science, no one knew what the conditions in the field would be. And sometimes "subdue" meant to stick a stake in the bloodsucker's heart!

Also, on the wall was a large variety of swords, which were useful for cutting off the head of an uncooperative monster. The sheer beauty and elegance made the Japanese swords a favorite. The three traditional samurai styles were available. Some preferred the wakizashi for its shorter length, allowing it to be drawn from a back-mounted scabbard. Katanas, the main fighting tool of the samurai, were too long to pull off that gag, contrary to what the movies have shown. But the length of these blades enabled the user to keep a healthy distance from an assailant. And the Tanto a short dagger. Knives of any kind were weapons of last resort when one was "backed into a corner."

Along this vein, there was an extensive selection of tactical knives. Some with single edges, others were double-edged, and still others came with serrations that had "nasty wound" written all over them. Mean looking machetes were in the mix, and that All-American favorite, the Bowie knife, whose blade was large enough to be considered a short sword. As in the ammunition for the firearms, silver-alloyed blades were the preferred metal. The exact chemical composition of the alloy used in all the sharp-edged weapons remained the secret of the bladesmith, descendants of the legendary Japanese Masamune family of the thirteenth century.

A small collection of bludgeon-style weapons, such as medieval maces, took up positions of prominence on the wall. Although there were more effective weapons, these really were kept in the armory because of the badassed nature of their appearance. A nod to methods used to hunt monsters of times past.

There was a selection of wooden stakes fashioned into sharp-edged knives. They made these from a combination of various hardwoods laminated together, then worked into what some would call beautiful pieces of art. It would be primarily used for skewering the heart of a sleeping vamp. At least, that was the hope. The multiple varieties of trees used for creating vampire stakes had more to do with cultural tradition rather than what was most effective. Some used ash for its strength. Aspen was supposed to have been the type of wood used to make Christ's cross. Blackthorn, hawthorn, and buckthorn were used in Croatia and Slovakia because of their visual similarity to Jesus' crown of thorns.

Curiously, there was one weapon that had no equivalent. It rested in a corner at the edge of the "Wall O' Hurt." There was only one of these. A wooden baseball bat. There was no indicator that this was something special. After being overwhelmed by the sheer volume of deadly weapons on display, it would have been understandable that if no one noticed such an innocuous item. But there it was. A baseball bat. No one could remember the last time anyone had taken it into the field.

Everyone assumed the bat was a joke, referencing the preferred weapon of choice in movies for fighting off zombies. The wood had a bloodstained appearance, suggesting it had been used for such a purpose, but they figured it was merely a prop, the notches showing kills, and the stains, over-the-top theatrics.

Terry was unclasping the third silver-mail neck guard he had tried and set it on the tabletop. "I think the second one was a better fit. Thanks." He grabbed the previous one he had tried on and placed it in the open rucksack in front of him.

"Now give these a try," Liz said, handing him a pair of mail wrist guards.

"Didn't have anything like this during my stint here." Terry examined one, trying to figure out how to put it on. "I suppose silver was considered too expensive. We used old-fashioned boiled leather."

"Nothing gives a vampire a better toothache than a mouthful of silver," Liz said with a devilish smile.

"Indeed. Yeah, these'll do." Now Terry turned to the weapons. "Wall O' Hurt. Nice. We just had a bunch of metal lockers lined up across this space. No fancy-ass display and no name."

"A lot of the weapons aren't in now, with the Action Teams and other agents out dealing with the full moon and free radicals. But I think you'll find a weapon or two that will serve you sufficiently," Craig said.

Stepping up to the Wall, Terry reached for a 9mm handgun with a flashlight mounted below the barrel. "This is nice," he said as he worked the slide. "Still, there sure are a lot of toys left to choose from, and so little time."

"Don't worry about not finding the right weapon," Craig assured him. "The mobile unit we'll be traveling in has its own smaller version of the Wall."

"Good to know." Terry's eyes scanned the weapons, marveling at the variety. "Again, way different from what we had... Hey! You still got Gibs," Terry said, as he reached for the bat.

"Gibs?" asked Liz.

"Yeah," he responded, swinging it back and forth as if he were warming up to play ball.

"You used this? For...,"

"Vampire killin' of course."

Craig looked up from packing his bag. "Never knew it ever was used. Always thought that it was a joke. The story is that someone had used it back in the seventies to knock some hippies around during a war protest or something like that."

"Well, you're looking at that guy." Terry patted the fat end of the bat into his left palm. "They sent us to San Francisco to root out a few free rads. They were holed up in an old Victorian. One of the few that didn't come down in the quake or burn afterward. Anyway, the neighbors didn't like the Hendrix blaring out in the middle of the night, and the sour aroma of death that hovered around the house kind of helped give them away. We got there and discovered a little tribe of bell bottom wearing, bead dangling, pot smokin' vamps. There were only the two of us. Why we thought there were only three of four of them, I'll never understand."

"SNAFU," Liz offered.

"More like FUBAR. We go in around noon. The windows were painted over, and all covered with tie-dyed sheets, and there they were sitting cross-legged in some sort of kumbaya moment. The smell of grass and incense was strong in the air. Patchouli oil *almost* masked the stink of death."

"How many more than three were there?" asked Craig.

"I could see seven in the prayer circle. We counted up to fifteen total."

"Two against fifteen? Holy shit!" Liz said in amazement.

"And the bat?" asked Craig.

"You both seem like people who may have found themselves in a do-or-die moment. So, you'll understand I really can't remember all that much. One moment we pull the macho 'surrender now and all will be good' thing and the next, all hell is breaking loose. Guns are firing. Vamps are flying around. Blood is everywhere. And somehow, when all was said and done, my partner and I were standing in a room full of imploding vampire husks. He with a couple of chair legs and me with this baseball bat." Terry shook his head, still not believing his own story. "Still don't know where that came from. Must have been in the room already 'cause I didn't bring it with me."

"And Gibs. The name of the bat?" Liz asked.

"Yeah, I named it in honor of Josh Gibson, the Babe Ruth of the Negro Leagues. Some say the best home run hitter of them all."

"Sounds like a crock of shit to me, Master Sergeant," Craig said as he turned back to his packing.

"And to me as well, Agent," Terry said, smiling and swinging Gibs one more time.

"You mean that story you just told was . . .," Liz felt someone had pulled the wool over her eyes.

"Like I said. I don't remember," Terry replied, still smiling.

"Fucking A," Liz said, unbelieving and reached for the bat. The brown stains looked like dried blood that had soaked into the surface. "There are hash marks." She counted them. "Fifteen, like he said."

"Still could be fake." Craig tossed out. "What happened to your partner? Where's he now?"

Terry's face lost the smile. "Turns out all the blood we had covering ourselves wasn't all vampire blood. Ken got himself slightly bit in the melee. Didn't catch it until we had hosed off. We were on the long ride back here when he told me about the wound. He asked to pull the car over so he could take a pee. I didn't see he had his sidearm with him when he walked into the trees."

Everyone returned to their work of getting ready to go to Portland. The silence spoke volumes about what they all had experienced and might very well experience again.

———◆◇◆———

CRAIG STOOD AT the side sliding door and shoved another bag towards the rear of the new command vehicle. Having to drive seven hours to Portland before they could even get their bearings and try to zero in on Vlad's exact location seemed a bit much. They all had the same question floating around the back of their minds—why couldn't they just hop an Air Force transport and arrive six hours earlier? So much for any form of a surprise attack on the bastard.

As long as he was asking unanswerable questions, Craig let his thoughts drift. If they only had known all this a day earlier, he would have just stayed in Portland, forgone the flight to Boise, and waited for the command unit to get to town. But no, he had to get back to Mountain Home and attend that meeting, be assigned the master sergeant, load up the van, and turn right around to go back west. Of course, he understood they needed this command center on wheels. The CSC wasn't like the FBI, with field offices in almost every city in the country. They had to take the field office with them. In fact, it was a field office, command center, armory, fast food delivery vehicle, and sometimes motel, all rolled into one.

This mobile unit was a first for the CSC, delivered just before the current budget issues that plagued the agency and threatened its very existence. The van was a prototype. Starting with a Mercedes Benz Sprinter, it carried a team of four. Though in a pinch, it could accommodate up to six bodies. The term "pinch" referred to how six bodies would feel crammed into it.

The layout included independent seating for a driver and a passenger riding shotgun with two more seats directly behind; all comfortably designed and could rotate to face in any direction. Behind the rear two seats was the Command Room function, with a wall of computers above a working desktop. Somehow, they'd even shoehorned in a tiny sink and one of those pod-style coffee makers. Hiding below the deck was a refrigerated compartment for food, accessed through a trapdoor between the front row of seating and the rear. At the rear of the van was the arsenal, a miniature "Wall O' Hurt."

The one design flaw they discovered was a lack of storage. They were piling up gear behind and between the back seats and the command wall, making it difficult, if not entirely improbable, for the computers to be accessed while in transit. *Why the hell didn't we have a roof rack installed?* Craig thought with frustration as he tried to find one more space for the team's first aid kit. All prototypes came with a certain number of bugs and poorly thought out features. He hoped this would be the last one he discovered or, at a minimum, the most annoying. Not that there was ever going to be enough money to provide a second of these babies to Con-West.

"That coffee maker is pretty slick," Paul said.

"Huh?" Craig turned to the voice. "Oh, hey Paul. Yep, caffeine's my life's blood." He gave the Keurig a tender pat. Then there was a moment's pause as it dawned on Craig that he had made a vampire pun, of sorts. "Sorry you guys can't come along, but someone needs to stay behind and keep an eye on the whole damned world. You know that, right?"

"Yeah, sure, I get it. But that's not what I wanted to talk to you about." Paul said.

"K."

Paul swallowed heavily. The meeting had just wrapped up, and before that, Craig and Liz had barely arrived back at the base from their trip to Eugene. There had been no time to tell him about going to Vamp Town and talking with Alex. He wasn't looking forward to this, and now that the moment was here, he was choking. He took a quick glance over to Ellie. She had been watching, saw him hesitate, and flashed a reassuring smile. "Go on, you can do it." The smile was telling him.

"Okay . . . You, uh, knew Cole sent Ellie and me to Vamp Town to talk with Alex. Right?"

Craig nodded. "Yeah. Couldn't be in two places at one time. Though next time you can go say hi to my mom and I'll chat with the vamps." Craig grinned.

"He wanted to talk with *you*, but Cole sent us. Obviously, because you weren't available. Which you just said." Nervously, he continued. "She, uh, told us that Ellie and I would be in your shoes one day and needed to learn how to deal with the undead on our own."

"So, what did Alex have to say?"

"Actually, not much. I'm confused by that. He lectured us about how immortals appreciated what humanity brought to the world—"

"And how, by happenstance, through no fault of their own, they had become blood-sucking monsters and shouldn't be held to account for how a vampire simply had to survive?

And how an immortal life wouldn't be worth shit without the arts and sciences, which only humans can bring to the world. Yes?"

"Yeah, something like that."

"I was afraid of that." Craig sat down on the deck of the van. "That was Alex's warm-up, shot across the bow, saying that he was done with the whole thing."

"You mean the treaty?"

"Yep. He was telling you, me, us, that if he couldn't be a part of our solution, then he was going to deal with Vlad on his own. Shit!" Craig stared through Paul and into pure space, everything that had been bothering him coming home to roost on his shoulders with this unwelcome news.

"One more thing." Paul removed his hands from behind his back. He was holding a well-worn plush toy duck and handed it reverently to Craig. "Alex. He, uh, said you might want this."

"That's Cindra's . . ." His voice trailed off at the realization that Cindra was dead.

"Sorry, man." Paul placed his hand gently on Craig's shoulder.

Chalk up another person to that pestilence called vampirism. "I thought that somehow—somehow a toy might help Alex with her transition. Foolish. Did he tell you how she died?"

Paul smiled slightly. "Sweet tooth. Apparently, she couldn't cross over to blood. She was hungry and got into that stash of old army rations in the back of the bar. He found her, what was left of her, surrounded by several open cans. She was holding an open tin of pound cake.

Craig rolled the yellow duck around in his hands. "She died resisting. Don't know of too many who could do that."

"Yeah, a real fighter."

"From what I see coming down the road, it's probably better things ended as they did for her." Craig wiped moisture away from his eye. A tear for the lost little girl. A tear for all those who would certainly die, or be changed, in the days and weeks to come.

THEY LEFT THE base a little after midnight, driving through Boise fifty minutes later. After another hour, they crossed the Snake River, the borderline of Oregon and Idaho, and drove on through Ontario, heading west towards Portland. The drive on Interstate 84 would have allowed the team to see some stunning high desert terrain if it hadn't been the middle of the night, made all the darker by the overcast, blocking out the stars and moon. Otherwise, a breathtaking landscape.

Unfortunately, in the dark, the only things visible were those ubiquitous road edge indicators, which monotonously ticked past the windows mile after mile. The blackness of the night made darker as the markers starkly reflected the vehicle's headlights back into the driver's eyes and seemed to be even brighter than the lights of oncoming cars. The only things that cut the eye strain were the occasional truck stops, which appeared to be floating islands of bright light in the night as if they were landing fields for flying saucers and, given this world, they might have been. Particularly if you considered the drivers of the big rigs in search of fuel and human contact—slamming down a cup of coffee, grabbing a shower and a quick nap only to hit the road again, towing two or three trailers behind them—as aliens.

After about four and a half hours of travel, they had reached Boardman. The sun had not quite risen, but if it had, the Columbia River could have been almost visible to their right. From this point on, the interstate would quickly align with the river, and together head west until they reached Portland, where I-84 stopped, and the Columbia continued to the sea.

Another hour and a half later, they passed through The Dalles, entering the Columbia River Gorge. Basically, a canyon, the Gorge was a gash cutting through the volcanic Cascade Mountains; marking the transition between the dryer, high-desert terrain of Eastern Oregon, and the wetter, temperate western side of the state typified by conifer rain forests.

This morning, their transition between east and west was going to be a wet one. Terry had to turn the windshield wipers from intermittent mode to the more frequent, normal setting. The increased use of the wipers had more to do with the road spray and how fast they were moving through the rain than how much water was falling from the sky. The weather report Liz read from her phone said that this was just the beginning of several storm systems coming down off the Gulf of Alaska, stacking up like airliners waiting their turn to land on the tarmac at PDX.

"Looks like we'll see some rain in Portland," Liz said, turning back to Craig, who was sitting in a reclined position.

He didn't answer, pretending to be asleep, but he was lost in his own thoughts. Thoughts an analyst might interpret as defeatist, but he knew to be bordering on fatalistic. He had a dark foreboding about what they were heading into, with no delusions of how bad things were going to go, and the dreary weather perfectly mirrored his feelings.

Liz shrugged and returned her attention to the front of the vehicle.

Craig watched their heads gently rock back and forth as the van surged on toward their uncertain fate.

Chapter 19

TERRY

B ICYCLISTS WHIZZED AROUND and past Terry
as he stood on the east side of the river, making him feel
more like a target than the tourist he believed he was. He was
looking west towards downtown Portland; the view framed
left and right by the Hawthorne and Morrison bridges.

This was an entirely unique vantage point of the city in
which he had grown up in the 1960s. And right now, it felt
as unfamiliar to him as Beijing or Nairobi. Since he had left
for the Army, he had not returned to the place of his birth,
save for a quick fly-in and out for his mother's funeral and
again for that of his brother. Still, he considered this place
his home, even if it was an, albeit estranged relationship.

But family was not the reason Terry left. It was that this
city was just not all friendly to African Americans. Until
WWII, Portland was basically an all-white town. They
had admitted Oregon as a state in 1859 as a compromise,
just before the civil war. The South didn't want another
free-state in Congress to outnumber them, and likewise,
the North refused to allow another slave-state to be added.
The compromise: no Negroes in Oregon free or slave. Of
course, there weren't any long, drawn-out debates about the
unfairness of such a policy. Most of the residents in the
petitioning region had no problem with a ban on blacks. The

long-lasting effects of that political decision resulted in the population of African Americans in Oregon in 1940 to be around one percent—amounting roughly 2,000 people in the entire state.

With the declaration of war in 1941, the US became focused on producing the machinery needed to win. Thousands of black and white workers from all parts of the country flocked to the Northwest to work in the shipyards at the urging of industrialist Henry Kaiser, attracted by the eighty-eight cents an hour wage, which was considerably higher than the norm of twenty-five elsewhere; swelling Portland's population by an additional 160,000 people. To accommodate this influx of residents, Kaiser built a new city of temporary housing—Vanport—on a floodplain between the two cities where he owned shipyards: Portland and Vancouver, Washington.

Vanport was unusual in its ethnic diversity, as all races were welcome to live in the two-story plywood, cracker-box, apartment buildings. Though there were black and white areas in the town, it looked thoroughly integrated from the perspective of longtime Oregonians.

Terry's parents met in the yards. His father, an electrician, was from Greensboro, North Carolina. His mother, a welder, came from Baltimore, Maryland. They took up residence in Vanport soon after their marriage, making it their home until the war's end.

After the shipyards closed, many of the workers who had flocked to the area for the jobs left, but not all. The Terrys, along with many others, remained living in Vanport until 1948, when the Columbia River flooded, erasing the city, and leaving its inhabitants homeless.

Losing everything, the couple lived in a succession of temporary and inadequate housing until his father could secure a loan to buy a house in the Albina district of Portland—the part of town begrudgingly ceded to the 6,000 blacks who had survived the flood.

The one-story Victorian was not much larger than the hastily erected apartments in Vanport. But it was sturdy and warm and just big enough. It was in this house that Jackie Robinson Terry (JR) was born in 1952, and his brother Satchel Paige was born four years earlier, in 1949.

Not that it was too obvious, but Terry's father was a huge baseball fan, and worshiped the heroes of the Negro league. He was especially proud of Jackie Robinson when he broke the race barrier in 1947 to become the first black to play for the majors when the Dodgers hired him. When Satchel Paige played for the hometown Portland Beavers during the 1957 season, his father dragged both boys to Multnomah Stadium to see as many home games as he could afford.

JR grew up as a black kid in a white city. On its surface, Portland didn't have the obvious signs of segregation like cities in the South. But the racism was always there, just below the veneer of polite society, and everyone lived by its unspoken, unwritten rules. In 1970, at 18, he enlisted in the army and got his ass out of town, never looking back.

In the Army, he lost his longtime nickname, JR, for another. The other guys in his unit came to call him 42. Jackie Robinson's—the ballplayer's—uniform number. As he rose through the ranks, those who knew him as 42 became fewer as he moved from private, to sergeant, to staff sergeant, and then 42 disappeared along with his given name, Jackie, when the promotions board awarded him the rank of master sergeant. From that point, he was only Master Sergeant Terry. No other name required.

Somewhere along the line after Nam, he "got noticed" by people higher in the food chain, eventually gaining the attention of the CSC, which invited him to join the highly secretive unit becoming a field agent in the containment of the global monster threat. They assigned him to Con-West and the role of overseeing RES SITE-ALPHA — Vamp Town. After a decade of babysitting vampires, they sent him back into the Army to run an enhanced training program intended to find and recruit the next generations of the CSC.

Now he stood on the banks of the Willamette River looking at his hometown—not recognizing it for all the construction that had gone on since his departure in 1970. The budget cuts that had been occurring since the great recession led to a policy of not replacing personnel as ranks thinned because of retirement and death. Officially retired from the army, Terry was still on the rolls of the CSC. Though he could easily wash his hands clean of the whole mess, he knew if he didn't help monsters would run loose again in the world. Besides, he really had nowhere else to go.

Terry squinted his eyes—trying to connect his past with what he was currently seeing. Everything about this city had changed. A bike bell trilled a couple from his rear as a rider warned him to get the hell out of the way. It seemed everyone rode those speed demon bikes. Terry hopped backward as the guy blurred by him, only to get yelled at by another cyclist whose path he jumped in, to get out of the way of the first. Yep, things certainly had changed. Even this viewpoint on the east side of the river had not existed when he was a kid. Just the freeway, Interstate Five. And that was barely ten years old when he had left in 1970.

Staring at the buildings on the West Side as they stacked up upon themselves rising away from the waterfront and up to the hills, he thought he could recognize at least a few of the remaining original cast-iron-front buildings that existed the last time Vlad had staked Portland out as his turf. The newer buildings he only knew from pictures online.

Vlad was here somewhere. That park over there across the river was the location of the original waterfront he had haunted. The changes must make this city even more foreign to Vlad than it was to Terry. The multi-tiered docks once lining the riverbank enabled ships to off-load no matter the height of the river. It also allowed for the creation of subterranean tunnels connecting the cellars of merchants to the boats.

The stories of how they used these passages ran the gamut; from the boring (extensions of commerce), to the nefarious (Shanghaiing sailors and opium dens), to the sensational (speak-easies and white slavery), to their complete non-existence.

As an agent for the CSC who spent many hours with Vlad, he learned the tunnels did indeed exist, and were not only employed for illegal human activities but also very popular with the undead set.

With the possibility of interconnecting tunnels still under the city, Terry knew that if Vlad were here in Portland, that is where he would be.

And then he remembered the promise made to his brother the last time they spoke—to look after his wife and daughter after he died. Of course, Terry meant it when he had said it, but his follow-through had left a lot to be desired. In fact, this was his first attempt. He fished a cell phone out of his jacket pocket and opened the contact list.

All the excuses played out through his head as he swiped at the screen, calling up the Terry name in the address book. He hesitated, finger hovering over the listing for Satchel Paige Terry, then stopped stalling and tapped on the green call button.

One ring, then the second and—

"Hello?" a female voice asked.

Terry hesitated. He was ashamed to admit that he couldn't recognize the voice as that of either his sister-in-law or his niece. "Um, hi. This is Jackie."

"JR!"

Relief. It was Satchel's wife, Martha. Naomi had never called him anything other than Uncle Jack.

"Now, what motivated you to call?"

"In town on a sort of business trip."

"Business? Thought you were in the Army?"

"They finally couldn't stand me. Retired last month. I, uh, picked up a side gig to supplement the retirement pay."

"Okay. Been a while JR." Her voice was somewhere between scolding and disappointment.

"I know. Look, I'm not the best at—"

"Oh, stop it. None of you Terry men were good at that sort of thing."

Terry felt the tension release from his shoulders. "How're things, Martha?"

"With me? Fine. I'm getting too old for teaching those sixth graders, but only one more year to go." She paused. "Now Naomi—that's another story."

"Something up? Want me to talk to her?"

"I would. She always seemed to like you, but she's not here."

"Maybe later."

"Not here—as in moved out," Martha said.

"Suppose it was about time. How old is she now? Thirty?"

"Forty-one. And yes, too old to still be living with me but—but it was a part of her diversion agreement."

He was thankful this conversation was happening on the phone. His face would have betrayed his feelings even more than the tone of his voice. "She on drugs?"

"Was. Now? Not supposed to be. Don't know. She's been gone for over a month this time."

"Listen, I'm sorry, maybe if I—"

"Told you to stop that talk, JR. Naomi isn't your daughter. The fault is mine."

"I could still talk to her," Terry said.

"Not sure anyone could say anything to her."

"I'd be willing to try. Couldn't hurt. Got a number you can give me?"

"Have her on my family plan. Hold on a second, and I'll send it to you."

Ping.

Terry's phone chirped at him, and he looked at the screen. "Got it. Thanks."

"Take care of yourself JR. Don't be so long in checking in again. You know you can call this number from wherever your side gig takes you. Doesn't necessarily have to be in the same town."

He could feel the smile in her voice and the loving warmth of her words. "Copy that, Martha," he replied softly. "If I talk with Naomi, I'll let you know."

"Thank you." And she hung up.

He looked at the number of his niece on the screen. His thumb hovered over it. Now was as good a time as any. He willed his thumb to move down and touch the screen, making the call, imagining that he could feel the micro-electric connection zap the skin as his finger touched the screen.

Ring. Ring. Ring.

"Bitch. Can't answer, leave a message."

Terry hung up immediately, not knowing what to say, stood up from the cold concrete wall and promised himself he would try again later. He turned back to look at the city. It was beautiful, even if it was no longer his home.

Where the hell under all that are you hiding Vlad? he wondered.

Chapter 20

HUNTER HUNTED

NAOMI SQUEEZED OUT of the crowded club and into the reassuring, cool night air. When she had entered, dusk was fading. The transition from day to night was a relief from the sun, even with the overcast which blanketed the valley filtering its intensity. Outside the rollicking venue, she could light a cigarette and assess the targets she had identified for him. There were so many to choose from. A myriad of possibilities. It was like a chocolate sampler. One piece might be cream filled, another caramel, or nut, possibly nougat. The trick was to stay away from picking the cherry-filled one. Those were never welcome, at least as far as Vladimir was concerned.

The cherry-filled ones were almost always a disaster. They were of no value to anyone. They would talk your ear off about nothing; informing you about the sale of cat food that was going on at Freddy's, or how the bus had to take a detour from its usual route because of the Blazer's game, and then go into painful detail about the potholes it hit along the way. Even humans wanted to kill these. The master would judge among the different varieties presented and select the best for a second life in his family or become a late-night snack.

Sometimes, however, a vampire would choose not to turn or drain a human. There were thousands of people who were

aimlessly looking for a place to belong in search of doing
something with a purpose. When combined with a natural
susceptibility to being mentally manipulated, this type of
human was the perfect candidate for becoming a "familiar"
to the vampire. A familiar learned to understand the needs
of the immortal whom she or he served. A vamp maintained
the close bond with a familiar, occasionally feeding off it and
sharing its own blood in pitying amounts. This created a
yearning desire to please for the familiar to please its master.

Vampires rarely, if ever, turned a familiar. It dangled the offer
of immortality out as a ploy to secure loyalty. The true value
of a familiar remaining human was that it could roam the
earth during the daylight hours doing the vampire's bidding.
The familiar's strong bond with its immortal master made it
susceptible, though to a much lesser degree, to some things
that really could hurt or kill a vampire. Daylight, garlic, holy
water, and crucifixes could affect them to varying degrees.
There were, however, familiars who had lost their immortal
patron. These unfortunates lived in constant search of a
new master to serve. Many walked the streets talking to, and
yelling at, imaginary, invisible masters. They teetered on the
edge of sanity, lives unfulfilled, never finding another.

Naomi Terry had been on the search for something more
in her life. She wasn't a stupid person, but everything she
tried ended up in a disaster. She had no intention of going
to college after graduating from Jefferson High, which was
fine because her dismally low GPA would have kept her from
following a path to higher education. At first, she moped
around the house until her father and mother forced her
to get a job. At least she could contribute something to the
family. She tried waiting tables. Gave the barista thing a shot.
Even signed up for a class at Portland Community College

hoping that would inspire her to continue, and actually get a degree.

Nothing seemed to take hold. Honestly, she didn't really want to try much of anything. Hanging out with her friends and smoking ganja was a lot easier. After a few good hits, she didn't care about anything, especially not the white people who gave her and her posse the dirty looks as they sat on the playground equipment. When she needed some cash, there were always strip clubs for her to perform in. If she got high enough before going out onto the stage, the experience would fade into a blur, and the old guy's drool disappeared as she grabbed the dollar bills from their disgusting paws.

Standing on the street corner now the sun had receded to a comfortable level, she gathered her thoughts for her report to Vlad. Taking a drag from her cigarette, she casually eyeballed one target that might be ripe for the picking tonight. Naomi felt her phone vibrate. Checking it, she found she had missed several calls, all from a number she didn't recognize. But there was one voicemail. Out of curiosity, she touched the screen to listen to it.

"Naomi. Hi. This is Uncle Jack."

Naomi dropped the phone to her side in surprise. Then she held it back up and looked at the screen again. The message had played out, so she hit the play button again.

"Naomi. Hi. This is Uncle Jack. I'm in town for a few days and would love it if I could buy you lunch or coffee or something. I . . . uh . . . your mother gave me this number and told me you might need a bit of help. Well, anyway, you have my number now. Call me. Okay? Love you, girl."

Well, of all the . . .? How long had it been since she had any contact with him? Not since her daddy's funeral. *Where have you been, Mr. Army Man?* She turned the phone off and placed it into her coat pocket, shaking her head. *Screw you Uncle Jack!*

———◆◇◆———

THE BACKGROUND SOUND of a slow drip was all that anyone could hear, aside from the heavy breathing coming from the two standing before Vladimir. Until this very moment, they believed they were going to some hip Portland party in the old Shanghai tunnels. Well, at least they were half correct. Upon entering the chamber, though, the realization this was no party set in quickly. Their inability to turn and flee, because of the mental grip Vladimir had on them, was enough of a sign that they would have no fun here tonight. And, if that wasn't enough, Stephanie was standing directly behind them, almost salivating from the anticipation of the kill. A genuinely unsettling sight, even through the jaded eyes of Naomi.

These two were the ones from the club Naomi had selected for her master. The female was barely twenty-one. New in town. One of those creative wannabes. Came to Portland because it's weird which sounded good to her. With a minor inheritance, she was under no pressure to find a job right away. She would just bide her time and maybe land something with one of the many ad agencies or tech start-ups. Or she might score a gig at Nike or Adidas. Naomi knew instantly that this woman could make an excellent addition to Vladimir's slowly growing family, should that be his choice.

The other was a slightly too old hipster—stocking cap, big full beard, ironic mustache with handlebars, red and black checked shirt, tight black skinny jeans with rolled up cuffs, immaculately clean handmade boots. She had heard guys like this being called a "lumbersexual." Probably had a bun under that knit cap. He kept going on and on about the Timbers and their style of play versus the Sounders. This one, she knew from the start, was a cherry-filled, destined to be drained and discarded. Hell, she would have killed him herself just to shut him up.

That was what he liked: two options. Not a vampire herself, Naomi could mix with the general population outside during the day without harm, though she found direct sunlight to be irritating, usually resulting in a kind of heat rash and headache. She adored Vladimir and would do his bidding for as long as he desired. Perhaps one day he would extend the hand of immortality to her. She looked forward to the once-a-week connection that brought the promise of infinite life as he gently pricked her neck with his sharp fangs. Never sinking them in too far. Not really piercing the jugular vein. He would take from her enough that she felt bonded to him and knew that this ritual secured their mental connection, but he never went all the way with her. Never biting into her throat to the extent she would turn or die.

Vladimir directed the hipster to take the remaining steps towards his perch. Naomi looked away, knowing what was about to transpire. She rarely looked at her master while he fed. It seemed so tawdry to watch as he performed such a personal yet necessary function. However, she didn't have the same problem watching when he turned humans to make them his. It was a profoundly intimate act, but one that didn't lead to death. It was something far more beautiful—the start of a new life, an immortal one.

When she again focused her attention on the master, he was about to start in on the girl. The slumped husk of the hipster lay discarded in the corner of the dark chamber. Stocking cap long since tossed aside. And just as she suspected, the dead white dude had a man-bun. Others were now taking their turn, licking and slurping up his remains. There was always something left for his family. Vladimir was an excellent master in that respect.

Naomi watched the girl's eyes open wide at the initial insertion of his sharp fangs. The surprise sensation, not dissimilar to a virgin's when a man entered her for the first time. A gasp of pleasurable pain and then submission. But Vladimir was acting strangely tonight. The girl, whom she thought would be a perfect addition to his family. He did not release her as he usually did with those he would turn. Instead, his mouth remained attached to her neck, drinking in as much blood as he could, twisting what should have been a tender moment into one of brutality. Then Vladimir offered the remains of this innocent to his second, Stephanie, who finished her with a ferocity Naomi had never seen before.

She looked away. Naomi had witnessed many other savage sessions, such as this one. Intellectually, she knew that a vampire's need to feed was comparable to all creatures' base desire to stay alive. But what Stephanie was doing was more than feeding, and she could no longer watch. She fished the phone from her back pocket, the one her mother had given her and the one her uncle had called her on earlier. She was tempted to replay his message, but opened the photo album instead and scrolled through the pictures.

She looked at the family photos her mother had pre-loaded, hoping Naomi might find some connection with images from happier times, pulling at heartstrings severed long ago. Naomi knew looking at them would cast doubt on her own choices. Despite her declarations, she cherished those earlier days, which was why she hadn't deleted them. Now they provided a much-needed distraction from Stephanie's overzealous feasting.

Stephanie always took great pleasure in not just drinking a victim's blood but relished tearing the neck open. Sometimes, decapitating the victim. Since Naomi had become a familiar to Vladimir, Stephanie had become increasingly brutal with all the food brought before her. The vicious act of destruction partially turned Naomi off. Mostly, though, it disgusted her knowing it fell to her to cleanup after the horrendous proceedings. It was her job as a familiar, after all. It was the same for interns and apprentices everywhere, taking on the dirty work to prove one's worthiness.

Photos from the past flew across the screen in a blur as Naomi brushed her finger across it. She was looking for a more innocent moment from an earlier life. A flash of pink made her stop and tap the screen for a larger view. There she stood, grinning in her pink ruffled birthday dress, white bobby socks, and shiny black shoes. The grin on her face revealed a missing tooth. The sparkly pointed party hat canted to the side of her head had the number seven in red on it. Despite the sickening sounds coming from Stephanie inhaling the last of the girl, Naomi grinned at the memory. That wasn't the last time she had seen her Uncle Jack, but it was one she remembered fondly. He sure was handsome in his uniform. She swiped the screen for another picture.

Vladimir had been perching on the rotten old armchair. He watched Stephanie devour the girl with a touch of regal pride, as a father might have for a daughter achieving a new developmental milestone. Then he noticed Naomi. "What are you so intently looking at, my dear?"

"Oh, nothing," she said, as she attempted to shut the phone down but couldn't.

"Please continue. I am curious to look at these pictures. Families are so important, don't you think?"

Vladimir had reached into her mind. He was seeing through her eyes the pictorial history of her actual family. He guided her hand to swipe across the screen, revealing one image after the other. Again, the picture of the little girl that no longer existed standing in the pink skirt appeared. Her hand stopped. The little grinning girl remained smiling on the screen.

Vladimir stood and casually walked to Naomi. He reached down and grabbed the phone from her hand. "Who is this standing next to you?"

The release of her brain was sudden. She stood and looked at the phone. "That's my dad and mom."

"Ah yes, I see the resemblance. A handsome man. A happy looking couple," he said as he swiped to another picture. "And this one? The one in the uniform."

"That's Uncle Jack."

"Your uncle?" A memory from the past struck him. "You say *he* is your uncle? Jackie Robinson Terry? Known as JR?"

"Yes."

Vladimir took the phone back to his throne and sat looking at the picture. He addressed the image. "Well, my friend. I have not seen you in many years . . .."

He let his voice trail off in thought, then looked at Naomi. "Did you say that he was in town and wanted to see you?"

"I didn't say." But she felt Vladimir poking around in her mind again and could hear the phone conversation with Uncle Jack being replayed as though it were occurring at the very moment. Vladimir released her again, and she staggered from the disconnect. "Um, why are you interested?" she asked with hesitation.

"Let me just say JR and I have had some shared history together." Vladimir looked thoughtful. "Stephanie, my darling. I believe it is time for Naomi to join our collective."

Stephanie let go of the crumpled shell of the girl. The dead body folded upon itself as it slid to the floor. A trace of blood caught at the corner of Stephanie's mouth, poised to trace down her chin. She seductively let her tongue slip out, brushed it slowly around the lower lip and catch the lingering red droplet before it made an escape. It was the one God-given talent she excelled at—both as a human and as an immortal. Stephanie loved the art of seduction and turning a human into a vampire was a very alluring act.

Vladimir rose from the throne and approached his familiar.

Naomi felt odd. Her head swam, awash with some form of intoxicant. It felt as though she was floating in the warm water of a sensory deprivation tank or a baby in utero. The room became a blur of images, sensations, sounds, feelings. Naomi's pulse quickened. She felt blood pumping through her system. Her heart was working overtime as it circulated the vital fluid up into her brain and down through her feet, and up again through her heart and back into the brain.

She could feel Stephanie behind, just barely touching her shoulders. Then suddenly clutching them in a firm grasp. Naomi could feel Vladimir reaching into her. He spoke. In her mind, she could hear his calming voice settling any anxieties, helping her to focus. *"Listen to me. No harm will come to you. You already promised yourself to me. I want you now."*

Stephanie's grasp became less intense as she reached around and cupped her hands upon Naomi's breasts. The sensation that Naomi felt bordered on wild sexual desire, but that was too simple, too vulgar. Naomi was aroused by Vladimir's long-awaited promise to make her one with him. In anticipation, she rolled her head to the left, exposing the length of her neck for him to bite into, inviting him to penetrate her pulsing artery.

The air changed as Vladimir moved closer to her. His proximity made the pounding of her heart even more conspicuous. It seemed like it would burst from her chest at the next beat. She felt his hand under her chin as he gently rolled it further to the side to expose the expanse of her smooth, chocolate brown skin.

Again, his voice echoed through her head. *"You are mine and will always be so."*

There was the usual stabbing sensation when Vladimir fed to maintain his bond with her. Then she gasped as he sank his fangs deeper into her throat than he had ever done before. He drank deeply, extracting her humanity. Suddenly, he stopped, and Stephanie took a turn. Naomi lost all muscle control, but the vampires were cradling her, holding her in a welcoming embrace, helping deliver her into an immortal life.

When Stephanie had finished, the two vampires stepped away from their newborn. Vladimir lifted his left wrist up and made a cut with one of the sharp, claw-like nails on his right hand. Blood erupted from the slice and Naomi could smell the coppery sweet liquid. She had an overwhelming urge to taste it, a desire that was fulfilled by Vladimir, who stepped to her and held his bleeding wrist out as an offering. "*Yes, this is for you. Do not hesitate. Drink my daughter.*" She heard Vladimir's words ring through her head and grabbed his arm, and clamped her mouth around the bleeding wound.

Naomi inhaled the master's life force, swallowed, and drank more. It connected her to Vladimir, her blood-father, in ways she never thought possible. When he tried to pull his arm away, Naomi would not release her mouth from the cut. She drank and drank. He had to pry her mouth off his skin. This sent Naomi into a spin of rejection and disappointment. But as she was about to wail in despair, Stephanie offered her bleeding wrist to continue the transformation.

"There now, my daughter. You are one of us, but you must not take in too much at first," Vladimir said out loud.

Naomi slowed her consumption and felt the soft hand of her blood-mother combing through her hair while gently suckling her newborn. As Stephanie pulled her bleeding wrist away, Naomi stood, lost between the vestiges of humanity and life as an immortal, blood-thirst quenched, for the moment.

The foggy reality that had been her life faded, and the world came into a sharp focus. The cataracts of humanity stripped away and Naomi now saw the underground chamber through eyes with enhanced vision. Everything she looked at was clearer, more defined. The shadowy corners popped to life as she now saw every brick and every line of mortar.

Next, she became keenly aware of the slow, incessant drip. Before, it had been nothing more than background noise coming from somewhere in the dark. Now Naomi could pinpoint its location. She watched the drip in slow motion seep out of a crack in the ceiling, track it as it let go of the brick, and follow its free-fall to a spot on the floor where it smacked the hard surface and exploded into a spray of smaller drops. Zooming in on a specific droplet, she found she could see into and enter it, like on a science show that disassembled things at a micro-level, observing organisms swimming about inside. It was as if the drop was an airborne aquarium falling down on the dirty concrete floor.

Then she viewed the whole cycle in reverse, tracking the drip up from the floor, across the brick ceiling, up through the crack, into the dirt above, around sewer pipes and fiber optic lines, up through a layer of cobblestone covered by asphalt into another crack at the bottom of a puddle, beneath the night sky whose stars obscured by city lights.

Naomi was losing her equilibrium and became dizzy. Her knees went loose, and legs buckled. She felt Stephanie holding her, guiding her to Vladimir's throne, and gently lowering her into it. Her eyes remained closed, afraid of other disorienting reactions. *"Amazing is it not?"* She felt Vladimir inside her head again.

Then the image of the little birthday girl in the pink dress came into her head. The focus shifted from the dress to the man to her left. Uncle Jack. "Your uncle. J. R. Terry. He is in town? Have you talked to him?"

"No, not yet." Naomi's answer was not verbal, but she heard herself respond.

"Send your uncle one of those word messages."

"Text, you mean."

"Yes, yes, send him a text, and invite him to meet you tomorrow night."

Total control of her own movements returned to Naomi. She picked up her phone and typed.

"Good. Your uncle is a hunter. He hunts me and all like me, including you. You will assist me in putting an end to this hunter."

"Yes, my master."

Chapter 21

TEXT

THE VIBRATION COMING from his pocket was annoying him. He had turned the afternoon outing, reconnecting with his former home, into an exploration of the Old Town where Vlad used to roam oh so many years ago. To say that even an eighth of the buildings still existed from the late nineteenth century would be an exaggeration. Heck, when he was a kid, he didn't even know the working wharf area of the 1890s had ever existed along this stretch of the river now known as Tom McCall Park. Back when he was a kid, it was a highway, Harbor Drive. He shook his head, trying to conjure up all the buildings where Vlad's "haunting grounds" had once been.

That turn of phrase made him smile, "haunting grounds" instead of "hunting grounds." He had to have been the first one to coin it. At least he'd never heard it before. Well, maybe he had, but he was going to claim it, anyway. The point was, he was as unfamiliar with this part of town as Vlad had to be. A further consideration was that any entrances to a tunnel system that existed back in the bad old days had to be very few today, given how many buildings were torn down under the guise of progress. Terry knew the underground had been Vlad's personal Shangri-La, and his gut told him if Vlad were in Portland right now, he would be below the streets lurking at this very moment.

Zzzzd. Zzzzd.

The phone vibrated again. It was damned annoying. Terry did not know how people could function with such a distraction, continually tugging at them. He had read an article about people who could feel their phones vibrating in their pockets when no calls were incoming. Even weirder, they felt the vibration when no phone was in their pocket at all. It was called Phantom Vibration Syndrome. A lifetime in the Army kept him away from such societal needs as constant contact with everything in the digital world. It suited him just fine.

Zzzzd. Zzzzd.

Crap! It had to be Craig or Liz checking on him again. He told them to not worry, that he wouldn't do anything rash should he accidentally bump into Vlad while trolling the night spots in Old Town. But there they were, checking on him, not trusting the old guy. Hell, he had selected and trained almost every agent in the CSC. Nearly all. How Craig had slipped past him was still a mystery he would unravel later. And he had the Vamp Town beat long before those children were even old enough to watch Dracula movies. So, for them to be all worried that he couldn't handle himself—

Zzzzd. Zzzzd.

Shit! "Okay! Okay!" He removed his phone and looked at the screen. Three missed calls, all from the dynamic duo and one text. Naomi! She'd returned his call. He tapped on the screen to open the entire message: *Hey Uncle Jack. You want to hook up?*

He tapped the screen to respond: *Sure do.*

Her response was quicker than he thought it would be: *Cool!*

He checked his watch. He had some time before he had to be back at the hotel for a Skype meeting with the team and base, which was scheduled for five: *How about a late lunch?*

Naomi: *Today? Busy all day but free at night.*

Terry: *Tonight? Sure. Where? When?*

Naomi: *Meet me at Shanghai Tunnel Bar. 2nd and Ankeny. 9.*

Terry: *Good. See you then.*

Naomi: *Love U.*

Reading that brought a smile to Terry. He'd been AWOL from the family for so long he wasn't confident he deserved her love. Not that he was sure what, exactly, he deserved, but he guessed he would learn more about that tonight. He couldn't miss the team meeting, so not in good form that, but he also had to see his niece. Nine tonight gave him plenty of time to do both.

He opened the map app on his phone. He recognized Ankeny as an old Portland name, one of the founders, he thought, but he needed the memory jog regarding the actual location of the street she had directed him to. He typed Shanghai Tunnel Bar and got the red arrow/dot thing pointing at the corner of SW Ankeny and Second Ave. just off Burnside, the main east/west boulevard. The bar was near the section of Burnside known as Skid Road. Not Skid *Row*.

It always bugged him when he heard the term pronounced incorrectly. And even though things had cleaned up some since the last time he was here, there was still plenty of evidence that life's hard-luck cases still congregated here.

As a kid, he stayed away from this part of Old Town. There was no end to guys down on their luck hanging out in doorways, passing a bottle in a bag back and forth. In a city that was no stranger to vice, this area had been its beating heart. The sad part was that he seemed to remember a lot of those lost men were Native Americans, who had left the desolation of their reservations only to get caught in a web of self-destruction, seemingly unable to find worth anywhere else but at the bottom of the proverbial bottle. To a young Terry, those drunk Native Americans looked to him to have gotten even the shorter end of the stick than the blacks in this white city.

Studying the map, he saw the bar Naomi picked for their meeting—reunion?—was not too far from the Chinese Garden he was standing near. Well, that made it easier for him to find later. In fact, the map showed he had been near the corner of Ankeny and Second earlier when he had stopped to check out that funky Voodoo Doughnut shop. He almost went inside, intrigued by the Pepto Bismol flavored icing on one offering, but tempted by the bacon slice on top of a maple bar.

He touched on a thumbnail photo of the bar at the bottom of the map, which opened onto a gallery of images. Terry scrolled through the pictures showing what the kids called a dive bar—dark, intimate lighting and a wall lined with booze bottles behind the bar. The description showed it was in the building's basement, meaning it was underground. The dark, below-grade aspect of it, along with the name, played off the stories about the old Shanghai tunnels and the map app located the joint close to the center of where they were supposed to have been. Aside from all that, it looked like a fun place to have a drink and reconnect with his niece.

Nevertheless, it was quite a coincidence, meeting in a place called the Shanghai Tunnel, considering why he was in town.

THE SKYPE MEETING with Control was a total waste of time. Terry didn't like meetings for that very reason. Sometimes, rarely, vital information was passed on. He had to admit live, face-to-face sit-downs made it easier to understand nuanced meanings through body language that satellite teleconferencing could not reproduce. So, meetings? Okay, not all were a time-suck, but this meeting? A waste.

He couldn't even remember what Cole had said, nor the conversation that followed. Maybe it wasn't the meeting, or Cole, or anyone else. All Terry could think about was the truly monumental meeting he would have with Naomi later. He spent most of the time letting the voices of his comrades filter into one ear, letting their words bounce around in his brain while weighing the good of such a "family reunion" against the terrifyingly bad emotional confrontation it could turn into.

Mercifully, the meeting ended around 7:30. It gave him enough time to freshen up before he headed back into the city. As he prepped, Terry felt his confidence waver, afraid his niece would judge him unfairly. Which shirt should he wear? Was his hair presentable? Were his teeth clean? He gave himself one last inspection in the room mirror and looked down at the new body cam sitting next to his wallet on the dresser. He hesitated before reaching out and attaching it to his jacket. If they had described how this gadget functioned accurately, he wasn't all that crazy about making his family life a public reality event for anyone to watch. But the rules stated he had to always wear the camera when outside of personal space, such as a hotel room. No exceptions. And what the hell, he might even run into Vlad on the streets? A longshot to be sure, but what if? It was night after all. Then he reached for the room keycard, grabbed the car fob, and he was out the door.

The drive back into town was less painful than he imagined. The late hour must have helped, but locating a parking spot was a horse of a different color. He circled the area a few times, getting totally confused by the one-way streets and the "NO TURNS" signs, not to mention the flocks of people rambling from bar to bar, crossing in front of traffic without a care in the world. Wasn't this a work night? Did anyone work anymore? Finally, he saw a car pulling out of a small surface lot not too far from the bar. Counting himself lucky, he gladly paid the extortionist rate and headed down the street.

Outside the bar entrance, he stopped and got a good shot of the name on the door. *Shanghai Tunnel Bar.* Who needed to use their cell phone camera when you had a body cam recording everything? Everyone at the Center would get a hoot over the establishment's name. Then he entered into a cozy, street-level bar and followed the signs down the stairs to the larger, expansive basement. The place looked just as the pictures online showed. It was dark. A wall of booze was prominently on display behind the bar top. Dramatically colored lights and Chinese lanterns illuminated the otherwise dark space. Loud music was blaring from the sound system, which was not shown in the photos. And a fair number of customers populated the tables and bar stools.

Terry stepped up to the bar and ordered a drink. He almost had to use his drill instructor voice for the bartender to hear, but she just gave him a nod, turned to grab some bottles and got to mixing. Waiting for his cocktail, he scanned the room. Aside from the music—Metal? Thrasher? He really didn't know what to call it—he liked the vibe of the place. Maybe they'd be open to some Ellington. Or not. *Wonder if she's here already?* He turned in the opposite direction and landed in the arms of a woman.

"Uncle Jack!"

MINUTES AFTER THEIR first contact, Terry could tell that something wasn't right. Words would not form answers to Naomi's questions. They weren't questions but a running monologue flowing out of her mouth, more of an attempt to satisfy curious onlookers than to communicate with her uncle. Whatever he was experiencing, he was powerless, unable to control the most basic of movements. When his body moved, it was not of his own volition, but like he was a marionette, hand lifting only at the pull of a string.

Fuck! He yelled at himself, berating the rookie mistake, as the realization of his position became clear and felt foolish at being caught so effortlessly. *Naomi! How could—*

Naomi grabbed his hand, and he involuntarily followed her through the semi-busy bar. They went down a dim hallway past a couple doors marked as restrooms, and past a few customers lined up waiting to relieve themselves. They continued down the passage now, almost devoid of light, until they came upon a door. Naomi took a key from around her neck, unlocked it, pushed it open. Rusted hinges whined as they were called to duty. She pulled Terry through and into a dark void, turning completely black after she shut the door behind them.

At least I got a shot of the bar exterior before walking into the trap. Hopefully, they'll see it, Terry thought.

Without the benefit of light, he could not see where they were going. All he knew was that he was moving and there was nothing he could do to resist. One step after another. Terry felt his body being directed around a corner and over some rubble he guessed was a pile of bricks and straight down another passage. There was another turn and a duck under something low overhead—beams? pipes?—and another turn.

This new section was damp and smelled of wet earth. The inky blackness clung to him like a heavy coat. He thought he heard dripping water reverberating faintly off hard surfaces. Then there was a muffled sound from above. *Thump, thump.* It sounded like a car driving through a pothole. His feet were wet from the many puddles he traipsed through as water had seeped into his shoes, which weren't as water resistant as advertised. And he still didn't know where he was.

How can Naomi see in the dark? Has she been turned? He asked no one but himself.

At one point, Terry's hand rubbed against a rough wall—rock?—then almost lost balance as the wall gave way into the open void of another passage. The floor took a decidedly downward slant. Terry was being pushed, pulled, compelled to walk further into the depths of an abyss.

With nothing to distract him, Terry was free to analyze his tactical situation, which he could sum up with some fancy military jargon, BOHICA—Bend Over, Here It Comes Again. *Stupid!*

But upon reflection, he could see the imminent possibility Vlad would have found his troubled niece in and amongst the lost and miserable people he preyed on. Terry recognized he shouldn't have been so trusting. It was a possibility for anyone in Portland to be one of Vlad's familiars, or even a vampire. After all, this was his domain.

Terry had let emotion lower his guard, something he learned not to do—the hard way—when he was in Nam. That pretty girl couldn't have been older than fifteen, with a basket of fruit, smiling as she approached the street-side cafe he and his buddies were sitting in eating noodles. One guy pulled out a buck and waved her over to buy some. She pulled a grenade out of the basket instead of fruit and handed it to the eighteen-year-old American. It exploded, killing them both, injuring the rest of them. Who could have guessed that kid was Viet Cong? From then on, however, everyone looked like VC to him.

He should have anticipated the possibility Naomi, as much as anyone, could have been swept into the vampire's orbit. She had been in search of something, someone, and monsters such as Vlad took maximum advantage of such wanderers. But Terry had let feelings cloud his judgment. He felt guilt for not looking after his brother's family as promised. *God!* Denial was more than a long river in Egypt, as the old saw went. And now the evidence was staring him in the face, as he had no other explanation for her ability to navigate these winding tunnels in the dark without light.

They made a right-angle turn. The floor had leveled out, and now he could see a dim flicker of light bleeding out from a break in the lining of the black tunnel. It looked like they had reached the end of the journey. And, he suspected, his personal end of the line.

As Terry was being compelled to walk through the opening, he heard himself chastise many of his trainees about emotional distractions.

"I am not training your brain to remember. I am training your *muscles* to remember. When you are in the shit, I do not want you to stop to think about what to do next. I want you to act without wasting time consulting your *goddamned* brain.

"*Muscle* memory, not mental memory. Your job is not about thinking, it's about *acting*!"

Not even remembering his own rant, Terry had dropped his guard and walked right into a trap. He saw the irony of his retirement ending so abruptly, and all because of a greenhorn mistake of underestimating the enemy.

Once inside the space, Terry's body came to a stop, rigid, unmoving.

The interior reminded him of pictures he had seen in the National Geographic of ancient catacombs with dark nooks and crannies and odd cut-outs into the side walls. The room layout did not appear to be a planned or purpose-built space. There was a randomness to it, like it was an unintentional cavity formed as the result of one building foundation angling into another and broken through by street maintenance and sewer repairs.

The walls of this chamber were a variety of materials: raw dirt, brick, cement block, and poured concrete—the imprint of 1x6 wood forms permanently cast into the surface. Columns or pilings sprung up from the floor, supporting beams and unseen structures above. A tangle of pipes hung from the ceiling and hugged the walls, presumably carrying water to faucets and waste to be treated.

The center of the space was aglow with oil lanterns and candles, the brightness of the illumination falling off into dark shadows around its perimeter, emphasizing the bizarre layout of the place.

Terry thought he saw the dark outline of bodies crouching in the shadows inching towards him, eyes aglow from the lantern light, declaring their corrupt appetite.

Naomi had entered the chamber in front of Terry, obscuring his view, and when he stopped, she continued forward, approaching a man. He was sitting—no, more like roosting—on an old, ratty armchair as though it were a throne from which he lorded over his cowering minions. She took his hand and kissed it as she kneeled before that motherfucker Terry had come to Portland to find. Of course, it was Vladimir!

"JR . . . or is it Jack? Or are you going by master sergeant these days?"

Vladimir placed his hand on top of Naomi's head and stroked her hair. "I enjoyed listening to your internal dialogue as your lovely niece brought you to me. I didn't want to ruin the surprise of our reunion. But really, 'Bend

Over Here It Comes?' You military types and the need for such vulgarities. It must make you feel more invincible."

Terry felt the desire to kill. He glared at Vlad, who merely looked at him with indifference.

"Ah, yes, I see it now." Vladimir gave a mental nudge, and Terry felt himself being compelled to walk towards the throne. "Welcome to my home, Agent Terry."

Terry stepped closer and had one thought, *Ah shit!*

Chapter 22

RED SKY IN
MORNING

A LAMP CLICKED on. Light filled the room, intending to deceive Craig's brain into thinking it was sunrise and time to wake up. His gimmick of setting a lamp on a timer to precede the obnoxious blare from the alarm clock by several minutes worked again. It didn't always. But this time, it did. As sleep gradually slipped away, he remembered a dream he was in the middle of before being harshly yanked out of it.

He savored these moments. Not quite awake, but also still not exactly asleep, either. The in-between moment of the morning where he wished he could remain for the rest of his life. Craig closed his eyes. A feeling of warmth washed over him as the pieces of the dream came back, then dissolved into the electrical flashes that made up conscious thought. The memory of embracing and kissing the woman felt real and comfortable, and he knew he would long for that feeling again, even if it was just a figment of his imagination.

Bleat! Bleat! Bleat!

The alarm broke through the hazy blanket of sleep. Then he remembered the woman who had been in his dream. His partner, Liz Adams. Now why the heck did he dream of her, and doing *that* with her? Damned subconscious BS.

The disturbing thing about dreams was that sometimes separate incidents within a dream which the conscious self knew was a staged show felt real. In between the fantastical activities and disconnected logic of time and place, there were moments, moments in which it all could seem so present. The colors and lighting. The tenderness of the touch. A passionate kiss that you still tasted after waking. The lingering memory you couldn't shake even a day later, possibly two. A dream so real it made you question if reality only existed once asleep, not during that interval, called "being awake."

These dream-state encounters could be with people from the past, or complete strangers. This group of performers remained hidden in the subconscious, waiting to be cast in the next night's dream-play. Why the mind selected certain people for specific roles was a mystery.

However, when a dream as real as this happened, and the encounter was with someone so familiar, even one you closely worked with, well, that can suggest certain things. Things usually buried in the dreamer's subconscious mind not to be exposed to the light of day.

He was *not* attracted to Adams. *No way!* So why the dream?

There was something else at the end of the dream. But in the first part, there was a vampire attacking him. No. A vampire was attacking him *and* Liz outside a nest. No. It wasn't Liz, it was Kathrine, his partner before Liz, and she was heading into the nest alone. He had yelled at her, "Stop! Wait for the team." But she ran on in, not hearing. He put the vamp down and charged into the nest after her. He saw her back turned. Her red hair blazing as rays of sunlight caught it coming through the cracks of the boarded-up windows. A vampire she didn't see was about to bite into her neck. He shot his weapon, and the vamp went down, and then another materialized, and he shot that one too. Then another came and another . . .

This continued for what seemed like hours. And yet they kept coming. He pulled the trigger over and over, never running out of ammo. Kathrine never moved to him. Finally, he emptied his magazine into the last of the bloodsuckers and only then did she turn to look at him. But it wasn't Kathrine.

Now it was Liz. She looked him in the eye. Tears of relief flowed down her cheeks. He had saved Liz, except it was supposed to be Katherine in the nest and he hadn't saved her. He had to put her down, bitten as she was. But Liz stood looking at Craig, her red hair cascading over her shoulders, and collapsed into his arms. He held her in a loving embrace, relieved that he had saved her, and they kissed. Then the timer rolled over to 6 a.m. with a *CLICK* and the light flashed on to life. The dream was over. Kathrine was still dead, killed by his own hands. But Liz Adams was alive and waiting for him in the mobile control van.

THE SIDE DOOR slid open with a smooth, rumbling swoosh.

"Got any ideas where your master sergeant is?" Craig asked, handing Liz a coffee.

Liz swiveled her chair around facing the open door, accepted the caffeine and took a sip. "He's not *mine*. And besides, I'm not in charge of his movements." She turned back to the computer screen and resumed looking through documents that Mountain Home had sent. "Anyway, he said he had some family business to attend to."

"When was that?" Craig asked.

"A few hours ago." Liz looked at the clock on the desktop. *7:35 a.m.!* "I mean, last night. Why? Isn't he here?"

"Nope. I gave his door a good hard rap or two. Figured the old guy needed to catch some extra Zs. Didn't answer his room phone either."

"Try his cell?"

"Nada on that too."

"Well, he's a big boy. He'll turn up soon."

"Soon was for our 7:30 get-the-day-started meeting, a time we all agreed to after our group Skype yesterday." Craig sat on the edge of the open door and leaned against the frame. "And before you ask, one of the rentals is gone."

"That only means he used it to go back into town to see his niece."

They had taken rooms at the Airport Hilton, located thirteen unlucky miles from downtown Portland. The airport was just off Interstate 84, which was the highway they had driven west out of Idaho on. They usually situated their command centers near the local airport, where they could always find hotels, cheap food, and other services such as car rentals, and bars. And, of course, the airport facilities themselves if they needed to fly in any reinforcements.

"Well, he should have been back by now for the meeting. Dude impresses me as having a permanent stick up his ass regarding procedures, especially being on time if not early."

"You could say something like that," she replied, smiling. Then paused and thought a moment. "But you're right. He would have at least called to say he was running late. Shit, now you have me a little concerned." She fingered the bottlecap-sized pin attached to the front of her blouse. "You say these things are always on and recording?"

"I didn't say, but the IT guy from D.C. did. Supposed to monitor everything we do in the field. It instantly uploads images to the cloud, and then the keyboard monkeys can review our actions later or watch us in real time."

"Let's see if anyone's awake back there." She typed, clicked, and moused sending a message.

Reply: *Good morning.*

Liz typed: *We seem to be missing one master sergeant. You got anything on him from his body cam?*

Reply: *Will check and get back to you.*

Liz responded: *Skype me when you find something. Thnx.*

She turned back to Craig. "So, while we wait, you have said nothing about the visit to your mom's."

"What's there to say?"

"Oh, something like: 'That was sure a delightful visit,' 'I miss her,' 'Should do it more often,'" she prodded. "Or: 'Thanks Liz for being there. Your presence really covered my ass.'"

Craig stared into his cup and said nothing. The cream still had not integrated entirely into the steaming liquid. Somehow, maybe, the dissipating swirling pattern might reveal the best response to the question he couldn't answer. "I guess you could tell it wasn't a comfortable experience . . . for her and for me."

This revelation softened him somehow, made him seem vulnerable, more human.

"Anyway, thanks for coming along. You did make it easier for me. I owe you."

"Well, I needed to get away. At least the weather was nice. Though you could have allowed more time. It was a quick turnaround."

"*That* was not my doing. Cole called for the meeting after I had told mom I was coming. Otherwise, I wanted to drive you back to Portland by going up the coast. It's a pretty drive."

She smiled. Was he hitting on her? "That would have been nice. Raincheck for another shot at it?"

"You got it. And rain is probably what you'll get too," he said, giving her a wink.

Chapter 23

REALITY TV

T HE NEW TECHNOLOGIES the CSC was using were supposed to offset the loss of funding on the human side of the organization, as if technology alone could monitor, contain, and search for all the monsters the agency had done since its founding. The prevailing theory reasoned that even though technology was pricey, it didn't need vacations, hospital stays, maternity leaves, pensions, or death benefit payouts.

As a result, Paul and Ellie, who were among the newest human assets added to the organization, were also among the fewest added in a very long time. They had to do more than learn how to hunt and fight vampires, lycans, and mutants. They also had to master the intel side of things and the new tech wizardry, all of which had been distinct departments previously. So, instead of traveling west with Craig, Liz, and Terry, they had to sit in the windowless, climate-moderated Control Center, locked away in a secret facility, inside the secured Mountain Home Air Force Base, in the middle of nowhere, Idaho. It was like being the babushka in the heart of a set of Russian nesting dolls.

On the big screen, Ellie and Paul were watching the feed from the body cams. The button-sized cameras also contained microphones and GPS chips for keeping tabs on an agent's movements.

Since they always turned the body cams on when in the field, every single moment in an agent's daily activity could be watched—live. And yes, *every* moment. Some genius had determined that giving agents the option to turn the device off would also provide them with the opportunity to forget to turn it on. So, no off-switch was provided. All material captured by these intrusive appliances uploaded continually and stored in the all-powerful cloud where it was accessible for after-action review. An ill-conceived procedural protocol, not to mention a tremendous drain on batteries, but one that came in handy when trying to find out what had happened to the master sergeant.

Fortunately, Terry was a stickler for following the rules. He was told to wear the camera at all times outside of his room. And wear it, he did. Because of the GPS signal, they easily located where he was. The disturbing thing about the signal, however, was that there was no sign it had moved since 9 p.m. last night, meaning the device was still pinging away from inside the bar Terry had entered.

The video playback would give them more specific information regarding Terry's fate. But not all technologies provided instant answers, and like this, required some moments to find and retrieve the correct files. When waiting to receive vital information regarding the safety of a friend, any amount of time it took was too much time, and Liz was becoming impatient.

"What's taking so long?" Liz demanded, glaring into the camera above the monitor.

"First, I'm new to this. Second, it's only been a minute. And third—" Paul stopped. "Okay, I've got the files downloaded from the master sergeant's cam and cued up. Ready?"

Before hearing an answer, the video playback rolled.

On the screen in front of Liz and Craig, an image of Terry appeared in a mirror after putting on his jacket in the hotel room. They watched him adjust the button cam to make sure it aimed in the right direction. A timestamp at the bottom right corner of the video said that it was 7:43 p.m. the night before.

"At least he's not so old school that he didn't pay attention to the tech briefing we gave him," Craig interjected.

Then Terry grabbed the room keycard from the dresser top in front of him and turned for the door.

"Fast forward through this stuff, Paul. Will you?" Liz asked, her voice tinged with impatience.

They then watched a sped-up version of Terry getting into the rental, driving on the freeway and into town, fight evening traffic, looking for on-street parking, and finally giving up, pulling into a pay lot.

"Paul, you have a location of that parking lot?" Craig asked.

"Uh, yeah, Google maps has it listed as Diamond Parking, Lot EP61. SW First and Ankeny."

The video resumed. Terry left the lot and was now walking past revelers, a couple of homeless looking for handouts, and a derelict drunk relieving himself on the side of a building. He stopped in front of a bar entrance and moved his body, trying to capture the name of the establishment. The sign read—*Shanghai Tunnel Bar.*

——◄O►——

LIKE VOYEURS, THE four watched Terry enter a compact street-level bar, but he did not linger there. They watched him continue down a set of stairs to the main bar in the basement. It was dark, low-ceilinged, and lighted by soft-colored, paper-shaded pendants. The wide-angle lens on the camera gave a distorted, one hundred eighty degree view of the surroundings. Several people were drinking and having a good time, but it appeared Terry hadn't seen the person he was trying to meet, so he walked up to the bar and sat at the empty corner. The bartender—hipster girl, multiple tats, and piercings, with half her hair shaved and the other half a deep purple fading out to white at the ends—approached, acknowledged his order, and gathered the ingredients to make whatever concoction he had asked for.

Terry resumed a visual sweep of the room, maybe to give anyone who was watching the lay of the land, but more than likely, he was just trying to see if his niece had arrived. Then he abruptly pivoted, and the camera showed the face of an African American woman just before the image went out of focus and blacked out as the two came together in a hug.

"Let's have the audio feed on this," Liz requested.

"Uncle Jack!"

"Hey princess," Terry paused, which turned into an awkward silence. "Look, Naomi . . . I'm sorry."

"It's okay, Uncle. No apologies." Naomi put her finger up to Terry's lips to silence him. It was an almost alluring gesture. "I'm a big girl now. I know how the world works."

"Don't be mad at your mother. She didn't ask me to talk to you. My idea."

Naomi looked around the bar. "Well, if talk is what you want, we should find a quieter spot." She flashed a beguiling smile, held out her hand for Terry to grab and she led him into a dark hall off the main room.

"What's she playing at?" Craig asked.

Liz shook her head in disbelief. "It looks like his niece is trying to . . . seduce him?"

Ellie's voice came over the speakers. "I wish we could see the master sergeant's face."

"Why?"

"I'm betting that his mind is being manipulated. Remember the Bucket of Blood in Vamp Town? The look on his face would give that away for sure."

"Fuck! You're right. Terry wouldn't go anywhere that might compromise his position. Not after drilling tactical awareness into our brains like he did," Liz said.

Paul added, "Unless he's being given a light touch, you know, Vlad just reaching into his head just enough to make him feel like he is doing something not against better judgment."

Craig wasn't so sure about the analysis. "Wow! Slow down there, cowboys. This is a big jump from meeting his niece, albeit under very weird circumstances, to some evil plan of Vlad's."

"Terry was on the SITE-ALPHA detail long before you got to the Asylum, right Craig?" Ellie asked. "He said that he coined the name Vamp Town. So, he knows Vlad."

"It's still a mighty big jump to connect Terry's niece with Vlad. Funky actions aside."

The lack of movement in the video drew their attention back to the screen. Naomi had stopped at a heavy metal door—one of those old fire doors with the multiple segments of sheet metal welded together. She pulled out an antique skeleton key and inserted it into a lock. After turning the key, she pushed on the door, swinging it away from them into a black void.

"Come on Jack, I won't bite." The temptress pulled him with her as she went through the opening.

Craig's heart beat faster. He didn't want to believe his partners, but he felt maybe they were on to something. "Wait. Go back a bit to where she said she wouldn't bite."

The video froze. Rewound. Then moved forward. "Come on Jack, I won't bite."

"Pause it." Craig got closer to the monitor, leaning over Liz's back. "Look! Her smile—"

"Holy shit!" Paul spit out.

Ellie asked, "Are those the tips of fangs?"

"That's what they are." Liz declared.

The door closed, and the image went black.

"Paul—"

"I got it."

The timestamp in the screen's corner clicking off seconds
was the only indicator the recorded image was moving at
all, let alone at fast forward. Then a flicker of light became
discernible.

"Continue at normal speed," Craig ordered.

A grainy image, barely visible because of the low light,
materialized. As Terry moved closer to the source, they could
see he had entered a chamber. Crossing through the entrance
was like dawn breaking for the light-sensitive camera, and
the screen burst forth in a bright white before it adjusted to
the new light level. An assortment of oil lanterns and candles
lighted the interior of this room.

While the illumination from the burning wicks provided
enough light for the camera to read most of the space,
there were still many dark shadows for anyone to be lurking
unseen in the gloomy perimeter. Naomi stood in front
of Terry, blocking the camera from seeing anything other
than her backside. Then she quickly stepped away from
her uncle and kneeled, revealing Vlad sitting on a decaying,
upholstered armchair.

The presence of that vampire sent chills down the spines of
everyone watching. They knew what Vlad was capable of
and had seen the horrible things he had done. Not one of
them believed his presence spelled out a fortunate outcome
for the master sergeant.

The position of the body cam Terry was wearing meant the
visuals were from his chest's point of view. The camera feed
was remarkably stable, suggesting Vlad had immobilized
him. The audio only contained background sound in

the chamber—dripping water, whispers, a giggle, heavy breathing. Nobody was talking. Then they heard Vlad's voice.

"JR . . . or is it Jack? Or are you going by master sergeant these days?" Vlad stroked Naomi's hair. "I did not want to ruin the surprise of our reunion, so I made no comment on your internal dialogue as came to me. But really? 'Bend Over Here It Comes?' You military types and the need for such vulgarities. It must make you feel more invincible. Ah, yes, I see it now. Welcome to my home, Agent Terry."

Then he lowered his hand from Naomi's hair to her cheek and caressed it lovingly. "My sweet. I think it is only appropriate that you get the first serving. After all, your uncle is our guest of honor."

She smiled. Stood and moved in close to Terry, completely covering the lens of the camera. Cut off from the ability to view what was happening, except for brief glimpses of Vlad grinning madly at the proceedings, they only had the audio portion of the event to listen to, which was, by itself, a disturbing experience. The seductive words and animalistic noises flowing out of Naomi's mouth might sound pornographic to anyone who didn't understand this wasn't sexual foreplay. It was something more associated with a predator animal toying with its prey before killing it.

Watching one more person about to die was too much for Craig. His breathing became shallow, and he felt lightheaded and nauseous. When he stepped back from the monitor, Liz understood. "Pause the video, please, Paul."

"Everything okay?" Paul asked.

"Just stop the damned video!" Liz turned around to check on Craig. He was taking a swig out of a bottle of water. "You good?"

"Yeah . . . uh, yeah . . . let's finish this." And they both turned their attention back to the computer screen.

"Sorry, Paul," Liz said apologetically. "Continue."

The feed resumed. It was still mostly audio, and now it was clear "play time" was over. The sickening sounds of Naomi feeding on her uncle left nothing to the imagination. And after what each of the viewers had personally witnessed, from the newest recruit to the oldest hand, their memories were more than sufficient to paint the gruesome details of the master sergeant's death.

Then they heard Vlad's self-satisfied voice. "Enough. We must save some for the others."

With that, Naomi stopped and stepped away, allowing the agents to see what the camera lens saw. In horrified silence, they watched the image move back and forth as though the camera was swaying in an unnatural breeze, as if Terry was held upright hanging from an invisible rope.

Naomi sashayed up to Vlad's side and stopped. She turned back to the camera with a look of sated satisfaction, her mouth red with the blood of her family. She bent down as if to give Vlad a kiss, but he flicked his finger up and took a swipe of the blood off her lips, licked it, and nodded towards Terry with appreciation. Then, out of the grainy gloom behind Vlad, Stephanie emerged and sidled up to his opposite side and draped herself across his shoulders.

Ellie let out a slight gasp at the sight of Steph, the only one from the bus to have been turned, aside from the little girl

Cindra. Vlad dramatically held out his right arm. With a flourish, he whisked his wrist around, pointing his fingers towards Terry as though the action was a command. The strings of mental bondage cut, and Terry's puppet body staggered. The image wobbled as the master sergeant seemed to fight to remain on his feet. Then his voice croaked out one word directed towards Naomi.

"Why?"

Abruptly, a group of vampires emerged from the dark niches of the chamber, flashing their fangs eagerly wanting their piece. They surrounded Terry, but before the video image became obscured by their bodies, there was one last clear view of Naomi. Did they see a hint of regret in her eyes? She licked her lips. Then the picture moved violently. A montage of blurry snippets played out, showing the ceiling, bloody faces, blackness, and the ground. The camera attached to Terry's coat dutifully recorded his body being dismantled. Dismantled was the most clinical word applicable. In reality, the hungry vamps tore him apart. And the agents watched hands and mouths frantically grab their piece of the great vampire hunter. It was like early tribal hunters eating the killed beast to absorb its strength.

At some point, the button cam seemed to move up, then down, then swing around as the now dead man's torso was being tossed about. Paul was sure he saw one vampire holding Terry's head above his mouth, draining blood from the brain, but he said nothing. Didn't need to. It was a repellent sight he knew all had seen.

In a state of shock, Ellie said quietly, "I . . . I think Commander Cole needs to see this."

Chapter 24

RESCUE

D IRECTLY AFTER TERRY choked out the last word of his life, Liz turned her chair away from the computer screen at the rear of the mobile command unit and made for the driver's seat.

"Whoa! What do you think you're doing?" Craig asked, surprised by her action.

Liz plopped down in the swivel chair and rotated it towards the steering wheel.

"Going to save him."

"Terry's dead."

"No, he's not. He's just captured."

"Just because you turned your head away from the screen at the moment of the attacked doesn't mean he's alive. There is nothing you can do for him."

Liz ignored Craig and looked around the dash. She flipped down the sun visor, then looked in the console compartment.

Craig held up a ring of keys. "Looking for these?"

"Give 'em!" Liz violently reached for the keys.

"I understand," he responded as he pulled his hand away from her fingers.

"What? What do *you* understand?"

"Watching a friend die."

This response stopped Liz. She pulled back her arm and sat for a moment until her breath slowed. Then her shoulders sagged in submission, and she lowered her head, resting her brow on the top of the wheel. Her back moving in spasms was all Craig needed to know. Liz was crying. He moved to the seat next to her and softly placed a hand on her shoulder. There was really nothing to be done to ease her grief. He had to trust that her core emotional strength would bring her around to see that now was not the time for sorrow, but for action.

"Look. We're going to go for Vlad, but I need you to be clear-minded and focused when we do. It'll be dangerous enough without both of us firmly in control of our wits."

After several minutes, Liz regulated her anguish and sat up straight. A few sniffs, a sleeve wipe across her nose, and she appeared to be ready. "Sorry," she apologized—fully aware that Craig had lost more than one close friend in the line of duty, putting them both down as well.

"Nothing to be sorry about," he replied with understanding. "It isn't easy. How could it be?"

Another sniff, "So . . . what do we do next?"

"We know what part of the city to start our search. Just don't know where Vlad is hiding under it."

"If we can pinpoint where Terry died, it would be a good start. Paul and Ellie can help us on that," she said.

"Oh, yeah! They can track his body cam." Craig replied not sure if they really could do that.

"Hopefully, Vlad is still in the same place," she replied, as she moved back to the rear of the van and sat in front of the computers. She got herself situated at the keyboard and hit the Skype call button. Ellie and Paul appeared on one monitor.

"Liz! You okay?" Ellie looked concerned.

"As okay as can be expected. We need to know if you can track Terry's movements once he entered the basement bar."

Paul scratched his chin. "Depends on a couple of things. I mean, as far as I understand how this system works, we won't be able to distinguish between the surface and the basement or any subfloors. Also, not sure how far below ground we can read the signal. Since we could watch his feed . . .," There was a moment's hesitation, recognizing that they had just watched the man die. "I'm assuming he was only one floor down since he entered the tunnels through the basement-level bar of the building. But that is only a guess, since most of what we watched was in the dark. Heck, he may have gone down some stairs or climbed down a ladder. No way of knowing how many levels there—"

"Yes, and?" Craig asked impatiently.

"We won't be able to map out any passages or rooms, the signal will just tell us he was somewhere inside the footprint of the building or near it, say if he were in a tunnel under the street. Now, if we had an accurate layout of the interior of the building and the tunnels, then we could pinpoint—"

"Got it," Ellie interrupted. "Sorry, had to let him ramble so I could do the real work." A satellite image of the building appeared on the van's second screen. "If we do a minute-to-minute review of his GPS signal, we can draw a line by connecting the red dots you see from the time he entered the building, walked through it down into the basement, then under another building, under a street and stops in the middle of this parking lot." Liz finished by pointing a finger at a red dot on the screen.

"Looks like a Family Circus cartoon where Jeffy wanders all around the neighborhood to get home using the least direct path," Craig said aloud absentmindedly.

Liz looked at him. "What the hell are you talking about?"

"Family Circus? Oh, never mind." Sounding more the man in charge, he continued. "Now that we know where to look, we'll take the second rental. This van will be too hard to park."

They didn't get away from the hotel until early afternoon. After a quick bite and transferring a few "toys" from the armory into the trunk of the Corolla, they were on their way. They had no plan. Craig knew this hunt would differ from any he had been on. Seeking a vampire nest in the heart of a city had the potential to go wrong in so many ways. They needed to make their insertion during the daylight hours. At least the sun would keep the vampires from escaping above ground and mixing with the public, they hoped. But they were flying by the seats of their pants on this and could not predict how this would turn out and how messy it could be.

The drive into town wasn't as bad as expected. This stretch of Interstate 84 between the airport and the city could get very congested, but it was still early. The only real problem came where it forked, giving the option of going either north or south on Interstate 5. Neither of them had ever driven into Portland, and this was where things got dicey. Craig said his map app recommended taking the south fork and exit over a bridge into downtown, take an easy right turn and, *bam*, there was their location—while the GPS in the car told Liz the north fork, exiting near the convention center, and going past the basketball arena was the correct route, which she took. She was the driver, after all.

Immediately after exiting the freeway, they found themselves caught in a messed-up maze of traffic lights and intersections where light rail tracks, buses, and trolleys all intersected with autos, pedestrians, and bicyclists going in a multitude of different directions. As luck would have it, all the mass transit options had arrived just as they entered the area, vomiting forth their passengers.

"I wonder what route Terry used to come into town. I bet it was my way," Craig prodded.

"It doesn't matter," Liz replied as she drummed her fingers on the steering wheel, watching the traffic light cycle to red again.

"Bet we could find out." He brought his phone up, pretending to dial Paul at HQ.

Liz shot Craig a stabbing glare that scared him, so he put the phone back in his pocket.

After a break in the congestion, they proceeded over the river and turned left into Old Town. From there, the GPS guided them straight to the Shanghai Tunnel Bar. Luckily, it was past lunch, and the parking in the area had freed up; allowing them to find a spot only a block away.

Liz parked. They got out of the car and went to the trunk to gear up. There were plenty of people still on the sidewalks, and the looks the agents got varied between curiosity to concern as they first donned tactical vests. A rough hacking cough came from behind. They turned, and Craig partially lifted his .357 out of the trunk at the ready, but what they saw was an old toothless dude sitting on a folding stool next to an overloaded shopping cart. He coughed again.

"Must be one hell of a party you two're going to. That stuff Kevlar you puttin' on?"

Not responding to the comment, they returned to the task at hand. Craig strapped on his belt with a holster and spare rounds. Liz did the same with her 9mm and a silver alloy tactical knife.

"Had me a couple o' them in Nam." The wino hacked out. "Knife wasn't as pretty, and the gun was a .45."

Craig lifted an HK MP5 out of the trunk and swung it around towards the voice as he put the sling around his shoulder in an intimidating fashion, just to scare the guy and maybe get him to shut up.

"Whoa. Calm down!" The wino hacked and coughed again. "Just tryin' to be friendly."

Liz placed a calming hand on Craig's back just before she pulled out a Mossberg 500 shotgun and loaded it. Pushing as many of the silver pellet-filled cartridges into the chamber as it would allow.

"That scatter-gun would have been handy down in the tunnels where VC hid," the wino hacked out, then turned and spit.

"Ready?" Craig asked.

"Yep."

"Then let's get to it." As Craig closed the trunk, he turned to the street guy. "And don't think of breaking into that car." He pulled back on the charging handle of the HK and let it snap back into place for emphasis.

"Whatever you say, general," the wino said, giving Craig a sloppy salute.

Then Craig tossed the guy a few bills out of his pocket and gave him a wink. "Thanks."

They walked cautiously along the block towards their target. People who saw them fearfully got out of the agents' way. Few wanted to get mixed up with whatever these armed strangers had in mind. But one guy approached them and asked curiously, "Where's the camera? Thought they stopped shooting *Grimm* last year. Oh, you're on *The Librarians*."

Craig responded, flustered by the question. "Just stay the hell—"

"You're ruining the shot. Could you please move away?" Liz interceded, accepting the cover thrown at them.

"Oh, yeah, sorry," he said apologetically, as he quickly left the agents to continue their "scene."

"What the fuck was that?" Craig asked, shaking his head.

"That was Portland."

"That was weird."

"That's what I hear."

Outside the front door of the establishment, they saw a "CLOSED" sign slapped on the glass.

"What do ya think?" Liz asked.

"Try the handle and see what happens."

Liz cautiously reached for it, while Craig stood at the ready. She slowly pushed her thumb down on the lever and pulled. Her eyebrows shot up, slightly surprised the door was unlocked, and continued to pull it open.

"Trap?"

"You said it."

They stepped into a small street-level bar. A youngish guy was working behind the counter, back turned to the door. Music was blaring out of the Beats headphones that seemed to be permanently affixed to his head. The music was loud. So loud, Craig thought he might even suffer some hearing damage from it. So loud that the guy didn't know the agents had entered the bar.

Liz and Craig stood for a few moments watching the guy mouthing the words to the unmistakable classic Stones tune about Satan being around at all the horrible moments in world history. The line about being in St. Petersburg when the czar and his family were killed seemed appropriate for hunting a Russian vampire.

After a few more seconds, Craig was tired of the performance. "Hey!" he yelled. And got no response, so he banged the HK on the bar top.

The man turned and saw the agents. "The sign says we're closed," he shouted, but cut short his protest when he saw the weapons pointing at him.

"Stairs?" demanded Craig.

"What?"

"Stairs!" Craig said louder.

"What?"

Craig pointed at his own ear with a wry smirk.

"Oh, yeah," the guy pulled off his headphones. But the music was even louder without his head to absorb most of the sound. "Sorry? What?" the man shouted back.

Exasperated, Liz barked. "Turn the fucking music off!"

"Oh, yeah." The barman pulled a cell phone out of its cradle, tapped the screen, and the music turned off. "Bluetooth." He stated as though anyone cared.

Craig raised his weapon slightly.

The barman's eyes widened. "Look, dude, I don't know what you're doing." He put his hands on the bar top in a gesture of being in charge. "But I don't want no trouble."

Liz saw two dots tattooed between the webbing of his right hand, between the thumb and forefinger—the mark of a familiar. She gave Craig a nudge and a nod for him to see.

"Look," Craig said, leaning on the bar, moving the barrel of the HK closer to the barman. "The silver in this bullet won't make you go all gooey as your body implodes on itself, but it sure as shit will kill you the old-fashioned, human way. So, point out the stairs!"

"B-b-back down the hall, see the sign?"

They both looked where the familiar was pointing and saw a large sign—"TO STAIRS." Before they went down to the basement, Craig grabbed the business phone that was sitting on the back bar and ripped it out of the wall. "Cell phone too," he demanded.

"Hey! That cost me a bunch. It's a Ten," the man protested as Craig snatched the new iPhone that had been the source of the music out of its cradle and dropped it to the floor.

"I hope you got the insurance," Craig said, crushing it under his foot.

"Now stay here and be good," Liz said as she zip-tied the guy's hands to a brass rail attached to the bar.

With that, Craig followed Liz through the hall to the stairs to the basement. She was halfway down when a loud ringing came clanging from the bar behind them.

"Shit!" Craig blurted out, running back to the entry.

The barman, hands still tied, was standing on the tips of his toes. He was awkwardly stretching his neck up as far as it could reach, teeth firmly clamped onto a knotted lanyard attached to the clapper of a brass ship's bell hanging above his head. He was vigorously rocking his head up and down, creating an alarmingly loud racket as he tried to signal anyone in the basement that trouble was on the way.

Craig shook his head, almost laughing out loud as he looked at the ridiculous sight. Drawing a knife, he came close to slicing the guy's lips as he cut the lanyard away from the bell.

"Really dude? You could strain something standing like that. Now do as the lady asked and, *this* time, be good!"

Craig then turned and ran back down the hall and down the steps. He jumped over the last two and landed on the floor in time to see a handful of customers scrambling down a dark hallway. One caught his eye as she turned and looked back before escaping. Naomi!

"Liz! Naomi in the hall," Craig yelled out.

Liz turned from the tattooed bartender and bee-lined to where Naomi retreated into the dark passage. A young man wearing a red flannel shirt and stocking cap flew towards Liz, trying to stop her, fingers curled with a set of extended claws ready to dig into the agent. Craig fired one round and nailed the kid. Vapor from the dying vamp immediately erupted from his mouth and nose, but Liz didn't turn or respond to the assault as she ran in pursuit of Terry's killer.

"Liz! Wait for me!" Craig yelled uselessly after her.

Now there was little doubt as to the coincidence of Terry meeting his niece in this bar at night. It was a vampire hangout. Vlad lured him here using Naomi as bait. The master sergeant didn't stand a chance.

Craig turned his weapon onto the remaining customers before another attack, and they quickly raised their hands.

"He . . . he was the last one. The rest of them went out the back by the bathrooms," a woman spewed out, pointing towards the hall Liz had chased Naomi into. "We're not one of them." She presented her tattooed hand to Craig. "See. We're all familiars."

"Better hope that's all you are. Up the stairs with the lot of you. Let the sun decide." He fired a burst into the ceiling to put an exclamation point on the statement. As the kids headed up the stairs, he heard one ask another, "What's a familiar?"

Honey trap.

Then Craig spun back towards the hall and followed Liz. At one point, he heard her shotgun fire once, twice. He came to a bathroom door. A dead vampire was propping it open, and he almost slipped on the slimy viscera, frothing out of it. A second restroom door was closed. Craig tried the handle. Locked. He stepped back and kicked the flimsy door into the room and was greeted with screams. Two girls were wedged into the single stall.

"Stop! Wait!" one of them yelled.

Craig approached them, gun at the ready. "Don't move." He pulled a flashlight from his belt and flashed its ultraviolet beam onto their faces. Neither girl reacted violently, showing they weren't vampires. "Let me see your right hands."

One complied instantly, hand quivering in fear. No tattoo. The other hesitated. And he poked her in the shoulder with the rifle barrel.

"Show me!"

She did, and he grabbed her hand, twisting it to look at the webbing next to her thumb.

"Ow!"

He saw two inked dots. Like a snake bite.

"Familiar." Craig pointed the barrel up to her head. "I should kill you."

"Familiar? What?" The first girl asked.

"Both of you get the fuck outta here." The familiar squeezed by Craig and out towards the stairs. As the other moved, Craig grabbed her arm.

"Stay away from her if you want to live."

Another shotgun blast drew his attention back down the hall.

Damn it, Liz!

"Go!" he yelled at the stunned girl, who didn't hesitate any further and skedaddled as fast as she could. Then he turned and went to support his partner.

At the end of the hall, the metal fire door they had watched Naomi unlock was open, leading into an incredibly dark void. Stepping into the blackness, he had to get his bearings. He snapped on the flashlight. Immediately, a purplish glow flowed out through its lens. The UV function might immobilize a vampire when pointed into its face but was all but useless as a means of illumination, except for highlighting things that phosphoresced in the violet beam. "Shit!" He clicked the button and switched to normal light.

There was another bang, and then the clatter of fighting up to his left. He pointed the bright white beam towards the sounds and cautiously moved forward, where the tunnel branched off to the left and right. He looked right into a blacker hole, then left, where he heard more noise of a ruckus and saw a faint light seeping out of an opening in the tunnel wall. The flash/bang from a shotgun blast told him all he needed to know. Shutting off the flashlight, he motivated himself down the passage to the door as swiftly as he could before he lost another friend. At the opening, he stopped and poked his head around the jamb for a quick look-see into the room to find out the situation, and then ducked back out of view.

Okay, two vamps down. One imploding. Another on the verge. Two still going after Liz. Was that Steph and Vlad in the shadows?

HOURS AFTER WATCHING the recorded video of Terry being brutally killed, those back in CSC Command were now following Craig and Liz, in real-time—driving into town, parking, and gearing up in front of a homeless guy. On the big screen, two video images presented slightly different perspectives of the same view. One showed what the camera attached to Craig was seeing while the other showed Liz's feed. As though this was an episode of *NCIS*, they watched the agents enter the bar and confront the bartender.

"What's that song playing?" Ellie asked.

"Stones. *Sympathy for the Devil*." Cole idly responded.

They watched Craig and Liz descend into the basement and their pursuit of Terry's niece into the mysterious tunnels below the city.

They heard Craig yell, "Liz! Wait for me!" Before he headed into the dark after her.

There were several moments when all they could see was darkness highlighted by flashlights or the burst of flame from gun barrels. The tension in the room was intense as they watched, unable to do anything but pray while the agents' individual dramas played out before them. All hoped the next surprise wouldn't be their friend's last. Then a cascade of events rapidly followed one another: Liz killing vamps and fighting Naomi, Craig entering the room, Vlad and Steph fleeing, Craig turning to Liz and her struggle with Naomi, Craig turning and leaving Liz to follow Vlad into a pitch-black tunnel.

"Why didn't he help Liz? What the fuck is he doing?" Ellie asked, close to panic.

Commander Cole responded as calmly as she could. "His job."

Chapter 25

ALL FALL DOWN

CRAIG STOOD FOR a long moment outside the chamber. Liz was clearly engaged in the fight for her life, yet his body had seized up. Panic was what he knew it to be. Another of his friends was about to die and it was going to happen in front of him. *What's wrong with me?* This wasn't like him. But he felt like he did in Utah, frightened into inaction. If it hadn't been for Liz, he'd be dead. Now, here he was again, half-convinced he could do nothing to change the outcome of what was turning into a failed mission. But the end of the story didn't have to be watching another partner, friend, die. Did it? The pressing fact, however, was if he didn't snap out of it right now, he knew Liz was a goner. And if the other deaths haunting him weren't his fault, then this time it sure as shit would be.

Taking a deep breath, he stepped back into the door opening. Liz had her hands full with Naomi and a hipster vamp clutching a laptop, which he was swinging as a weapon. This triggered one of those weird thoughts that always popped into his head at the most inappropriate moments. For example, the words hipster and vampire just didn't quite fit into his understanding of such things, not that it should have surprised him much. But the vamps he had been dealing with were old, some extremely so. And the idea of them using computers—well, that just didn't compute (terrible puns, apparently, were also allowed at these times). What would vampires surf the web for? And just what did vamp porn look like? Shaking his head to clear away that stupidity, he still wondered why a vampire would need to use a laptop as a weapon at all. Didn't he have claws and fangs? All questions to be answered later, if at all. Questions that had arisen in the fraction of a second between seeing and acting.

He made one last assessment of Liz's situation. She had just inserted a wood stake in the hipster's heart, who was imploding, oozing steaming innards all over the floor. The smell was disgusting. And in this confined space where no fresh air had ever entered, the stench of bloating vamp combined with the years of mustiness and rotting death was all but debilitating.

Now Liz was fully engaged with Naomi. Craig couldn't tell whether she saw Vlad morph into his smoky/wispy self and escape through a gaping black hole in the brick wall. But at this moment, he had to make sure Steph didn't join in the fray. They'd find the rogue vamp again someday, and hopefully with a stronger force.

Craig raised his .357 aiming it directly at Steph, a warning not to get involved in the fight. The look he saw in her eyes was one of calculation. Steph looked at Craig, then at Naomi and Liz. Then, with no further hesitation, she turned and followed Vlad into the void.

Now Craig had a new decision to make. He wouldn't have been able to follow Vlad through the dark passage in his amorphous state. But Steph was still too young an immortal to pull *that* magic trick, meaning he had a chance of following her to Vlad's next hidey-hole. It also meant he'd have to leave Liz behind to handle Naomi on her own.

And they both knew stopping the rogue vampire had to take priority. There was no time for feelings and emotions at this stage. Besides, Liz obviously could take care of herself.

As if underscoring that thought, Liz brought her left leg up in a round-robin spin, connecting with Naomi's jaw, and sending her reeling back into a post. The agents made the briefest of eye contact. Craig gave her fancy footwork an appreciative smile and thumbs up gesture and then a more serious look, apologizing for having to leave. Before she could blurt out, "Don't you dare follow them by yourself!" Craig had disappeared into the pitch-dark tunnel.

Turning in the direction he saw Steph exit, Craig took only a few paces and immediately slammed into a brick wall, blocking his path. Thinking that he may have been wrong regarding Steph's ability to turn into wisps of vapor, he reflexively reached for the flashlight and clicked it on. The tunnel had not ended where it seemed, but it abruptly made a right turn.

Craig pointed the light in front of him to keep from finding another painful obstacle. He saw this section was short and ended at a gap in the wall supported by timbers like those used to keep mines from collapsing. Rubble—brick, concrete chunks, wood, and piles of dirt—lay strewn around the surrounding ground. The opening was a rough-cut hole that someone appeared to have created with a pickaxe and sledgehammer, which explained the scattered debris.

He approached the irregular opening and aimed the beam of light into the black emptiness. The light revealed a narrow passageway that wasn't at all like the brick-lined tunnels behind him. It was more like an overly large cement pipe, such as a sewage pipe or utility corridor. Whatever it was he had stepped into, the rough-cut hole was an improvised connection from the old Shanghai tunnels to a more contemporary underground system of sewer pipes and service passages.

Before he proceeded further, Craig stopped and listened for Steph.

Thump. Thump.

He heard what sounded like a vehicle above his head probably driving over a pothole, then silence, and then, there, footsteps splashing away off to the right!

With light in hand, and gun at the ready, Craig continued the chase and headed down the musty tube. Electrical raceways, gas lines, and various sizes of pipes (he hoped the ones leaching a strange-colored discharge around the fittings were for water) ran along the ceiling of the passage. Strung in and around the pipes was a tangle of cords, wire, and other cables held to the wall with an assortment of porcelain insulators. Exposed light bulbs affixed to the ceiling looked like they might have come straight from Edison's workshop. Of course, were functioning.

He had to duck several times to avoid entangling his head in some low-hanging cables and smacking it on a large metal conduit. To Craig's unstudied eye, this was an old utility corridor that had not been accessed very often, if not abandoned altogether.

Further down, he stopped again to listen. There was more muffled traffic noise from a street above and more silence. Then he caught it! A distinct splash of a foot stepping in a puddle. And not too far in front of him, either. The beam from the flashlight revealed the corridor gently curving to the right. Craig extinguished the light and cautiously, but swiftly, moved in the sound's direction.

As he rounded the bend, he saw a flicker of illumination coming from a junction. Then a body stepped out from this opening. The shapely silhouette was that of a woman, Steph. She was looking to see if he had followed her. Satisfied, she turned back toward the light, took a step, and disappeared.

Craig's heart pounded, recognizing this as an obvious set-up. The whole thing, from killing Terry to luring him and Liz into these tunnels, was a trap. He fingered his mother's silver rosary hanging around his neck—a gift with the unspoken acknowledgment that her boy needed protection. He made a quick sign of the cross, kissed the crucifix, something he hadn't done since he was a kid, and tucked the silver beads back under his collar. Giving the rosary a pat for luck, he cautiously walked through the doorway towards uncertainty.

Steph stood in the center of the chamber next to a decaying armchair. She was facing the door waiting for Craig, ready to pounce, yet did nothing. He took a hesitant step towards her, gun at the ready. Then there was a flash of movement to his left, rushing towards him from a dark recess. Craig turned and fired the weapon once into the attacking shadow, dropping it. Before he could assess the situation, another figure, directly behind the first, charged aggressively toward him. He fired two rounds into this vampire, ending it as well. Then he quickly spun back towards Steph; sweeping his eyes around, looking for any other bloodsuckers who might be hiding.

Seeing none, his eyes fell back upon Steph still patiently standing next to the chair. A wisp of dark vapor formed, swirling around her. Its black tendrils wove themselves together into an increasingly dense shape of a man standing in front of the dilapidated piece of furniture.

"Welcome, Agent Wright," Vladimir said after he materialized into flesh next to his dark-haired follower. "I am flattered by so many important visitors." He sat on the rotted fabric of the chair that could have been off the set of *Dark Shadows* and perched in regal majesty as though the dripping, brick-lined chamber was his throne room. Steph stood by his side, his loyal consort, or royal guard. Or both.

Again, Craig had an inappropriately timed thought at how hackneyed the entire image before him was—an ancient vampire sitting in a dank underground cell on a rotting armchair, his lightly clad vixen next to him *and* with the clichéd name of Vlad to boot! The only things missing were his red-velvet-lined cape and coffin.

Craig took another step into the room, gun now leveled at Vlad's heart, determined to take him down. He took another step and another and—then he stopped. It felt like he was suspended in acrylic, like the fabled ant preserved in amber.

"You are under arrest." Craig heard himself say stupidly, but only as an echo in his mind, his jaw and lips not moving.

I'm so fucked! he thought.

Another voice arose in his mind. "Yes, Agent Wright. It appears you are fucked. But not in a good way. As the joke goes. No?" Vladimir said, lips not moving. "And it seems it is I who has arrested you." Vladimir laughed at his own play on words.

Then Craig felt something else inside his brain, something unnatural. Vlad had reached into his head; intruding into the dark recesses of his mind, fingering through the stored memories he had locked away.

"Ah. You know of the master sergeant's fate." Vladimir said out loud. "It is a shame that, like you, I could not trust him to become a member of my small circle. A boy scout as a youth, a boy scout as an adult, and in my experience, a boy scout as an immortal, always striving to do the right thing. I learned from my blood-father that grudges can carry from the mortal to the immortal life. Thus, I am compelled to end your continued existence as I have done to JR." Vladimir sat back on his throne to reflect. "It is interesting the way you Americans like to use initials to shorten names. JR for Jackie Robinson. Your postal service using OR for Oregon. I believe I just might shorten my name to simply V." He nodded towards Stephanie. "What do you think, my darling?"

Craig felt his finger try to pull the gun's trigger. In his mind, he fired once, twice, again, and again, until he emptied the weapon—all hits to Vlad's heart.

"Nice shooting, Tex." Vladimir laughed. "If I had not reached into your consciousness, I would be a smoldering heap of goo."

"You motherfuck—"

"And . . . I see that you have some severe mother issues that need working through."

Craig wanted to act. But he couldn't move or raise the firewalls in his memory to block Vlad from further hacking into a life best kept away from others, especially himself.

"Such a horrible thing about your father. Parkinson's is devastating to the victim and his family. Immortals have no disease. Oh! And I see the other friends and co-workers you have lost. The beautiful one, with the red hair, Kathrine. She went down with so little fight. And then you pulled the trigger. You must hate immortality so much that you are willing to kill your beloved. Her wound was such that she might have turned, not an easy transition without one of us to help her along, but you could have been together forever. Hate is such a potent emotion. A shame." Vladimir clucked his tongue and shook his head slowly.

"But I see a new one in your life, red hair as well. You are an easy one to read, Agent Wright, even without probing your mind. I wonder if she has the same thoughts for you. If she were lying here, wounded, would you make the same decision as you did with the others? Would you put her down like some spent animal as well?"

If this were a scene in a bad film, Craig would be tied to a chair with a gag in his mouth and every time Dr. Evil made a new probing pronouncement he would have wiggled and squirmed and made muffled noises of indignation as he desperately tried to free himself from the bindings. But then this was no movie, and Vlad had an iron grip on Craig, fixing him in place, clamping down on his physical processes. He couldn't move. He couldn't even yell out a damning invective. All he could do was watch as Vlad manhandled his most private thoughts.

Steph stroked the back of Vlad's neck and whispered into his ear.

"Ah, Agent. It seems you have another female admirer," Vladimir said with a smile. "I hope you don't mind if she isn't a redhead."

He wanted to move, fight, run! But Vlad's mental grip still held him immobile. Stephanie walked to Craig, slowly, provocatively. His eyes flared wide as she sidled up close to his body. It felt as though his heart was going to beat right out of his chest.

Then Stephanie stepped away and gave him a thorough once over, like someone inspecting a horse before auction. Approvingly, she moved back in close to him and nestled her nose into the hollow of his neck, where she could feel his veins pumping. She inhaled deeply and licked her lips at the scent of his warm blood.

"I think she likes you, Agent Wright," Vladimir observed. "I believe she is considering you for an eternity of togetherness. But unfortunately, my dear, I have told you this one will have to be destroyed. Do not fret. We will find you another pet. Now finish your dinner."

Obediently, Stephanie did as she was told. Seductively, she moved her mouth close to Craig's, her lips hovering near his but not touching. He expected to feel the warmth of her breath, but it was ice cold. Her tongue was like a popsicle as she whisked it against his lips. Steph looked at Craig, disappointment in her eyes, and smiled, revealing her fangs. Then, she summarily opened her mouth, clamping it over his pulsing throat, and drove the sharp points deeply into his artery. Craig felt a rush of pain masked by the feeling of extreme pleasure.

Stephanie raised her right hand to clear his collar out of the way so her lips could get a lock against his skin. As she did, her fingers touched the silver beads around his neck. Horrified, she staggered back. The violent reaction caused her fingers to get entangled with the holy necklace, ripping it away from Craig's bleeding throat. Frantically, she flailed about, desperately trying to free her hand from the searing effect of the blood-covered silver.

Surprised by this turn of events, Vladimir let his grip slacken on Craig and turned to help his disciple. Craig's body collapsed. Death, or worse, was not far away now. He wanted to grab his .357 and end things, but even though Vlad no longer had a stranglehold on him, his hand would not move. He was spent. His body had no ability to function, all his energy draining away onto the stained concrete.

Vladimir easily removed the rosary from Steph's fingers. He gently brought her blood covered hand up to his mouth and kissed her burned skin. "There now, my sweet. All better." His tone was that of the concerned parent placating a child after a fall. "I have told you that these trinkets have no power over me," Vladimir said, holding the rosary in the air. "Say your prayers, *Agent*!" He spat out contemptuously. Then he tossed the silver beads with a sneer toward Craig.

The taste of Craig's blood on Stephanie's fingers stirred Vladimir. He rose to his feet with a stern air of a headmaster and said to her, "Now, return to the task you started, finish him and be not wasteful."

Gingerly, she crawled to where Craig lay, paying special attention to avoid touching the rosary again. She hesitated before continuing and looked back at Vladimir as though he were asking her to eat a pile of garlic.

"There is nothing further to fear from that one. Besides, his blood will help your hand heal more quickly. Now drink!"

The fury in Vladimir's voice sent her immediately down onto Craig's neck, at first licking, then lapping up the blood.

With renewed vigor, Stephanie clamped her mouth over the wound and sucked with all her might.

A clattering sound of debris scrapping across the cement floor echoed from outside the chamber opening. Distracted, Stephanie looked up from Craig's bleeding neck and saw Liz standing in the doorway, gun pointing right at her. Stephanie let a primal, territorial hiss escape through her red lips, warning the interloper this was her kill.

———◆———

LIZ FIRED THE last of the silver-coated rounds into the vamp attacking with a laptop. Then Naomi flew at her with savage fury, fingers extending elaborately painted nails as weapons to rip into Liz's face. Baby fangs were barely noticeable in her open mouth but ready to do damage. That there had been no time in her brief life as a vampire for her claws and fangs to develop fully was not the issue. The genuine concern was this newly turned female had the strength of at least two normal humans. Combined with a passionate desire to fight to the death for her master, she was a formidable force that could easily take down the biggest and strongest of agents.

Before Liz had time to think about what to do to stay alive, instinct kicked in. She dropped the useless, empty sidearm. Then, with her right hand, she reached across her chest to her left shoulder, found the handle of the tactical knife strapped to her back, and pulled it from the dark confines of its scabbard. The polished silver and steel alloy blade flashed in the lantern. Its reflection seemed as bright as the sun as it absorbed the lantern light and then, with an amplified brilliance, threw it into the eyes of the attacking vampire.

The bright light blinded Naomi for the briefest of moments, sending her a pace or two back towards the chamber wall. It was long enough for Liz to swing the blade in a sweeping arc up to her left shoulder. When the tension in her muscles released, the knife's edge cut down across the vamp's neck like the beam of a trebuchet being released, launching its load.

Naomi's eyes opened wide with surprise as the razor-sharp edge made its initial slice and, without stopping, continue to cut deeply through her throat. Unheard words gurgled from her lips, but the hatred that Liz saw in her eyes spoke volumes. Naomi's body bloated. Her boiling internal organs frothing out the opening of her severed neck should have to push her head to the ground. The only reason her head did not fall off entirely were the tendons still connecting the skull to the spine. The remaining tissues served as a hinge, allowing the vampire's seething innards to burble up from her gut and out the throat, making her head bob up and down like a deranged novelty toy.

Naomi did not, could not, understand her newly immortal body was in its final death throes—a fact the recruiting posters must have failed to mention. Then Liz saw something new in the dying vamp's eyes. Naomi was pleading for help as her body ballooned out to the brink of explosion and then, with the release of one final gaseous eruption, imploded and collapsed in a gush of syrupy, red steaming liquid. The anguish Liz saw in Naomi's eyes caught her off guard. For a passing moment, Liz even felt sympathy for her, but was certain that even if she had the power to save the woman, she wouldn't have, not the person who had killed her friend.

During her fight with the two vampires, Liz's mind had registered Craig entering the room and then running off after Steph as she fled into the maze of dark tunnels. What was he thinking? Hadn't he been insistent on remaining a team in such situations? She was really going to tell him off when this was all over.

With no time to deal with her stained blade, Liz quickly returned the knife to its scabbard, picked up her dropped 9mm, and loaded a fresh magazine of silver death into its handle. The hipster had knocked from her hand the flashlight with his laptop, but she quickly found it aimlessly lighting up a brick wall where it had fallen. One last survey of the dead to make sure they weren't capable of following, as if piles of gelatinous muck could do much of anything. She took a deep, steadying breath, and then headed off into the dark tunnel after Craig.

In the inky blackness, Liz slowly inched her way along the passage, sweeping her light left, then right, keeping her back to the damp brick lining. This was no time to be jumped from behind. But that might have been slightly better than having a vampire master materializing in front of her out of smoke and mirrors. She quickly reached the rough-cut opening into the old cement pipe and paused, not knowing which direction to go. Looking left, then right, she saw no signs showing which way to go, so she swallowed and guessed, and cautiously proceeded left. After about three steps, she stopped to listen. Nothing. Then—

Thump. Thump.

Just traffic noises from the street above, so she kept moving. Another three steps and another pause. Still no sound. She moved again.

Bang!—Pause—*Bang! Bang!*

Gunfire. But coming from the opposite direction, she was heading. Reversing course, Liz moved faster, though still wary of the possibility of attack.

Ahead, Liz saw the pipe veer off to the right in a gentle, sweeping arc and slanted downward, deeper underground. There was no way to see much ahead, but the gunfire meant Craig was being assaulted. She picked up her pace and proceeded with less prudence than she should have, recognizing that Master Sergeant Terry would throw verbal thunderbolts at her for such erratic behavior.

One step after the other, Liz progressed around the bend, heart throbbing as she headed into the complete unknown. Then the sweep of her light caught the edge of a break in the pipe's cement lining, revealing a junction or doorway. The brightness of the LED flashlight had temporarily interfered with her night vision. All she could see was a bright white spot surrounded by darkness. She clicked off the light, closed her eyes, and counted. *One one thousand, two one thousand, three one thousand.* Then she opened them and saw the flickering of lanterns outlining the edges of the door.

Raising the 9mm, Liz moved towards the light source, prepared for an attack. She stumbled over some bricks but recovered as she entered a chamber and saw someone bending over Craig's prone body. Peripheral vision caught Vlad standing in the background. The person hovering over Craig looked up and let out a primal hiss. It was Steph, blood dripping from her lips.

Without a moment's hesitation, Liz pulled the trigger and fired it again and again straight into the vampire's face. The back of her head exploded in a horrid eruption of blood and brains, splattering the nearly dissolved feet of Vlad as he turned himself into hazy black tendrils wisping away from the carnage. Liz swept the room with UV light, looking for signs the errant vampire wasn't lurking in a corner or tucked up above a sewer pipe. Satisfied for the moment, she turned her attention back to her prone partner, and saw his actual condition for the first time.

"Oh my God!"

Craig's throat was a red mess. The carotid artery was pumping out blood onto the ground under him. He might have been dead already, but when he brought his arm up, placing a hand on the wound, she knew he wasn't, at least not yet. Maybe he would not die at all. But if he didn't die, the fact he had been bitten foretold the unacceptable alternative of his becoming a monster.

Her mind quickly went back to her first day with the CSC. Eugene Evers, lying on the burned-out patch of grass that was a park in Vamp Town, pleading with her to finish the task a vampire had begun. Not sure he was going to die and not wanting to risk becoming one of them.

Liz's duty was onerous but clear. Whatever the fantasy was of something going on between her and Craig ended when Steph bit into his throat.

Chapter 26

NEW NORMAL

L IZ STOOD PANTING as she watched Steph's body melt into a festering brew on the floor, out of breath from the exertion of taking out three vampires. "Double, double toil and trouble; Fire burn, and cauldron bubble," Liz said, remembering the witch's chant from Macbeth. Then she fired another round into the "burbling cauldron." "Bitch!" One last ingredient for the crone's potion, hoping to see a better future for herself beyond the immediate one she already knew about.

She had not looked at Craig trying to forestall admitting a horrible truth. He was dead or on his way to becoming a vampire, and for just a little while longer she refused to think about it and what her duty demanded. What she *needed* to do next.

Agency protocol stated a wounded operative had to be bluntly said: killed. There was no way around it. Even a scratch from sharp vampire claws could transfer toxins that could turn a human into a vampire. This quarantine procedure further stated the deceased team member must have her/his head removed, then the body had to be incinerated. They could only bring home their ashes. This mitigated the chances of a fallen agent—slight as that may be—of being revived, not as a human but as a vampire, spreading the infection inside the CSC headquarters itself.

The discovery of eighteenth-century burial sites in Eastern Europe where they interred suspected vampires vividly illustrated there had been a valid concern about the spread of the vampiric contagion from those supposed to be dead. Within these graves were beheaded skeletons with metal spikes driven through long-since-decayed chests. Stones were wedged into mouths to keep fangs from biting, and iron cages were placed over graves to keep the dead from rising and walking the earth. All such measures were taken to ensure the dead stayed dead the living remained human. Superstitions aside, the wisdom of the past had informed the agency regarding the necessity of such Draconian action.

The stench of Steph's body steeping and soaking into another stain on the concrete floor brought Liz back to the reality of having to complete her duty. She knew she had neither the tools nor the strength to cut off Craig's head. First, however, she had to pump a silver-clad bullet into his heart, something she didn't have the will to do. But his pleading eyes gave her the strength to pull the trigger. They both knew it had to be done. And while she did not want the task, she also knew Craig didn't want to be in this situation either.

She checked the magazine. One bullet left. Then she kneeled next to her friend. His throat was too savaged for him to speak, but his eyes said it all. And what he was saying was too unbearable to contemplate. Those eyes full of sorrow, desperation, and love revealed a lifetime of being together, a future that could not be, all flashing by in the time it took to chamber the last silver round.

Liz reached down and brushed his hair back as she imagined his mother might have done when he was a child. Choking back tears, she kissed Craig on the lips and looked into his eyes one last time.

"I love you, Agent Wright."

Then Liz delicately placed the muzzle of her 9mm against his chest, aiming at his heart. Craig stared up into her eyes. He gripped the muzzle with both hands, helping maintain her resolve, then he winked and smiled, showing that he was ready.

Liz closed her eyes and pulled the trigger. Then she stood, eyes still shut tight. The gun's loud report was all she could handle. Seeing the effects of a bullet, her bullet, on Craig was too much to bear. As it was, she knew the sound of the gun would echo through her head till her last day.

Looking at the destruction of life on the floor, Liz doubted her role in the CSC. Maybe for the one-hundred-year history of the organization, there had been few deaths associated with it, but for the brief period she had been an agent, there seemed to have been more than enough. Liz was tired of it. Especially the part in which she had to kill teammates and now her friend.

Brain swimming in self-doubt and regret, she lowered her head. The silver rosary Craig's mom had given to him just a couple of days earlier lay at her feet. She bent to pick it up. There was a fair amount of blood on it. Whose she didn't know, nor care as she fingered the beads. She brought the crucifix up to her forehead, and through long ingrained muscle memory, she used it to cross herself. Touching one bead, she prayed, "Hail Mary, full of grace . . .," Who was she kidding? Prayers don't help situations such as these.

She wanted to blame God for what had happened. Without a doubt, she needed to understand how God could have even created these monsters. If He hadn't, then who or what did? And if not God, then didn't it follow that there was no God at all? But this was no time for philosophy. All she could think about was the death of her partner and maybe, conceivably . . . Well, who knew where that might have gone? She knew he remained emotionally distant because of the death of a former partner—former because he had to do to her what Liz just did to him. No, this was no way to live, wallowing in self-pity and doubt. Liz slouched in defeat, shoulders hunched, arms hanging at her sides, the useless silver necklace dangling from her left hand, forgetting Master Sergeant Terry's admonitions to remain focused and tactically aware of her surroundings.

From a dark recess of the chamber, she heard clapping. At first, it was soft and could have been the rhythmic drip, drip, drip of water seeping in from the city above. Then the clap, clap, clap became more pronounced and the recognizable sound of two hands beating together was obvious.

Liz looked at the source of the applause. A man materialized and emerged from a shadowed corner. After a moment of surprise, she recognized the reality of her situation. The time of feeling sorry for herself had come and gone.

"Vlad. You piece of shit."

"Oh, Agent Adams. I am offended by such language." He looked down at the once beautiful body of Stephanie, now a smoldering pile, leaching into the cracks of the floor. "And after my ovation to you on your performance." Vladimir shook his head in a sad, dejected fashion. "Such poor manners." He took another step closer to her.

Liz tensed, preparing herself for what would happen next. She had seen it before during her first day as a field agent. They had sent Liz and Craig to Vamp Town to rescue any humans who still might be alive after stumbling into the town filled with vampires. She had watched Vlad hold Craig off the ground by his throat like a rag doll, slowly choking the life out of him. Craig could not resist because Vlad reached into his mind and controlled his every action. Liz tried to help, but Vlad just swatted her aside like a bug that had landed on his sleeve. No mind control required.

The 9mm was useless since she had used the last round on Craig. Cautiously, she reached for the tactical knife at her back. Liz's arm was about halfway across her chest when, suddenly, she felt him touching her mind. Her arm stopped moving. Vlad had shut down her ability to move.

"Now, now, Agent. Let us have a fair fight. Yes? A show of abilities. No need for weapons."

Then Liz's arm continued to move up to the knife. She was Vlad's plaything now. Her hand touched the handle and grasped it. The blade eased out of its scabbard, down across her chest, and stopped with the tip pointing under her chin, drilling into the skin. She was powerless to stop. This was it. With one casual thought, Vlad could have Liz thrust her own knife up into her brain. Fight over.

His smile was that of a mischievous child. "Please. Do you think me to be so dishonorable as to take the easy path? We shall fight, but without weapons."

Then Liz felt her arm sweep out, moving the blade away from her neck. Her hand loosened its grip, and the knife flew out into the dark shadows clattering to the ground. Vlad withdraw his presence from her mind and she could again freely move.

"I wish to show you the type of leader I truly am."

"What do you mean?" Liz asked, surprised.

"Agent Adams, I require your respect and trust as you become a member of my family."

Startled, Liz shook her head in dismay and backed away from Vladimir.

"You cannot defeat me, though you will try. However, you will join."

———◦———

LIZ'S MOUTH WENT dry. She knew that help was too far away. But they had to know. They had to. After watching Terry die, the Center had to know what it was up against. Craig was right. They should have brought Alex into the agency. Vlad was too powerful for any human to take on. She knew this show of fair play on Vlad's part was precisely that: a show. She was doomed. Not to die, that would be too easy. She had been condemned to life as one of the undead, to roam the earth in search of her next victim. And presumably to be under the thumb of this deranged vampire.

Panic set in. What to do? Flight was out of the question. There was only one way out, and Vlad was standing in front of it. Besides, once out, she didn't know where to go in the maze of tunnels. It was time to take control of this situation, no matter what.

"Why do you want me in your bloodthirsty family? What could I possibly add? This is about something bigger, isn't it?" Liz was fishing, stalling.

"You can ask all the questions you desire. No one will rescue you. Or at least arrive in enough time to alter the outcome." Vladimir resumed his seat on the armchair. "When we first met, I saw you had a strong sense of justice. You have a precise definition of what the correct thing to do is. You convinced Agent Wright dropping that bomb on our heads was the wrong thing to do, allowing him to question the morality of keeping us imprisoned for simply being who we are.

"No immortal asked to be converted into freaks of nature," he continued. "That mad monk wasn't doing either my brother or myself any favors by turning us into the creatures we are today. But there is no going back for us, no matter how much we wish.

"Alexei tries by playacting the role of a human. Like the ancient Greeks, he dons the character mask and costume of jeans, boots, and plaid shirt, pretending to be as American as your apple pie, which he could never eat. Human food does not digest so well in our guts.

"You will learn, as your system becomes adjusted, such foods you find enjoyable will only make you violently ill, even kill you. Just another reminder that you should accept what you have become. You will discover a vastly superior self than who you are today." He sat back on his throne and crossed his legs.

"You are correct in ascertaining I have something more substantial in mind. *We* have been unfairly pursued and locked away. Of course, some people had to die over the years. People always die. It is a natural process. Hunt and being hunted. But I am finished with allowing myself and those who follow me to live according to how humans see the world.

"We are living intelligent beings with rights of our own. No more negotiations. No more treaties in which we get the losing end of the arrangement. From this point forward, we shall dominate as we should have all along and stop cowering in the dark. I have sent my demands to your CSC, and they will comply or—"

"Or what?" Liz countered, taking a step towards him, feeling emboldened. "Or you will drop some big ass bomb on us? What?"

"You have a great sense of humor. A bomb? Where would I get such a device? And why would I use it and destroy the very world I live in?" Vladimir shook his head. "No. No bomb. Something much more devastating and long-lasting. Either humanity allows us to live without fear of being murdered, permits us to hunt as we need, and guarantees a steady supply of blood for my growing family *or* when the time is right, we shall conquer the world and claim it as our birthright. Humans will be the ones locked away. You shall become our chattel. You will serve the undead in all ways. You will be kept in herds and bred for the exceptional qualities of your blood. We shall argue the finer distinctions in the flavor between corn-fed or free-range humans. Ha! Either way, humanity will step aside as the top predator."

Liz tried not to show any emotion, but her eyes burned angrily, revealing a powerful urge to kill.

Vladimir stood and walked to Liz. "I require your help in this conquest. I need an adviser who understands the humans of today. Your sense of fair play can only help to mollify my desire for complete revenge. Your knowledge of the CSC will be indispensable." Vladimir looked into her eyes. He brought up his hand, seductively touched her cheek, and brushed his fingers across her lips. "Of course, there are certain pleasantries you will discover that are incomparable to anything you now know."

Seething with rage, Liz curled her hands into battle hammers, ready to strike. The intensity of the action helped her remember the rosary she still clutched in her left hand as it embedded itself into her palm.

Immediately, she thrust the string of silver beads into Vlad's face. He became enraged as the figure of the crucified Christ on the cross burned into his cheek. He grabbed her by the throat, picking her up, feet dangling.

"I told you, charms cannot stop me!" He squeezed harder. "I believed I could help you see what is best for both races. You could have been an important adviser to me as I moved forward. I do not want to wage war on humanity. You would have helped me stay on the path of doing the least harm to mortals. I only want what is fairly ours."

It seemed like Vlad's fingers reached all the way around Liz's slender throat, palm pressing against her Adam's apple, allowing air to enter her lungs only through sharp, deep bursts. He was choking her to death!

"Such a shame, too. You had the potential to save your people from my darker self. You were going to be the good angel on my shoulder, always keeping me in check from the horrors I will bring down on those you love." His grip tightened.

Liz could feel consciousness slipping. It wouldn't be long. The fingers on her right hand brushed something on her belt. One more ragged gasp of oxygen and her brain cleared from dimness to a fuzzy lightness. Her wood knife! Craig gave it to her on their way to Vamp Town—a lamination of three species of hardwood (ash, aspen, and linden, all purported to have vampire killing properties), carved into a sharp stake with a cross at the hilt.

Barely able to make her finger joints follow her commands, she grabbed the knife's handle, brought it up between their two bodies, and plunged the tip as close as she could to Vlad's heart. The surprise in his eyes told her she had made her point felt. Craig appeared in her oxygen-starved brain and grimaced at the lousy pun.

Vladimir's eyes went wild, taking on a beastly glaze. He did not move. His left hand still had a stranglehold on Liz's throat, but the grip had relaxed slightly. He brought up his right hand and grabbed the wrist of Liz's hand, which still drove the knife into his chest. He squeezed and twisted with enough force to break it, causing her to let go. Then he dropped Liz to the floor, where she lay gasping for oxygen.

Unable to do anything, Liz remained on the ground and watched Vlad jerk about madly as he tried to remove the knife from his chest. She was going to enjoy watching him implode. But he didn't. She could tell he was wounded. His lack of focus on the puny human sprawled at his feet hinted at the fact he was concerned for his own survival. He desperately tried to remove the knife, but one side of the handle guard that formed the cross appeared to have entered the wound and had caught on the inside of the incision. Vlad roared with pain and hate. The more he tried to extract the stake, the further it seemed to dig into his chest. As he flailed around, Liz could see she missed his heart by fractions of an inch. Maybe an unrecoverable wound, but no steaming pile of inside out Vlad innards either.

Vladimir clutched his side with blood slipping out between his fingers, the knife protruding from his body. He made a sweeping movement, wincing from pain as he brought his arm up across his body. She watched him gesture and make a face she was unfamiliar with. He did it a second time, apparently expecting something to happen, like a magician tapping the brim of the top hat. "Ta-Da!" But there was no rabbit inside.

After a third attempt, she thought she could see his body fade, becoming transparent. His feet and lower legs appeared as thin wisps of dark smoke, but then they swirled together, becoming flesh once again. Furious, Vlad gave Liz a kick. But even that action caused him intense agony. The schoolyard bully not getting his way. He turned and staggered from the chamber, dribbling blood as he fled into the black tunnel.

With the shock of the ordeal subsiding, Liz awkwardly climbed to her feet, pushing against her right hand, but the pain from Vlad almost crushing her wrist was too much, and she collapsed back to the floor. Other than a bruised throat and sore wrist, Liz didn't think that she had any other injuries. Despite that, she did a general scan of her limbs and torso before attempting to stand again. All seemed okay. So, using her left hand this time, she struggled up to her feet. A wave of vertigo greeted her as she stood upright, but it passed as quickly as it came on.

Still not convinced that she was injury-free, Liz pulled out her cell phone and opened the camera app. She walked to a lantern and used the flickering light to examine her face and neck, using the selfie mode as a mirror. Nothing.

She knew it was a fantasy to expect to have any signal strength to make a call for help, but she checked anyway. Well, sometimes fantasies could be real, the existence of vampires, for instance. Hopefully, the body cams got it all and help would be coming. Her job now was to get out of this labyrinth of tunnels and out into the world of fresh air and life.

God, I feel like crap, Liz thought and exited Vlad's throne room.

Chapter 27

W T F

F INALLY, OUT ON the street, Liz leaned against
a building to stabilize herself after another wave
of dizziness. She ignored the line heading into Voodoo
Doughnut for a late-night sugar rush, and they ignored her.
To them, she was just another partier who couldn't handle
her liquor. She gulped in the fresh night air as deeply as her
sore ribs would allow, not discounting the other body parts,
also screaming in pain.

Exhausted from fighting and subduing how many vampires?
Three? Four? And tussling with the baddest, motherfucking
one of all. Liz considered herself lucky to still be alive.

Terry was dead and at the hands of his niece. His own blood.

Craig. Damn it! Craig! Her knees buckled as she saw the
vivid replay in her mind's eye of the moment she pulled the
trigger. They were looking into each other's eyes, and she
knew at that moment he loved her and . . . and she loved him,
too. "God damn it, Craig!" She cried out; tears came to her
eyes. *Why didn't you tell me? Why didn't I tell myself?*

She imagined hearing a throat unsympathetically being
cleared. It cut through the pity party she was throwing for
herself and snapped her back to the actual situation she was

facing. She recognized the unmistakable note of disapproval right away. Master Sergeant Terry had a way of making one feel personal problems amounted to nothing when it came down to the job at hand. Liz straightened up to near attention. The embedded Master Sergeant Terry in her head was right. Now was no time to lose focus. She may have killed three vampires and possibly mortally wounded Vlad, but this was the heart of their home turf in Portland, and the time of day during which vampires thrived. Right now, she had to get back to her base and contact the CSC. The grief would always be there for her to wallow in.

She gave her pants a quick pat down, looking for the car key fob, and found it safe and snug in the right-side pocket. Fortunately, she had insisted on driving from the hotel, knowing that Craig had had no rest since before visiting his mother. Oh, God! His mother. Not now. Later. Liz looked around to get her bearings, then headed toward the parked car. Her body continued to ache, especially her right wrist. She rotated it a couple of painful times but couldn't remember injuring it. *Must have fallen on it awfully hard when Vlad dropped me.*

The pain intensified when she reached for the door and then was surprised at how weak her hand was, barely able to grasp it. Then there was another stabbing jolt as she lifted it to pull the door open. Once inside, she realized her mouth was dry as wool. She grabbed a water bottle and took a long swig from it, and swished it around before swallowing. And repeated the process a couple more times. Then the back of her tongue reacted to a feeling that welled up from inside her stomach. She knew what was going to happen next from a succession of freshman year parties that all ended up the same way. She threw open the car door and leaned her head outside just as she violently vomited up all the water she had consumed and some dinner as well. Liz continued retching until nothing remained in her gut. Still, with nothing left to vomit, her muscles spasmed for several minutes after. People walked by, taking no note of something they saw night after night in this part of town, the entertainment district. Finally, she sat back in the car, face clammy, lungs desperate for air, but breathing hurt after straining her stomach muscles from puking. A fresh bout of wooziness attacked her equilibrium, and she closed her eyes, hoping it would pass soon.

Then she heard a loud banging on the car window.

Bang! Bang! Bang!

Slowly, she opened one eye. Then she opened the other eye and saw the old homeless guy they had parked near. He was peering at her through the glass, a look of concern clearly visible on his face. He was about to knock on the window one more time, but Liz rolled it down.

"You okay, lady?"

"Yeah . . . I think so. Thanks."

"I been there, and I tell you I know how it feels. Well, you take care now. But if you need help, I'm just over there," he said, as he jerked his thumb towards the overflowing shopping cart behind him.

"No, I'm fine. Thanks." Liz rolled the window up and firmly grabbed the steering wheel. Not knowing what had happened to her, but feeling a calm settle over her body, she depressed the brake and touched the ignition button.

Ring. Ring. Ring.

Her cell phone. "Adams," Liz answered weakly.

The voice of Commander Cole spilled out of the speaker. "Liz! Are you alright? We watched the whole thing."

Liz closed her eyes tightly, fighting to control her feelings. "Yeah. Great . . .."

"Do nothing further until help arrives."

"No worries there. I gotta get some rest. Feel like crap. Wait. What help? I thought you couldn't spare anyone else. You aren't sending Ellie and Paul? They're too green. I barely made it out myself."

"Not many options. The Action Teams are all tied up for the next several days, what with the full moon and all. The lycans are just too hands-on during this time of the month. But you're right, those two aren't ready to be out on their own." Cole left that hang, then added, "When some bodies free up after lycan detail, I'll send in a cleanup and recovery unit to handle Craig's remains and see if there are any clues where Vlad is. And Adams."

"Yes?"

"I'm also sending someone with experience who can help you. Hopefully, you won't need it, but better safe than sorry."

"Fucking wonderful," was all Liz could croak out, ending the call.

Liz had to force herself to focus on driving the car. The simple motion of shifting into gear was almost too difficult. She could not remember the last time she felt as sick and as weak as this. Her head swam and eyesight blurred. This was the worst case of the flu she ever had.

Then all went black.

———————◄O►————————

MIRACULOUSLY, LIZ MADE it through the call from Cole without throwing up. That much she could remember. After that, nothing. She had no clue how she made it back to the hotel—whether she drove, took a cab, or sprouted wings and flew. But here she was, spread out on the bed in her room and didn't know how long she had been asleep. She *did* know, however, that she felt like shit and needed water, but could not muster the energy to move. Then she tensed up. Something didn't feel right. There was another person in the room with her.

Slowly, Liz opened her eyes. The room was dark. No lights were on, and the curtains were completely covering the window. The only illumination was the daylight sneaking in around the edges of the fabric and through the vertical slit where the two panels came together. It hurt her eyes. The light stabbed into her eyeballs with the pain of a white-hot poker. She never had migraines before, but this was how others had described them. *First time for everything,* she thought.

The sound of the bathroom faucet being turned on confirmed that there *was* someone else in the room with her. Craig? No. Craig was dead. She had killed him. Then who? She looked to her right towards the bathroom. The glow of light from the window inside it was enough to see that no one was in there.

"Sit up, Agent Adams," a familiar male voice said.

Startled, Liz snapped her head to the left. A shadow of a man sat in a chair close to her.

"You must drink a little of this."

He was holding a glass, but before he handed it to her, he pricked his wrist with the nail of his little finger and dripped some blood into the water. There was enough light for to see the red filter down through the clear liquid like filaments of string or smoke. It reminded her of how Vlad . . . Vlad! She bolted upright; reaching for the 9mm she always kept under her pillow when on assignment. That it was, there was a good sign. At least she remembered to do one thing right before passing out.

"Agent, you do not need to fear me. I am trying to help."

She pointed the gun at the intruder. "Tur—Turn on the light."

"But it will hurt."

"Do it!"

The shadow man reached for the base of the lamp on the nightstand and switched it on.

Liz, squinting, eyes in pain, lowered her weapon when she saw the face of Alexei.

He offered the red-tinged water, "You must drink this. It will mitigate some symptoms you are feeling."

She looked at the blood in the water, then at Alex. "No. I'm not drinking that."

"What you are now feeling will only get worse."

"How is your blood going to help me with the flu?"

"Because you have been infected."

"With the flu." Then another light went on but in her head this time. "You mean I've been bitten? Where!" Liz jumped up and stripped off her coat and ran to the mirror to inspect her neck. Alex stepped next to her. She saw him out of the corner of her eye, but his reflection did not appear beside her. She craned her neck to inspect as much as possible. "I don't see—"

"Look at your wrist. There, the right one."

She did. But there weren't any bite marks, just the scratch.

"Oh shit!"

"Your body is dying. It is craving blood. Without blood, you will go mad with desire for it. Then you will lash out at the next human you encounter, and your transition will have begun."

"Kill me!" She screamed, pleading with Alex for help. "I don't want to become a . . . a . . .,"

"Monster?"

"Just kill me." She went back to the bed and picked up the gun. "Shit, I'll do it myself." She said, wrapping her lips around the barrel and pointing it up to the roof of her mouth.

"Before you pull the trigger, perhaps you will indulge me a moment longer to explain your new, ah, situation. Please?" Alexei asked. His experience with Cindra had sharpened his feelings concerning life and death. And while the contrast between immortals and humans was night and day, he knew there had to be ways of accommodation on both sides of the spectrum, though he was at a loss for how that might happen.

Liz hesitated, then slowly withdrew the barrel from her open mouth. She looked at him. "Okay, explain."

"Under circumstances such as yours, in which a human is scratched, there can be a transference of infectious material, a toxin, much like a virus, that begins turning a mortal into an immortal. The transformation is slow and exceedingly painful. Often, the person infected is unaware of her predicament, and nothing is done. Throughout days or weeks, vampiric urges manifest and, if left unattended, the cravings become uncontrollable, and the infected becomes a raving animal."

"Really? That helps. Thanks for the explanation," Liz said dryly, raising the gun back to her mouth.

"Let me finish." Alexei said, placing his hand on the gun and gently directing the barrel towards the floor.

"Okay, continue."

"The infection can be allowed to run its course. This usually leads to a messy death. It can be redirected towards turning the contaminated into a vampire, though a weak, undisciplined one. Or, if caught early enough, the transition and its effects can be put into something like what you might call stasis, a type of suspended animation. You can remain as you are right now, indefinitely."

"Indefinitely?"

"Yes. Well, almost. Eventually, death will come to you at some point, but not until after you have outlived all those you know, unless you are the victim of an accident or violence. Otherwise, you remain human . . . relatively."

"How?"

"Drink the Nostrum," Alexei said, holding the glass up. "It is an ancient potion of water mixed with blood, created by a medieval monk, as I have given to you, but not exactly. I dripped only a tiny amount of my blood into regular tap water just to revive you. Nothing more. Vampire blood will only do harm depending upon the amount consumed and how long you have been drinking it."

"Great," Liz said sarcastically. "So, what other kind of blood is there to save me?" Then the truth dawned on her. "Oh, wait . . . No. No!"

"You need human blood. The amount will vary depending upon how you feel, but let us say, as a start, a ten percent solution each day. Then, as your body adjusts, you can cut the amount of blood required in half. You may eventually discover that as little as a few drops in a glass of water may be all that you will need. But that will be many years from now."

"That's a lot of blood."

"You have a very virulent infection."

Liz kept a firm grip on the gun but let it rest on her lap, trying to process this information about how her life had suddenly changed. "And this special water?"

"Holy water, along with a crushed clove or two of garlic, aconite, also known as wolfsbane, and a hint of a couple of other ingredients. It may surprise you to know that I do not have a ready supply of these ingredients," he smiled hesitantly.

For a moment, her dire situation dissolved, and she blurted out a snort of a laugh at Alex's joke. "So, where, how?"

"There are people here, in Portland. They . . . assist immortals during the day. One I trust is, at this moment, shopping for the crucial ingredients. One of your CSC blood banks is in Old Town, conveniently close to the Downtown Chapel and a Chinese herbalist shop. Commander Cole has smoothed the way with both the attending nurse and the pastor. The herbs only cost a few pennies. Until my 'assistant' returns, you must drink this." Alexei moved the glass of water and blood closer to her. "Then rest."

"A familiar?"

"Yes."

"Terry's niece was one."

"At first, but Vladimir turned her to ensnare Master Sergeant Terry."

"Why kill Terry?"

"I believe my brother decided it advantageous to eliminate your best hunters. In his time with the CSC, the master sergeant had proven to be a tactical equal to Vladimir. Their chess games took on epic proportions. Vladimir couldn't afford to let Terry continue to live and challenge his plans. Checkmate."

Liz remained on the edge of the bed fingering the gun, feeling grounded by the coolness of the black metal. There was too much for her mind to digest. Too much new information was being presented. It was like her first day on the job when they sent her with Craig into Vamp Town. She had no idea what she had signed up for then, and now she had to make a snap decision concerning her life based on . . . alchemy?

"The commander described to me what had happened," Alexei said almost apologetically. "I am aggrieved by Agent Wright's passing."

Liz considered Alex's words. "And Cindra? How come this potion didn't work for her?"

"She had been bitten, which injects the toxin deeper into the body than a scratch. More importantly, she was too far along in transition. I . . . I am sorry. I thought I could help her through the process and into acceptance of her new life. But her human nature was too strong. She defeated vampirism. If you could bottle her desire to live and love and go outside and feel the warmth of the sun, then you would have a powerful vaccine."

Alexie took the gun from Liz and set it on the dresser away from her immediate reach and again offered her the blood-tinged water.

She looked at it and accepted the glass. Touching the rim to her lips, Liz felt the urge to retch rise again.

Chapter 28

BROTHERS

A LEXEI LOOKED DOWN at his brother. Vladimir didn't appear to be invincible now. Sitting in a chair, which was undoubtedly a stage prop he used to project an image of unstoppable dominance. Alexei shook his head and mused. Ever since his brother had brushed shoulders with Anton Chekhov at a party in Moscow, he considered himself to be quite the thespian.

After helping Agent Adams past her crisis point, Alexei knew it was time to find and confront Vladimir before the CSC did. He had a rough notion of where his brother had secreted himself. Back in 1896, after fleeing New York and Police Commissioner Theodore Roosevelt's vampire hunters, Vladimir had retreated to a little back-water city on the far side of the continent referred to as Stump Town. Portland, Oregon. It had gained the nickname because of all the stumps left after cutting down the trees to build the place. Vladimir liked dark and dank recesses from which to work and the young town's ever-growing maze of below-grade passages provided the sine qua non—essential ingredient. He most assuredly was somewhere under Portland.

Before leaving Liz, Alexei made her drink as much of the Nostrum as she could hold. Her condition required she consume the better part of a unit of blood mixed with several quarts of holy water for a first time dosage. As her life progressed, she would refine the blood-to-water ratio required to maintain equilibrium. For the next couple of weeks, however, she would down far more human blood than she would like, while her body adjusted to its new reality.

The potion made Liz gag. The thought of ingesting human blood was antithetical to all she believed was right. Consuming human blood was regarded as cannibalism, which was one of the foremost taboos for mortals. Without the other ingredients that made the concoction taste extremely bitter, she may not have been able to tell if there was blood in the holy water. The coppery flavor could always be thought of as one of the many minerals found in any municipal water supply if her eyes were closed. Along with the queasy effects of consuming the Nostrum came the powerful urge to sleep, which her body desperately required to heal. But before she became lost in dreamland, Alexei had her recount how to find the entrance to Vladimir's lair. Of course, his gentle touch on her mind helped immensely in learning what he needed to know.

With the setting sun, Alexei's familiar called Uber to take his master directly to the Shanghai Tunnel Bar entrance. From there, Liz's memories, combined with the shared genetics of brotherhood, served as a homing beacon enabling Alexei to navigate the tangled web of passages and chambers under the city leading to this room where his brother sat, slumped over on the dilapidated chair. Ragged breathing told enough of the story. But drainage from the chest laceration was the real indicator of Vladimir's precarious condition.

If his brother hadn't been on the verge of death, Alexei would have laughed at an image that popped into his mind. A vampire Santa Claus, red-stained white beard, on an ornately carved gilt throne, hungrily calling out to the elf at the door. "Send in the next one," as he wiped the red blood off his lips from the last hapless child, empty husks of little bodies in snowsuits scattered on the floor. But this was no time for idle amusement.

Bullets and blades containing silver have been standard vampire-killing tools for hundreds of years. But wooden stakes fashioned as spikes, rods, spears, and knives have been in use since before the invention of gunpowder and forged metals. Effective vampire-killing stakes have always been made from a variety of hardwoods commonly found throughout Europe: oak, hawthorn, rowan, mountain ash, holly, juniper, and linden. Individually, any of these hardwoods created quite potent tools for killing the undead. But after years of experimentation, they discovered laminating several of these woods together added a lethal layer to these weapons, with many being fashioned into the shape of a cross for added measure.

It was with such a carved implement that wounded Vladimir. It took minimal deductive reasoning to figure this out. A portion of the cross-shaped knife handle protruded from his brother's chest. The remainder was buried deep in his gut, and with each depleted breath, Alexei could see his brother inching closer to death.

"Brother," Alexei finally said.

Vladimir raised his head at the words. He was drenched in sweat. His internal organs were on a slow burn, already consuming his body from the inside out. He gave a weak, sardonic smile, spit blood from his mouth, then answered,

"Brother." It was more exhalation of breath than a spoken acknowledgment of the being standing in the room with him. The exertion from speaking one word was enough to make him pass out. Yet he hung on.

Alexei moved closer to his younger brother. He reached out a hand and brushed Vladimir's hair from his face, a gesture of comfort for his dying sibling.

"Your compassion is your weakness," Vladimir coughed.

"Yet, it is not I who appears weak at the moment."

Vladimir snorted out an agonizing laugh. "You call this weakness?" He gestured to the knife handle. "Your sense of humor has not improved by your exposure to the Americans." He took in a ragged breath then spit out, "Dullards."

"I thought it more ironic than outright funny."

"Yes. Ironic in so many ways." Vladimir fought to take in a shallow breath. "Mainly because it appears you will have won, again. I suppose you and your CSC lords will round up all of my people and take them back to that . . . internment camp," he coughed.

"That town is finished."

Vladimir arched his right eyebrow at this.

"There are no more immortals left in the reservation. I released them of their obligations to me, to anyone claiming leadership of the families. From now on, there will be no Khan."

"What? You think that a single pronouncement can end a centuries-old behavior? That you can, with a mere flourish of the wrist, stop me from gathering my people into a force to be reckoned with?" Vladimir coughed more. The exertion of still trying to defy his older brother was too taxing.

"Most have never believed as you," Alexei replied. "Yes, they resented the treaty. I now understand the hatred and frustration. I admit it was a mistake to use my power as Khan to force acceptance." Alexei paused and waited for Vladimir's reaction. "I believe if given a choice to live out eternity in a quiet, low-profile life, versus one of aggression and vile hatred, only a tiny few immortals will follow you." He looked at his brother's condition again. "Or should I say, *would have* followed?"

Vladimir coughed again. "Enough with the bad jokes. I doubt most are prepared for the constant fear of being hunted."

"Being hunted is a part of our lot. Just as for some humans, being prey is a part of theirs." Alexei conceded.

"And what of the Center for Specter Control?"

"Lycans, mutants, and budget woes. We will always be in their sights, as you have suggested. I will try to mitigate the fall-out."

"It sounds a lot like an option I suggested several times. Live and let live. You rejected it, I recall." Vladimir said, ending in a violent, coughing spasm.

"And I'm sure the church will more than likely resume its inquisition, seeking our kind and hunting us with renewed vigor. But I didn't come here to rehash old quarrels and decisions. As you say, I am too compassionate. But the fact remains, I am still your brother. I promised to look out for you."

"A mortal's sentiment."

"That mortal was our mother."

Vladimir snorted out more blood and steaming goo. His internal organs were quickly stewing. "I am dying," He spat out the next word, "*Brother.*" He coughed again. "There is nothing to be done about it."

"Oh, but there is."

Vladimir tried to lift himself up in his chair. "You would do this for me?"

Alexei stepped back from Vladimir and rolled up his shirt sleeve. "As I told you, I made a promise."

"One, I doubt I would keep for you in reverse circumstances."

Alexei drew the razor-sharp nail of his little finger across the skin of his exposed wrist. Blood spurted out, pooled around the cut, and dripped to the ground.

Vladimir's eyes brightened. Alexei moved his wrist to his brother's yearning mouth. Vladimir swiftly grabbed the blood-soaked arm, clamped down on the offering of salvation, and greedily drank. The dying man accepting the outstretched hand of life. With each swallow, he could feel the fire being quenched inside and vitality returning to his depleted body.

Alexei could also feel his brother regaining health. He tried to disengage his wrist from Vladimir's mouth, but it was firmly attached like a leech. His brother was going to drink him dry. Was his brother trying to kill him or was he just weakening him sufficiently to keep him in check? Either way, this had to stop and stop now. Alexei reached for the knife handle still protruding from Vladimir's rib cage. The handle burned his hand and the harder he gripped it, the more he could feel the acidic bite of the wood on the flesh of his hand. Nevertheless, he ignored the discomfort and gave the stake a wrenching twist.

Vladimir's reaction was immediate. He howled, releasing the suction on his brother, and instinctively grabbed at the source of the pain. Alexei gave the handle of the knife one last twist, causing steaming liquid to spill out, further staining Vladimir's shirt. He looked up accusingly at his older brother.

"Oh, I thought you were finished," Alexei said acerbically. "Do you know," he paced around the usurper's throne, "I actually thought you might love me, despite what you said or did." He stood in front of his wounded brother. "As children, I believed hidden behind your visual display of resentment, you loved me as I loved you. But now I see you never did. Nor do I believe you even liked me."

"You just tried to kill me. Is that your idea of brotherly love?" Vladimir hissed.

"And what of your attempt to deplete me? Were you trying to kill *me*? Or just weaken me so you could make your escape easier?"

Vladimir sat back and arched his neck, so he could look up at Alexei. He held a hand covering the seeping wound and firmly clutched the arm of the chair with the other, white knuckles revealing the pain he was fighting. "Father always fawned over you. You, his little general, could do no wrong. And you followed through with that moniker, ordering me around like a soldier in your little army. An army of one."

"I have always suspected you had an ulterior motive for taking me into the old monk's lair," Alexei said as he paced around his brother. "It is strange how we have never discussed that, even once. You thought Lazar would drink me dry. Consume me. Toss my drooping body to the side and then give you everything. But that did not happen. And when he passed on the power and knowledge enabling me to become Khan, you saw that as the final straw.

"The last time I came to fetch you from this city, to fulfill the terms of the treaty, I knew you were resisting my call and my physical presence was required. But even with all the fresh blood at your disposal here, you weren't able to draw up enough strength to break the imprinted code that would have allowed you to defy me, your Khan, and off to the reservation you slunk in defeat. How that must have galled you the most."

"But I have broken the imprint. I rose and challenged. You backed down." Vladimir contested.

"Yes. Vamp Town. So, it appeared."

"Appeared? Hah! I defeated you."

Alexei took in a breath before he revealed the truth to Vladimir and to himself as well. "I became complacent. I found a comfortable niche to live in but ignored how others were not content and chaffed at the confines of the agreement with Roosevelt. I restrained you all from obeying natural urges. I spent my time in pursuits that made me feel . . . human: stargazing, literature, music. I drank the blood provided, but I did so infrequently and without relish. I became weak. When the bus passengers found our town, you took advantage of the fresh blood, which strengthened and emboldened you," he paused. "You did not defeat me. I defeated myself."

Enraged, Vladimir tried to stand, but his weakened state made the attempt at forceful indignation seem pathetic.

"Farewell, brother. I leave you as you wanted, on your own, the master of your own domain." Alexei turned to leave.

"You cannot leave me with this dagger sticking out of my chest . . . I will die."

"Perhaps, or maybe, you drank enough of me to weather this storm. One day, you may regain your strength, but it will be a long time before you can carry out anything near the ultimate solution you planned for humanity."

Vladimir grit his teeth and spit out, "Let us hope we do not meet again. If we do, I will finish you! Ah!" The pain was too much, and Vladimir collapsed back against the chair.

"Yes, possibly. Then again . . .."

Chapter 29

WHAT NOW

"HELLO CALLER, THIS is Dr. Gwen. You are on the air."

"First-time caller, long time listener—"

"Yes, yes, I get that a lot. What's your name?"

"Bret from Portland. As in Bret Maverick. From the TV show?"

"Yes. Have we talked before?"

"No. First time like I said."

"I cut you off the last time, Bret."

"Swear to God. This is my first time calling."

"Well, Bret, how can I help you?"

"I know your show isn't about this kind of stuff—"

"Tell me, and I'll decide."

"Okay. I saw something strange earlier tonight, and it freaked me out. This swirling black cloud, like a mini tornado, appeared across the street from me in the shadow of a building."

"I believe what you saw was a dust devil."

"This wasn't no dust devil, Doc. As it twisted around, I could see through it, but the more I watched, the less transparent it became. Then, in a matter of a few seconds, the tornado turned into a man!"

"That is not possible."

"And then it stepped out of the shadow and—"

"That'll be enough! I know all you frat boys seem to think that my show is some kind of joke, but I am trying to help—"

The door at the back of the control room buzzed open. Paul immediately clicked off the radio show.

"Craig liked that show, too."

Paul and Ellie shot up from their chairs and turned to great Commander Cole.

"Just listening to something to pass the time."

"No, I understand. The night shift can seem a bit long." She looked at her watch. "But I see the sun must be up somewhere outside these walls."

"Quittin' time!" Paul said enthusiastically and started gathering up his belongings. Then he looked back at the boss. "I mean, not that I don't love working in this coffin . . . Eh, box . . . Oh, you know what I mean, ma'am."

"Yes. Yes, I do." Cole stepped down to the workstation. She looked around the otherwise empty room. Then, as if she suddenly noticed, she said, "Our ranks are getting thinner."

The obviousness of the statement left Ellie and Paul with nothing to add except awkward silence as they stood with their commander. Without further acknowledging the agents, Cole silently continued to look around the room, lost in an introspective loop, flashing back to the busy command center this place once was.

"We're sorry you lost your friends, ma'am," Ellie said softly.

"Thank you, though I can't rule out that Liz hasn't survived. Since I asked Alex to help, I have heard nothing from him, and the Action Team hasn't reported in since they arrived in Portland. Though I must admit, it isn't looking so good." She took in a deep, steadying breath. "They should be back soon with the remains of the master sergeant and Agent Wright. It's possible that they found something regarding Liz's fate while clearing out the tunnels. But until we have something definite, we will continue on with the idea she's MIA."

The phone on Ellie's desk buzzed. She answered and hung up.

"The front gate says the Action Team has arrived and is heading straight here."

"Any word on Liz?"

"Nothing. Just said they drove up in the mobile command rig Liz and Craig took to Portland, followed by the team's Humvee."

The remaining CSC staff wandered into the control room as if summoned by an unheard signal sent throughout the asylum. They quietly gathered around the perimeter and stood motionless, focused on their commander.

Cole smiled, shaking her head, "The master sergeant, and I went way back, and Craig—" Cole set a small brown bag on the top of the desk, "—and that potty mouth Craig . . .." She reached into the bag and removed a yellow bathtub duck, caressing it once just hard enough to make it squeak ridiculously before setting it down on the desk. "Fucking goddamned Ducks," she said wistfully.

"Ma'am?" Ellie wondered.

Almost under his breath, Paul said to Ellie. "Craig was a Ducks fan, and Commander Cole's a Broncos fan."

"Uh?"

"College football. Oregon Ducks and Boise State Broncos."

"Oh! Sorry."

"I never want this moved. Or there will be shit to pay," she said, lips cracking into a smile. "Copy?"

"Copy, ma'am," the two answered together.

And still more people entered the room. Ellie considered the growing size of the crowd might appear to a random observer that the agency was not as deficient in personnel as had been painted. But these were the worker bees that made the hive hum. The reduction in force size was most apparent in how attrition had thinned the ranks of field agents and Action Teams. With the deaths of Craig, Terry, and likely Liz—three in one hunt alone—it was clear the line of defense between humanity and the monsters had weakened immeasurably.

The door buzzed open again, and four somewhat scraggly looking people entered. They seemed exhausted as they made their way down to Cole. The first time Ellie had met these operatives, they were rescuing her and Paul from the vampire town. Back then, their faces were flush from the rush of battle, adrenaline flowing through their systems.

Now they just looked beat up. After several nights of making sure the lycans remained contained at RES SITE-DELTA, they were sent directly out to Portland for clean-up. It had to have been demoralizing to retrieve the remains of three of their own, and in the prescribed manner called for in the regs. It wasn't really any wonder they kept silent after their gruesome task of incinerating piles of congealing vampire viscera and then removing their comrade's heads before their remains also were torched.

They gathered around the workstation, looking defeated. Heads hung low, standing quietly in an almost protective formation around commander Cole.

"If you'd pardon my unrequested input, ma'am, but we've got something to say," Sergeant St. Jean said quietly, breaking the silence.

Cole looked into the eyes of this Action Team. So many of its original eight members had been lost. First Swanson some months ago at DELTA, then Timmons, Evers, and Todd, trying to save those from the lost bus in RES SITE-ALPHA. Four out of eight. A terrible toll.

"What've you got to say, sergeant?"

"We . . . want to get Vlad."

"What do you mean? Get Vlad?" Cole was confused. "I watched Agent Adams stake him in the heart. He had to have been one of the piles you scooped up to burn."

St. Jean just shook his head. "Sorry to tell you this, but there was no sign of either him or Alex. I mean, not that we could scientifically say for certain. You know? Aside from clothing, that is."

Cole looked at their faces. Something wasn't adding up. They weren't telling her the whole story. "I said nothing about Alex being there."

The defeat and exhaustion that was drawn across the faces of the Action Team slowly turned into slight grins and smirks as though they were holding back on some private joke.

"What the fuck is going on here, sergeant?" Cole demanded.

Most everyone looked down at the floor, inspecting shoes, not wanting to come into eye contact with an overly agitated commander.

The buzzer at the back sounded, breaking the tension of the moment. The door leading into the control room slowly opened, and a figure of a woman filled the void. She wore black slacks, a black flight jacket that was zipped up to her chin, and black leather gloves. A tactical scarf with a woven black-and-white middle eastern pattern—what was called a shemagh or keffiyeh—wound around her head and face and protectively covered her neck, with the rest draped off the shoulders, showing off its hand-tied fringe rather elegantly. A pair of large-framed Jackie O type dark glasses covered her eyes.

"This looks like quite the pity party," the mystery woman said, stopping in front of Cole. The woman unwrapped the scarf, revealing the lower half of her face. Then she pulled the fabric completely off her head, and a thick mane of red hair spilled out and down onto her shoulders. She put a hand on her glasses but stopped. "Could you lower the light level a bit, please?"

Paul touched the lighting control on the desk in front of him, and the room dimmed. "How's that?"

"Thanks, Paul, this is perfect." Then she removed her glasses, and—like a butterfly emerging from its chrysalis—Liz Adams fully revealed herself. Smiled. "I'm not dead yet," she said in her best Monty Python voice.

Those watching the whole incident play out would always remember Commander Cole's reaction. No one had ever seen her smile in such a genuine manner. Even those who had shared a moment in the lounge with her, watching the Broncos beat up on a supposedly better team, had never seen such unreserved joy. And then to see her embrace Liz in an affectionate mother-child-like hug was too much to have been expected.

Cole opened her eyes in mid-embrace and saw the room full of people watching her in awe. But they were also sharing in the relief of seeing Agent Adams alive. Then she saw the operatives smiling broadly and Sergeant St. Jean had the biggest grin of all.

The shock, joy, wonderment, and thankfulness of the moment quickly dissipated. Now it was back to business. Cole straightened and put her "commander suit" back on. She let her hard gaze fall upon St. Jean—all starch and polish. He lost the smile and felt the heat from her eyes burn into his.

"I, um, I . . .."

Liz stepped between the two. "Sorry, ma'am. The surprise entrance was my idea." Liz grinned weakly.

St. Jean touched Liz's shoulder and eased her to the side, exposing himself to the wrath of Cole. "You're right to be mad, ma'am. We were all just so happy to find Agent Adams alive, and she was so happy to see us we thought a minor diversion would help ease the hurt of losing Terry and Craig. In hindsight—"

"In hindsight, I should loosen up more." Cole cut in with an apologetic smile.

"What I said still stands, Commander. We want to get Vlad." The sergeant said with determination and a sense of deadly purpose. "Ma'am, you can lock us up for eternity if you want to, but there's no stopping us. We're going to erase Vlad and any other vamp who gets in our way."

"Ultimatum?" Cole asked.

"If that's how you want to read it. I prefer to call it a promise we four made to ourselves and our friends," St. Jean responded. "You can lock us up on the dark side of the moon for all I care . . . *after* we finish."

Cole considered what she had just heard. "St. Jean. Huh? You know, I don't recall what your first name is. Don't think that I ever knew it."

"Well, I don't think that it's very important right now, considering. It's in my personnel file."

"And that is back in the HR office in D.C. If I'm going to be bullied into letting you run around the countryside like vigilantes, I think I should know the name of the bully. *Now.*"

St. Jean's face flushed immediately. He looked around the room. All eyes fixed on him. Even his friends, his team, were looking at him squirm.

"Hey, yeah. What *is* your name there, sarge?" Chris Okada asked.

The others chimed in as well.

"Yeah, come on."

"What is it? Ronny?"

"Don't be so bashful."

Taking a deep breath, Sergeant St. Jean, former marine recon, the oldest member of this Action Team, afraid of nothing and no one, closed his eyes and exhaled. "Norbert."

"Oh," Matt Ortega let out.

A little snort shot from Torri Ellingson's nose, choking back a laugh.

Commander Cole maintained a straight face while everyone else in the room couldn't help but laugh.

"Stupid goddamned family names . . . Norbert Gaylord St. Jean . . . the third," he ground out. "Happy?"

"Wow! There are three of you?" Ortega blurted.

The room erupted.

"Thank you—Norb," Cole said with a wink. "If I'm to let you hunt vampires, then I need you four to become agents. Your time as CSC muscle is now over. It's time to put those brains to work. But not before a little classroom time." She looked at the others lining the walls. "And I believe that the rest of you still have work to do around here, or am I wrong?"

The gathered staff, knowing when discretion was the better part of valor, filed out and quickly emptied the room.

"Welcome home, Agent Adams," Cole said to Liz. "But you have some explaining to do. My office. Now."

⸺◆⸺

COMMANDER COLE SHUT the door firmly as she entered the office behind Liz, signaling there was going to be some serious talking going on. Cole touched the dimmer control and raised the overall lighting level in the dim space; causing Liz to shade her eyes.

"Sorry ma'am, but do you think you could keep the office a little on the dark side?" Liz almost pleaded.

Cole stepped behind her desk and looked at Liz, studying the younger woman whom she had assumed was dead. "There's something about you I can't put a finger on. You seem healthy enough, but you look pale. How do you feel?"

"Um, the lighting?"

"Sure. Sorry. How's that?" Cole asked as she complied with the request.

"Thanks. I'm fine." Liz answered, rubbing her eyes. "At least I think I am." She smiled weakly.

Cole scrutinized her subordinate, trying to ferret out the truth. "We watched you and Craig go after the master sergeant into the tunnels. Saw the fight you had with his

niece. Watched Craig with Vlad . . . and how you . . .."
She paused, not wanting to scrape at the still-raw trauma
of Craig's death. "We watched your fight all the way until
you confronted Vlad. Then something went wrong. We lost
visual. After Vlad threw you down, the feed went dark.
The body cam must have been damaged when you hit the
ground."

"Did you see me stab him?"

"No. Your bodies were too close to see much of anything."

"I stabbed him, ma'am. Think I got him good, which is
why he tossed me aside. He had to focus on getting the
dagger out." Liz closed her eyes, trying to remember. "After
I plunged the stake into Vlad's chest, things get fuzzy. I really
thought I stuck it into his heart, but . . . I recall nothing after
that. St. Jean says they didn't find anything in that could have
been Vlad, so I have to assume he's still alive."

"Or he went and died somewhere else in those tunnels.
Poisoned rats do that."

"Or that, yes. I buried that knife deep into his rib cage.
Wouldn't surprise me if he's a pile of sludge down there, but
the Action Team did an extensive search, probing even into
areas I didn't go into, and still they found nothing."

"Tell me about Alex," Cole said.

"Yeah, what about Alex? Did you send him to help? I
thought he couldn't be a part of the CSC."

"And he's not. Never can be. But sometimes 'The enemy of
my enemy—'"

"Is my friend. I get it."

"So, tell me. How did he help you? Or did he?"

Liz took a moment to gather her thoughts. "That is the question, isn't it? Did Alex help me? Well, I'm alive." She weighed that statement, then continued. "And I guess that is a good thing. But it all depends upon the *type* of alive I am."

"That's something you'll have to tell me because you're talking in riddles." Cole sat up straight, alarmed. "You're not a vampire, are you?" Then she realized it was the middle of the day and sat back. "Of course you aren't. I'm no good at Pictionary either, so you'd better spell it out for me."

"No. Not a vampire, but not a human anymore, either."

"Here we go again."

"Sorry, but if you think you're confused, then you gotta understand this is my life here, and I'm just coming to grips with it."

"Why don't you tell me what you can about Alex?"

"Okay, let's see. I made it out of the tunnels and to the car. You called. I threw up more than once. Then I woke up on the bed in my hotel room. I guess I drove. I don't really know. But Alex was there in the room, too."

"I told him where your hotel was."

"Then he had me drink a glass of water with several drops of his own blood mixed in." Liz showed her injured wrist and shook her head. "Vlad gave me a nasty scratch with one of his claws. My dizziness resulted from vampiric toxin being absorbed into my body. The process of my becoming a vampire had already begun."

"And Alex fed you his own blood diluted in water to . . . to help you transition? But you just said that—"

"Right. I'm not a vamp. His blood was a quick fix to get me over the hump until the other ingredients arrived."

"Holy water and human blood." The pieces fell into place, though Cole should have had it figured out earlier. "That's why he asked me to help get access to the church and blood bank . . . the Nostrum."

"Yep."

"That sounded like pure quackery. I thought Alex was feeding me an old wives' tale." Cole admitted.

Liz spread out her arms in a "here I am" gesture. "Guess the old wives' weren't all full of shit. And see my wrist? Almost healed."

Cole opened the desk drawer near her right hand and removed a Smith and Wesson .44 Special and placed the stainless-steel revolver on the desktop, barrel pointing towards Liz. "So, are you all right?" asked a concerned commander. She placed her hand close to the gun handle.

Liz darted her eyes at the gun, then raised them and gave Cole a firm look. "Do you see me as a threat?"

"You say you aren't a human, *but* you aren't a vamp, either. I assume that means you can't ever get back to being a pure Homo sapien. Why shouldn't I end you now before you turn? Or should I also assume that the Nostrum is keeping you from becoming a vampire?"

Liz pulled out a flask-sized bottle from her coat pocket. A clear liquid with a pink hue was visible in the glass container.

She unscrewed the cap, placed the bottle to her mouth, took a big swig, exhaled, and grimaced at the bitter taste, setting it on the desk in front of her. Then the look on her face changed as she coughed and gagged on the fluid. Quickly Liz reached down, grabbed the trash can, and brought it up to her mouth as she fought to keep the Nostrum in her stomach. A few sketchy seconds passed, then she gingerly set the waste bin back onto the floor and wiped her mouth with a corner of her scarf. She smiled sheepishly. "Sorry, I'm new at this." She again leveled her gaze at the commander. "So, to answer your question. Yeah. I guess you could assume that. As I long as I keep drinking this vile brew."

Cole relaxed a bit and sat back in her chair, thinking. "No urge to bite someone?" She probed. "Or the desire to drink blood?"

"Ma'am, the only craving I have is for a shot of whiskey. No, a double."

"You actually think that this solution is permanent?"

"If I don't believe it, then you may as well shoot me now 'cause I don't want to be one of them."

Cole made a quick move, reaching for the revolver. Her hand hovered over the handle as though she were making a big decision. Then she grabbed the black grip and deliberately returned the gun to the drawer and shut it with a determined thud. "Tell me about it."

Liz exhaled, not sure what Cole was going to do. "I have to learn the proper dosage and then, when, and how often I will need to take it. One thing I know for sure, I have to drink this stuff at least once a day. Like a diabetic on insulin."

WHAT NOW 333

Cole leaned across the desk and reached for the open bottle. "May I?"

Liz nodded.

Cole looked at it, then took a big sniff. "Whoa! Gotta like garlic."

"Over time, I'm supposed to be able to regulate just how much garlic and wolfsbane I will need per dose, according to how I feel."

Commander Cole could only look at Liz with sympathetic eyes. "So, what does all this mean for you?"

"Alex told me I would have no blood cravings like that of a vampire, as long as I drink the Nostrum. I will maintain a limited ability to eat human food, though experimenting to find what works for me will be an uncomfortable process. And then, of course, there is the issue of life itself."

"Yes. You are alive, and I'm happy about that."

"Not just alive—pert near immortal."

Chapter 30

AWAKENING

T HE SUN HAD set behind the West Hills, and though the last of its light lingered, it wasn't anything for a vampire to fear. Especially for one as old as him. In this twilight moment, Alexei strolled by many homeless who had planted themselves along the curbs or in some ungated alcoves of Old Town for the night—begging for money, making deals, passed out, livers shot, or just disoriented by what life had dealt them. Aside from the misery of those clinging onto society's fringes, it was a pleasant, early spring evening, and the sidewalks were full of the luckier half of society in pursuit of the best happy hour fare.

When Theodore Roosevelt was president, this city had recreated itself from a frontier village to a major seaport in the Pacific Northwest. Then it coasted along until the Second World War when it saw another boom. Then coasted again, awash in post-war prosperity, plateaued, coasted again. Now, it was recreating itself one more time. In such periods of rapid growth, the established residents always see those from elsewhere—people drawn to its vitality—as a threat to the status quo. His brother saw these new arrivals as perfect marks—new to town, with no local connections to question where they were, or where they might have gone. University towns were good in this way as well, though their smaller populations made it hard to hide one's nocturnal compulsions, creating the need to keep moving so as not to attract attention.

These were concerns Alexei had not considered for a long time but was coming to grips with them in his new reality. And the cities of today? A far cry from before the treaty, but presenting the same challenges and opportunities in which to hunt as those he had been accustomed to. He thought wistfully of New York when Theodore was police commissioner. Talk about a homelessness problem! But undeniably an ideal place in which a vampire could gorge itself.

Vladimir had the perfect situation in a city packed with an endless supply of humans that could have sustained him and his nest for years, with no one caring—the dregs of society, the unwashed masses, and the mass of immigrants who poured in almost daily. But his tendency towards living life in excess brought the attention of society upon him, and thus the eyes of the law. The vicious way they killed created a cycle of fear that was said to rival Jack the Ripper in London. This sensational comparison only fueled Vladimir, whose killing spree gained the tagline: The Night Stalker Murders. With the crosshairs of vampire hunters firmly trained on Vladimir's heart, he had to flee.

Looking around at the few buildings that still existed from that time, Alexei understood why Vladimir had fled here. Long before the time of mass media, his brother could resume his hunting with impunity. Of course, Vladimir loved Portland. It was, and still is, a cornucopia for the dramatic tastes of one such as his brother.

Alexei paid no attention to where he was walking; allowing the flow of the crowd to direct him. He had gotten wrapped up in the sights and memories of a time long past. At a street corner, he stopped and surveyed his surroundings. It was totally dark now, dark if one didn't consider the glare of the LED street lights. An unfortunate twenty-first-century addition to cities. He liked the moody quality of gaslight that cast a warm glow on the ground in a ring around the shade of the lamppost, then faded out after several feet into the beautiful darkness of black shadows.

The old buildings around him were mostly new since his last visit to Portland when he had to come to pry Vladimir loose and drag him to the reservation. Yet they had a comfortable quality that made him feel as though he knew them. Alexei stopped being a tourist for a moment and found himself in front of the corner entrance of a bar. The sign identified the establishment as Jake's Crawfish. The interior of worn wood and nicotine-stained walls lined with pictures and artifacts of an earlier time appealed to him, a place that could have been around back then, so he entered and sat on a stool at the bar. The raspy/husky voice of Louis Armstrong played over the sound system; confirming he had entered the correct establishment.

Moments later, a silver-haired man wearing a white jack and sporting a black bow tie approached Alexei. He placed his hands on the bar in a welcoming way. Few would notice the two dots, a tattoo, applied in the webbing of his fingers between the thumb and pointer finger, looking like a snakebite. But then, the tattoo wasn't there for just anybody to notice.

The bartender's engaging smile drew all focus away from anything else except his sparkling eyes. "Name's Pete," he said, adjusting his glasses. "What'll you have?"

BLOOD CITY

Alexei's eyes shifted from the smiling face down at the two dots and back up to Pete's eyes. Recognizing the tattoo, Alexei returned the smile, allowing just the tips of his fangs to show below his upper lip.

Pete winked.

"I think I have just what you're looking for." The barman turned, opened the cooler behind him, and reached into the very back, past the chilled glasses and the bottles of craft brew. He returned to Alexei with a dark green glass bottle and presented it. The handwritten label was uninterpretable—*A halandók véres szívéból.*

"From the bloody hearts of mortals," Alexei read quietly. "Hungarian."

Pete pulled the cork out and smelled it to check if the contents had turned. Satisfied, he poured a dark, rich-looking red liquid into the wide-mouthed Bordeaux-style glass and set it on a napkin in front of him.

Alexei swirled the liquid around and took a sniff. "Nice."

"It's a blend, but I believe you'll find it to be an excellent vintage, Mr. ah . . .?"

"Alexei . . . Rurik."

Upon hearing the name, Pete gave a low bow of recognition, a gesture of deference showing he knew who was sitting in front of him, the Khan of all the families. And while he was merely a familiar, he knew royalty when it showed up in his bar.

Alexei signaled for Pete to lean in close, so he could say something in private. "There is no more Khan. Those days are gone. Follow whom you will."

Pete winked in acknowledgment and poured a bit more into the glass, pretending to be working.

A middle-aged woman, sitting a couple of stools away, looked at the drink in front of Alexei. "I thought you weren't supposed to chill red wine." She said in a tone that grated on Alexei's ears.

Re-corking the bottle, Pete said, "This is quite special and old. Refrigeration is the only way to store it, so it'll keep."

The woman's eyebrows arched up. "Really? That special, huh? Can I order a glass?"

Pete replaced the bottle in the cooler. "It's reserved for special customers."

"What's so special about him?" she asked, looking at Alexei. "No offense."

Alexei looked at her as he swirled the red liquid around in the glass and smiled pleasantly. "None taken."

The woman picked up her glass and took a sip. "I don't know anything about red wine. I'm a white zin kinda gal if you can't tell. Oh, Pete, could you drop a couple more pieces of ice in my wine?"

The bartender rolled his eyes, looking at Alexei as he complied.

A mischievous smile formed on Alexei's face. "Would you like a sip?" He asked, pushing his glass towards the woman.

Pete stopped to watch, not sure what was going to happen.

The woman smiled and took the glass. "Why sure. Always be open to new experiences, is what I say." She put her fingers in her mouth and pulled out a wad of gum she had been hiding inside and placed it on a napkin. "If it's that good, I don't want to spoil the taste." She smiled coyly.

"First rule. Always hold the glass by the stem." Alexei instructed. "Now swirl it around and let it wash up the sides of the bowl. There, that's correct. See how it clings to the glass? The longer it takes to flow back into the bowl, the better. It's called 'having legs,' and this has excellent legs." He gave Pete a conspiratorial wink. "Now place your nose inside the glass and take a quick sniff. Smell anything?"

She stuck her nose inside the opening of the glass as instructed and sniffed. She did it a second time. "No. Am I supposed to smell something?"

"I detected hints of dark loam and copper," Alexei said.

The woman took a quick sniff. "If you say so," she said.

Alexei looked at Pete again, but said to the woman, "Now take a quick sip."

She tipped the edge of the glass to her lips and took a tiny amount into her mouth.

"What do you taste?"

"Nothing. I taste nothing." She said with red-tinged lips.

"You need to educate your palate."

"So, how much for a glass of this?"

"You couldn't afford it," Pete answered.

"Too rich for my blood? That it?" She sat up straight on the stool, tensing a bit. "Well, I wouldn't pay a plugged nickel for that tasteless swill. And I can afford quite a bit."

"That's okay. I wouldn't sell it to you no matter how much you could afford."

The woman's face clouded over. "The hotel said that this was a great place." She opened her purse and pulled out a few bills. She tossed them on the bar towards Pete. "I can't see why? Rude staff! I'll be telling them about this!" And then she stormed out of the bar.

Pete leaned into Alexei, "She looks like she could be a tasty morsel if you could shut her up for long enough."

Alexei inhaled the aroma of the red elixir and took an appreciative sip. It had reached room temp and had opened nicely.

"She's not on my menu tonight. Besides, I suspect that she might have a rather sour aftertaste."

Pete slammed his hand down on the bar and gave a snort of a laugh.

"Order!" the cocktail waitress called out.

"Sorry, sir. Looks like I have a paycheck to earn. Call if you need anything else."

"Thank you. I'll be fine," Alexei reassured him and returned to his drink. Watching the action in the room, he pondered his decision not to follow the woman and do what Vladimir would do without compunction. It just didn't seem right to him anymore. That woman may have had no sense of humor, and she was annoying, but did she really need to die?

An excessively large man on the other side of Alexei gave another man to his left a nudge. "Hey, look at those guys carrying on over there in the corner," he said, referring to a group of three happy, buoyant young men wearing a mishmash of campy secondhand-store clothes who didn't fit the profile of the other customers. Some might say that they were deliberately crying out to be noticed.

"Yeah, fags," replied the other.

"I'm surprised that Bill lets *those* types in."

"Bill doesn't own the place anymore."

"Oh, yeah, that's right."

"But I'm sure he wouldn't have cared. Money's money."

This conversation should not have surprised Alexei. Humans prejudged, based on surface appearance. That group was flamboyant, but he could see that their flair was a personal expression and one or more of them were probably struggling artists taking advantage of the late night cheap Happy Hour eats. The two next to him continued.

"Are you visiting?"

"Here on business. Got a product presentation tomorrow with the city."

"Good luck with that. This town is full of fuckin' liberals."

Alexei had been wondering about his place in a world without the constraints of the treaty and the CSC. Sitting here, listening, and observing, helped him to arrive at a moment of understanding, acknowledging the inescapable fact of his life. He was a vampire. Taking a human life to sustain his life would always bother him. Perhaps it was the Christian commandment, "Thou shalt not kill," that still resounded from some hidden piece of his lost humanity. But his primary goal was to survive, and consuming human blood was necessary to do that.

An idea gelled. Being selective regarding which humans he would feed on might assuage his negative feelings concerning killing, and help humanity by eliminating those that brought nothing positive to the world. Was his calling to thin out the hateful people from the human herd, making room for the creative and enlightened?

His gaze drifted back to the two obnoxious gentlemen who were shooting off their mouths. After so many years of drinking bottled blood, his mouth salivated at the thought of biting into a warm, throbbing throat. His addiction, for that's what it was, had slapped him in the face and he knew he could no longer fight it. He gave the two blowhards sitting near him a more studied examination, like a hunter looking through a rifle scope. One caught his eye and Alexei smiled and raised his glass in a silent toast as though he agreed with their vile words. They were mortals, and he was a bloodsucking killer, or soon would be again this night. He had to live, right? He knew his friend Craig, had he survived, might understand his choice. Well, did he actually know that, or was he making excuses, still hoping to be accepted by the mortals? Liz probably wouldn't understand, but she still had a few things to sort out. Perhaps later.

"Yeah, heard that, but the boss says he wants Portland as a customer," the large man said as he signed his credit card slip.

He shoved his hand over to the other. "Well, gotta go. Nice to have met you. I'm Frank."

The two shook hands. "Harvey."

Alexei took another sip of the luscious drink. He looked at the three artsy men enjoying themselves. Vladimir's people had better not be around for their sake. They had a look his brother sought for late night entertainment. His brother was on a long road to recovery, and he needed every drop of fresh blood he could suck down to rebuild his strength.

He flagged the bartender and indicated he wanted the check. Pete placed his tattooed hand on the bar and said, "All covered."

Vladimir had been right about the reservation. Vamp Town. His brother had chaffed at the life Alexei had forced them all to live, while pretending to be mortal, doing human things like driving a Jeep, and watching the moon come out as though it was the early morning sun rising, longing for its warmth on his face. He had been fooling himself, but not at first. Alexei convinced himself he had chosen the honorable path to save his people from extinction. But the law of unintentional consequences had to have its way.

Right now, he saw his path forward. Alexei knew he had to keep his brother from wreaking havoc on humans while also satisfying his own need for blood. He felt confident with a little due diligence he could find deserving targets for his lust.

Alexei smiled and thanked Pete. Then he slipped off the stool and followed the self-serving prig who had just left.

Now, taking in the chill evening air, he knew his brother wasn't wrong in opposing the document that locked them away from the world. Alexei had no illusions, however.

Vladimir never wanted to walk down a city street and take in the ambiance, enjoy the music, and appreciate what humanity brought to the world. All he wanted was to feed.

Alexei reassured himself that the original intent of the treaty was, at the core, a good idea. Keeping humans and vampires apart was good for both species. It was no way to live, to be in fear that the person you met might want to slash your throat and drink your blood *or* that they might find you as you slept and get staked through the heart. Alexei and Vladimir had different approaches to how to handle the issue.

Vladimir envisioned a world dominated by vampires, one in which humans were submissive, herded like sheep, and cultivated to provide an eternity's worth of fresh, warm blood. In that scenario, war with humans was inevitable.

Alexei saw a different path. Humans still would be needed for sustenance, of course, but done in a more sustainable way. He smiled, thinking about the farm-to-table food culture. Not that he imagined farms full of humans being raised for slaughter, as his brother had. On the contrary, Alexei's developing vision was less obvious and more deliberative.

The equation was simple. Immortals needed blood to exist. Humans provided the blood. Therefore, vampires would forever hunt humans. But for vampires to continue following this centuries-old path, they must do it under a new paradigm.

Immortals had to drift back into the shadows, stay out of the limelight, and return to the status of legend and myth. They must focus their nocturnal hunting only on those humans that no longer added to the collective good. Humans could not make those choices, morality getting in the way, but vampires had no such issues. Killing humans was not a problem.

This approach could mean a smaller population, but the race would remain. Perhaps humans might come to understand and accept this new way. Maybe even embrace it. Who knew?

And then the ongoing hunt and destruction of vampires could taper off and, with some luck, eventually cease.

The big loudmouth from the bar stopped at the corner waiting for the traffic to pass, then he crossed the street and entered a dark parking garage.

Alexei looked to see if anyone was watching and then followed the man into the shadows.

Chapter 31

EPILOGUE

Spokane, Washington 2018

T HE THROBBING IN his head was becoming more incessant. It had been quite some time since he had felt this way. The resulting headache was not the fun side of drowning your problems in a bottle.

Pound! Pound! Pound!

"Ouch!" He would have to deal with this. The pain in his temples was becoming implacable. Attempting to open his mouth, it felt as though his lips would flake off in large dry pieces, and that his tongue was glued to his upper pallet.

Cottonmouth.

Pound! Pound! Pound!

"Ugh!" Aspirin. He needed aspirin. He pried open one eyelid. Before him on the table sat the mostly consumed fifth of whiskey. Next to the empty pint of vodka. *Did I sleep here sitting up?* he thought. Trying to move his head, the pain in his stiff neck told him definitely yes, though passed out was probably more accurate. The crust on the corner of his mouth testified to that fact as well. Drooling was the least attractive aspect of an older man who had passed out, that and the snoring. Snoring didn't bother him. But the sore neck from sleeping with his chin to his chest did. Really? Almost a fifth and a half of booze?

Bang! Bang! Bang!

The haze in his head thinned as the pounding morphed from the throbbing head to the front door.

Bang! Bang! Bang!

"Please, Thomas, let me in."

Who is that?

"Just break the son of a bitch down you want in so bad." He half yelled.

Pound! Pound! Pound!

"Ouch!" That hurt.

Bang! Bang! Bang!

"Thomas!"

"Okay, okay…." Thomas said to the door as he lifted himself up from the chair onto rubbery legs.

Bang! Bang! Bang!

He stumbled towards the door and threw it open. "Yes?" he asked groggily to the person standing in front of him. Then his eyes widened. An uncontrollable urge to vomit overwhelmed him. Covering his mouth with a hand, Thomas made haste to the kitchen sink, where he spewed out the contents of the previous night's bender, making the countertop and the stack of dirty dishes collateral damage with a messy over-spray as he tried to hit the intended target.

The man followed Thomas into the tiny house. He scanned the dirty room with disapproval.

Still leaning over the sink, Thomas's stomach spasmed. He lowered his head deep into the filthy basin and wretched again, and again, and again. Finally, when nothing more came up—except what felt like the lining of his stomach—the uncontrollable convulsions diminished, he cautiously raised his head, turned on the faucet, and slurped down large gulps of water. When he finished washing out his mouth, he looked down and shook his head as he splashed water around the sink in a half-hearted attempt at flushing away the puke.

With the water still running, he went to the refrigerator and grabbed a large jar of a clear, red-tinged liquid, got a glass from the drainer, and filled it. As he gulped down the contents, he reached for a switch on the wall and flicked it up. The disposal whirred into action, chewing up the vomited contents of the night's weakness. Turning off the disposal, he opened a cupboard and pulled down a bottle of aspirin, put the open container to his lips, and swallowed several tablets, followed by more reddish water. Next, he grabbed a bottle of Pepto and took several large gulps of the unnaturally pink peppermint concoction.

The man watched, saying nothing.

Thomas turned from the sink, another full glass of red water in hand, walked past the man and over to the sofa, placed the glass on the coffee table, and dropped onto the worn cushions.

"Hmmm." He rubbed his temples, trying to give the aspirin some help. "I thought for certain that Spokane would be far enough off the radar for you not to find me."

"Alcohol does not always lead to the most clear-headed thinking, Thomas. Gonzaga is a Jesuit institution, is it not? And the Holy Father, being a Jesuit himself, keeps in close contact with his brothers in Christ," he said with a wry grin.

Too weak to respond, Thomas just arched his eyebrows. Damn, even that hurt. "He wasn't even Pope when I left the service. It was one of those Italian ones . . . Oh, what was his name?"

"Come on Thomas, you may have thought you left the service of the church, but the Holy Father had always reserved the right to recall you. I think the American military calls it the ready reserve. Yes? And you do have a special relationship between those we hunt and those we protect."

Thomas closed his eyes, partly from the hangover but mostly to mask his thoughts.

The man waved his arm around the room. "Look around you. Do you see what you have allowed yourself to become?"

"When did the Swiss Guard recruit mothers?"

"What? Your mind is addled."

"You judge me as though you were my mother, Hauptmann. You are Swiss Guard. Ergo, you are a motherfuc—"

"Being profane will get you nowhere, Father." The man, known to Thomas as Daniel Glanzman, captain of the Pontifical Swiss Guard, admonished.

Another swallow of the reddish liquid was followed by a long, painful sigh as Thomas let the throb of his aching head dull the moment.

Glanzman picked up an empty potato chip bag, allowing a few remaining crumbs to escape onto the carpet. "It is none of my business Thomas, but aren't certain foods and . . . drinks . . .," he said, pointing out other snack food wrappings and the empty alcohol bottles. ". . . considered bad for someone such as yourself?"

"Are you genuinely concerned, or are you compiling information for your report back to Rome?"

"A bit of both, I must confess."

A weary sigh came out of Thomas' mouth. "Yes. The list of menu items that do not assault my gut is not extensive. My tolerance for food leans towards the rarer of cooked meats. Bloodier the better. Certain bland vegetables are digestible. Rice, potatoes, and pasta with no sauce are boring staples. Onions play havoc on me. Alcohol? As you have observed, it tears me apart, but without it, I cannot keep the monster inside my head at bay."

"And chips?"

"I like salty snacks when I drink," he shrugged, "And I pay for it," Thomas acknowledged while taking another swallow of the crimson water. "Besides, it's not as though bad food will kill me."

"That appears to be true. It seems like nothing can kill you."

Thomas gave him a self-deprecating shrug. "It is my cross to bear," he grinned weakly, "One I can't seem to escape." He sat up straighter, put a hand on his forehead, and rubbed his brow.

"You have sacrificed much, my friend. But this is no way for the famous Father Tomislav Lovac to spend his life."

"And it appears you are here to save me from all this."
Thomas waved his arm around the dirty room.

"The Holy Father has requested—"

"I know. And I am the only one with the skills, and so on and
so forth." After a pause, he added, "I thought the Americans
had the issue under control."

"That was true until about six months ago. But you always
knew 'under control' does not mean 'eliminated.' And while
the Holy Father allowed you the fantasy of believing the
vampire threat had been diminished so much as to be almost
nonexistent, we all knew, even you, that one day your services
would be required again."

"When was the last time we saw one another? The last time
they sent us out on a hunt?"

"Those Finnish murders."

"Yes, 1960. Ghastly affair. But no evidence of a vampire
feed." Thomas looked at the man who had interrupted a
perfectly awful morning. "And so . . . why are you here, now,
after fifty-eight years?"

"He's out," Glanzman let that sink in. "He took several
others along with him."

For a moment, Thomas was back in New York City,
helping to eradicate a nest. He had entered the basement
of an overcrowded tenement and hesitantly entered a room
reeking of death. His first hunt. Someone came upon him
from behind. He had no time to react, could barely hold his
arm up to protect his neck. When the monster's fangs shot
out, one penetrated his shoulder. Then Roosevelt's detective
squad engaged the monsters, hacking and shooting. They

killed all the parasites except the one who injured him. That one got away.

Ever since that day, Thomas had to drink the vile potion—the Nostrum. Holy water laced with human blood and other assorted ingredients. The taste was heinous but kept the infection from taking hold of his entire being. How it worked? He did not really know, except he had faith it would prevent him from turning into a vampire and for over 100 years, it had not failed.

"Vladimir . . .," Thomas spoke the evil one's name and rubbed a spot on his left shoulder where he had been injured.

"According to the Americans, Vladimir and a group from their reservation had consumed a very fresh supply of human blood," Glanzman replied.

Thomas' eyes arched open in surprise. "But from where? How? I thought they provided the vampires with packaged blood. Unless—" Thomas focused on the Nostrum he was holding.

"Unless some living humans found their retreat and became unwilling donors, which is what happened. A bus broke down close to their reservation. The passengers blindly stumbled into . . . what do the CSC agents call it?"

"Vamp Town."

"Yes. Out of the ten people who entered the town, two got away unharmed and joined the CSC, one female passenger and a little girl were turned, and the rest . . .."

"Supercharged food for Vladimir, allowing him to challenge Alexei." Thomas twirled the jar around, agitating the fluid, creating a red whirlpool in his hand.

"Yes."

"What of Alexei? Is he dead?"

"The Americans say he is alive, though they do not know where he is."

Thomas waited for the maelstrom in the jar to settle.

Glanzman continued, "The Center reached out to the Vatican, informing the Holy Father of Vladimir's escape and possible collapse of the treaty. The Pope, in turn, activated the Cacciatori—the Hunters."

"Unit composition?" Thomas asked as he slipped into tactical mode.

"Twelve. Just as it has always been since Pope Clement originated it."

Thomas let out a wry chuckle. "Clement's 'Twelve Disciples.' Too bad Jesus didn't have a few more apostles. Twelve men were never enough to fight those demons."

"Who, besides the two of us, remain of the Cacciatori?"

"Sergeant Major Merriman. He retired from the Swiss Guard twenty years ago, but it seems training a new group in the art of the hunt is more exciting than sitting on his empty farm and watching the grass grow over his wife's grave."

"So, we have Michele, an eighty-year-old sergeant major. A seventy-year-old captain." Thomas nodded to Glanzman. "A one hundred fifty-three-year-old Jesuit priest afraid of his own shadow, and nine Swiss boys still wet behind the ears. I'm certain Vladimir will quake in his boots when he sees the likes of us."

"You may be one hundred fifty-three years old, Thomas, but you do not look a day older than thirty. If a bit green around the gills."

"Thank you. But today I swear I feel like sixty."

They both shared a smile with that meager attempt at a joke.

"But there is one correction to your list."

Thomas arched a brow, silently asking what he had gotten wrong.

"I am a major now," Glanzman said, with a cocky smile on his face.

"Are you bragging? What did our Lord say about pride?"

Glanzman looked a bit chagrined.

Thomas gave his old friend a wink. He had never held his position of monsignor as a spiritual cudgel over his comrade's head, but from time to time, it was always humorous to catch him off-guard, just to see his reaction. And as in the old days, Glanzman fell for it. Not that Thomas cared much anymore what God thought. In fact, he wasn't sure he still had faith left in the existence of God, any God, especially a God who could have created the monsters he had hunted in the church's name over the years.

"Do not worry, my friend. If Christ cannot overlook a simple human emotion, such as pride in one's accomplishments, how do you think he judges me?" Thomas started picking up empty liquor bottles to emphasize his own lack of perfection. "So . . . what are our instructions?"

"You are to go to the CSC and ally with them. They are expecting you. I will return to Italy and join up with the

Cacciatori at a papal estate where Michele is training the recruits. We will join you when they are ready."

Thomas set the bottles down on the kitchen counter. He leaned against it and rubbed his pounding head. At least he could stop boring students in the Eastern European Folklore seminar he was teaching. If he was fortunate, he might confront Vladimir again, and maybe this time be put out of his misery permanently.

"On the bright side," Glanzman said, "The CSC is within spitting distance, as the Americans say. Just over the border in Mountain Home, Idaho."

Thomas lifted the Nostrum to his lips and took another healthy swig. "Yes, I am a lucky man."

Author's Note

I've been told by those who seem to know such things that writing one novel is an accomplishment. Two? Well, then I must be some sort of superhero. The fact is, I know finishing one book is just a drop in the ocean of creative expression. And two is a start. I have a long way to go before I feel comfortable calling myself a writer.

Before I started **Blood City**, I had doubts about a storyline, let alone finishing it. Now I start the same process with book number three (working title, **Book # 3**), and I kind of fear I will find myself facing the same situation. But after a short break, I will plunge headlong into it and see if I can't pull it off one more time.

I want to thank my BETA readers. I know it is a lot to ask for one's time and I really appreciate your help. Thank you to Janet Tapper for her story editing. She asked the questions and spotted the flaws in the logic that kept me focused. And Grant Byington for his copyediting skills. Thanks to Brian Green for his help building my website. And a hearty thanks to Steve Cridland for taking my promotional photos.

A special thank you, again, to my brother, Brian Seats, who designed the cover for both **Vamp Town** and **Blood City**.

Please visit my web page: **www.jeffseats.com**. Sign up for my mailing list. I promise not to bury you in tons of emails, just will let you know when something new is on the horizon. If you enjoyed this, please consider leaving a review on Amazon.

About the Author

Jeff Seats lives in Portland, Oregon, where he has worked in the entertainment industry as a scenic designer, set decorator, and production designer for both stage and motion pictures. You can visit **www.jeffseats.com** to see some of his past work as a designer and photographer.

Currently, he is in production on the audio version of ***Blood City***. Book three of the ***Monster Keeper Series*** is hiding somewhere in his head and when it begins to leak out, he'll start on that too.

Bonus Material

Scan the QR Code or visit **www.jeffseats.com/bc-bonus**
to see maps and period photos and explore links for further
reading about the region's history.

www.ingramcontent.com/pod-product-compliance
Lightning Source LLC
Chambersburg PA
CBHW051323250626
47155CB00007B/2427